C000170784

# IN JUST ONE DAY

HELEN MCGINN

Boldwood

First published in Great Britain in 2021 by Boldwood Books Ltd.

Copyright © Helen McGinn, 2021

Cover Design: Alice Moore Design

Cover Photography: Shutterstock

The moral right of Helen McGinn to be identified as the author of this work has been asserted in accordance with the Copyright, Designs and Patents Act 1988.

All rights reserved. No part of this book may be reproduced in any form or by any electronic or mechanical means, including information storage and retrieval systems, without written permission from the author, except for the use of brief quotations in a book review.

This book is a work of fiction and, except in the case of historical fact, any resemblance to actual persons, living or dead, is purely coincidental.

Every effort has been made to obtain the necessary permissions with reference to copyright material, both illustrative and quoted. We apologise for any omissions in this respect and will be pleased to make the appropriate acknowledgements in any future edition.

A CIP catalogue record for this book is available from the British Library.

Paperback ISBN 978-1-80048-359-0

Large Print ISBN 978-1-80048-348-4

Hardback ISBN 978-1-80280-205-4

Ebook ISBN 978-1-80048-362-0

Kindle ISBN 978-1-80048-361-3

Audio CD ISBN 978-1-80048-354-5

MP3 CD ISBN 978-1-80048-355-2

Digital audio download ISBN 978-1-80048-358-3

Boldwood Books Ltd
23 Bowerdean Street
London SW6 3TN
www.boldwoodbooks.com

*For my sister, Alex, and my brother, Tim.*

# 1

There was nothing Flora loved more than a good wine atlas. Well, apart from an actual glass of the stuff, obviously, but when it came to studying the subject of wine, she could get lost in a book of maps for hours. And given the current state of the wine shop – not a single customer in sight – she did indeed have all the time in the world to pore over the contours of the hills of the Côte-d'Or or get lost, on paper at least, in the vineyards of Piedmont.

The sound of the bell signalling the door opening made her jump. She quickly closed her book and shoved it under the counter.

'Hello, Flora!'

'Oh, hi, Colin.' Flora's heart sank a little; then she immediately felt guilty. Colin was a very sweet man, always dressed in matching jumper and trousers, sometimes mustard from head to toe, sometimes red, sometimes blue but never mixed. He was a regular in the shop, visiting perhaps twice a week, each time to pick a bottle of wine. But choosing that one bottle involved a lengthy chat, and much of that was Colin telling Flora how much he knew about wine rather than an actual conversation. Flora thought maybe he was just a bit lonely, and if coming in to talk wine to her meant that he wasn't, just for a short while, then she was happy to help. Even if her mind often wandered over to her mental to-do list as she listened.

'How are we today, Flora?' Colin beamed at her, brushing down the front of his – today, light blue – jumper over his round tummy.

'Very well, thank you, Colin. So what are you in the mood for, wine-wise? What's on the menu tonight?' That was the other thing with Colin: he knew *everything* about cooking, and would recount in detail how each element of the dish was sourced, then cooked.

'Tonight I'm pushing the boat out, Flora. Tonight,' he paused for dramatic effect, 'I'm making pie-yay-yah.'

Flora looked at him quizzically before remembering that he took on the country of origin's pronunciation of words for added effect. 'Ah, paella! How delicious...'

'Exactly, how delicious. And let me tell you the secret of a great pie-yay-yah.' Another pause.

Flora racked her brains. 'The saffron?'

'Oh, no, my dear. The ingredients are the easy part. The secret is in the *socarrat*.'

'Carrots in paella?' Flora thought back to the last time she'd eaten paella, ready-made and hastily heated up from Marks & Spencer. She didn't remember it having carrots.

'No, not carrots. So-kah-raht. It's the lightly toasted rice at the bottom of the pan. It sort of caramelises and goes crunchy. And there are certain ways of getting the crust.' He looked at her over the counter. 'Shall I tell you the best way?'

Just then the doorbell went again. Saved by the bell, thought Flora. 'Mack, you're back!' She greeted him a little too enthusiastically. 'I'm so sorry, Colin, I'm going to have to go. But I'm sure Mack would love to know your paella secret.'

'Your what?' Mack hung his coat up on the wall behind the counter and turned to face them both. His thick white hair stood up at crazy angles, half-moon glasses perched on his nose with bright blue eyes twinkling behind them.

'Pie-yay-yah. It's what I'm making tonight, Mack.'

'Seafood or traditional recipe?' Mack fixed Colin with a stare over the top of his glasses.

'Er, seafood.' Colin was suddenly a little less verbose.

'Well then, you'll be needing a bottle of this to go with it.' Mack walked across the shop to a shelf on the other side and reached down for a bottle. He turned and held it up.

'Rosé? Really? I'm not sure I…' Colin took the bottle. 'What is it?'

'Spanish Garnacha, from Navarra. Just the right balance of fruit and freshness, not so heavy that it'll drown out the flavours in the dish, but with enough weight to match it. Made by a lovely producer – he farms organically and makes the best paella I've ever eaten.' Mack walked back over to the counter.

Colin studied the bottle. 'Well, if you say it's worth trying, I'll give it a go. I'm not really a rosé man, to be honest, but…'

Flora busied herself stuffing her books into her canvas tote bag and picking up her handbag. 'Mack, if you don't mind I've got to run.'

'Yes, of course, Flora. I'll see you tomorrow.' Mack started wrapping the bottle in tissue paper for Colin.

'How did it go?' Flora asked Mack quietly as she passed.

'I'll tell you in the morning. See you then.' He smiled at her, clearly trying his best to make her think there was nothing to worry about.

'Thank you kindly, sir.' Colin took the bottle from Mack. 'Bye, Flora, see you next week.'

'Yes, and you can tell me how the paella went. And what you thought of the wine...' She smiled at him. No doubt Colin would be an expert on rosé by then.

* * *

'Is that you, Flora?'

'Hi, Mum.' Her mother, Kate, looked up from Flora's sofa, the floor of the small sitting room covered in books and toys. With her flowing red skirt and multicoloured cardigan, she looked like a fabric rainbow.

'Oh, darling, you do look tired.'

'Wow, thank you...' So soon, thought Flora. Her mother usually left it at least a couple of minutes before getting a dig in. Flora had been up late the night before, studying. Again.

'Sorry, darling, I just mean... I worry about you taking on too much. What with the shop and everything.'

Flora suspected what really bothered her mother was the fact that she worked in a shop. 'Mum, how many times do I have to explain? Having a job that fits in, most of the time, with school hours is a godsend. It's not like I have to commute for miles and I'm not stuck in an office for hours on end. Not to mention that I'm doing something I really love.'

'But, darling, don't forget the children need you, too.'

'Oh, Mum, please don't do this now. I'm there for them *most of the time*. And Johnny is really supportive, so I don't see what the problem is.' Flora knew that one mention of Johnny and her mother would zip it. Kate adored Johnny. 'Anyway, thank you for picking the kids up. Normally, they'd go to Tilda's after school today, but one of hers is sick.' Tilda had been one of the first friends Flora had made when they'd moved to the area. She lived five minutes away and, with both of them working and having children roughly the same age, they helped each other out as much as they could.

'Oh, anytime. You know I love seeing them.'

'Where are they, anyway?' Flora looked out through the French windows into the garden but there was no sign of the children. She suddenly clocked how quiet it was.

'Upstairs, I think. They went to go and clean something.'

As if on cue, water started to slowly drip from the corner of the ceiling onto the cushion next to Kate.

Flora looked up. 'Oh my God! What have they...?' She was halfway up the stairs by the time Kate stood up.

Flora ran into the bathroom to find water overflowing from the sink, cascading onto the old wooden floorboards and pooling in the corner by the bath. 'Pip! Tom!' Flora shrieked, feeling both relief that they were clearly fine and fury that they'd been up to no good. She turned the taps off and threw as many towels as she could get her hands on onto the floor.

'We're in here!' Pip called. Flora raced to Pip's room to find her sitting in her wigwam with Tom, their faces lit up by the light of a screen.

'Where did you find the iPad? You know you're not supposed to help yourselves. And what *have* you done in the bathroom?'

Pip looked horrified. 'Oh, Mum, I'm so sorry. We were trying to clean Tom's comic. He'd drawn on it and wanted to rub the pen off. So we tried to wash it but it wouldn't come off so we... we... then it started to fall apart in the sink...'

Tom stood up. 'But it's OK, Mama, because Granny gave us this to watch instead.' He held out the iPad. 'I'm really sorry.' Tom swiped his blond hair with his other hand, his enormous brown eyes looking up at her.

'Oh, for God's sake… well, that was clearly a stupid thing to do, to wash paper in the sink. Come on, Pip. You should know better.'

'I'm really sorry, Mum. I'll go and clear it up.' Pip looked up at her mother, her brown eyes peering through her thick dark fringe.

'No, I'd rather you went downstairs and helped tidy up, and we'll say goodbye to Granny, too.'

Kate appeared at the door. 'Well now, you two. What were you doing up here?'

Flora bit her bottom lip. She was so cross, but she knew it wouldn't end well if she reminded her mother that the time to really worry was when the kids were quiet for too long.

'Oh, you little monkeys, I told you not to let Mummy see you with the iPad! It was supposed to be our secret!' Kate winked at them.

Flora thought she might actually taste blood if she bit her lip any harder. She took a deep breath. 'Mum, it's OK. You go. I'm going to clear up the bathroom. The kids can help me.'

'Are you sure? I'd probably just be in the way. I'll get going, then. Let me know when you next need me to step in…'

Flora resisted rolling her eyes. 'OK, thanks, Mum. I will.'

'Bye, darlings!' Kate blew kisses to Tom first, then Pip. They both waved back and thanked her in unison. 'I'll let myself out.'

'Bye.' Flora sighed. She looked back at the children. 'Right, let's sort this mess out.'

* * *

'Flo, wake up, my love.' Johnny tried to wake her without giving her a fright, by gently prodding her arm.

Flora was at the kitchen table, her face flat against the

foothills of the Andes on the pages showing maps of Argentina's vineyards. She opened her eyes, adjusting to the light. She wiped at her mouth and sat up, blinking. 'What time is it? I must have...'

'It's just past ten. I'm so sorry I'm so late. Trains were a nightmare tonight.' Johnny looked down at her, his tie loose at his neck, his face pale with tiredness.

Flora rubbed at her eyes then stretched her arms out wide before wrapping them around Johnny's waist. 'There's some leftover chicken pie in the oven, if you're hungry?'

'Ooh, yes, please. Have we got any baked beans?'

'I'm sure we have.' Flora held on to him for a moment before letting him go, taking in the warmth and smell of his skin through his shirt.

He ruffled her long brown hair. 'Thank you. How's it going?' He walked over to the oven and peered inside.

'What, this?' Flora looked down at the pile of books, the files of work and stack of notebooks. She sighed, pulling her hair back and tying it into a messy bun on top of her head. 'Sometimes I worry that I'm doing all of this work and when it gets to the exams, I'm not going to remember a thing. I can barely remember where I left a cup of tea half the time, let alone what Burgundy's best Chardonnay clone is.'

'Chardonnay what?' Johnny grabbed a tin from the cupboard.

'Oh, don't worry, it's very boring, really. Unless you own a vineyard in Burgundy, of course. Anyway, Mack had his meeting with the bank today.'

'How did it go?'

'I don't know yet. Colin was in the shop...'

'Colin's always in the shop.'

'Yes, but unfortunately we cannot run on his custom alone. He only buys a bottle a week, two at a push.'

'Shame.'

'Tell me about it. Anyway, we couldn't really talk so Mack said he'd fill me in tomorrow. Honestly, I think he's hanging on by a thread. I've told him to let me go, that he doesn't really need me, but he won't.'

'He knows how much you love that job, that's why. And it wouldn't be much fun sitting in an empty wine shop all day on your own, would it?'

'I know, but still. I do feel we're nearing the end of this happy arrangement. And that makes me really sad.' Flora sighed. She closed her makeshift pillow and piled it up with the other books.

'Well, see what he says tomorrow. There's nothing you can do about it now. You need sleep. Go on, go to bed and I'll be in as soon as I'm done here.' Johnny poured a glass of water and passed it over to her. 'Here.'

'Thank you.' Slowly, she got up and started climbing the stairs.

Johnny waited until she was gone. He let out a long breath. He'd meant to tell her as soon as he came in. All the way home on the train he'd been planning how to break it to her. But telling her he'd just been made redundant face to face wasn't nearly as straightforward as he'd imagined.

# 2

Flora hadn't ever actually planned to get into wine in a serious way. It had all happened rather by accident. She'd spent the first five years of her working life in advertising with a number of large London firms. She'd loved the pace and glamour of it at first – she'd once flown to New York *for lunch* – but after a while something began to gnaw away at her, a sense that what she was doing didn't really matter, at least not to her. Around that time, she'd met Johnny. He was a friend of a friend and they'd met at a party, both taking refuge in the kitchen to get away from the karaoke in the other room. Flora had not long extricated herself from a long-term relationship with someone from work – her boss, in fact, not the smartest move she'd ever made – and getting into another relationship definitely wasn't the plan.

But then meeting Johnny wasn't in her plan either. Previous boyfriends included a musician (disaster) and a before-he-was-famous actor (also a disaster). Johnny just seemed so uncomplicated compared to her usual 'type', and as the months passed he continued to pursue her with gentle persuasion rather than grand gestures. Before long her resolve to stay single for a while was forgotten and Flora had never been happier. Everything was perfect, in fact, except for her job, which, by now, she hated.

It was Johnny who suggested one evening over noodles at their favourite local restaurant that she might look at evening courses at a local college.

'To do what?' Flora spoke through a mouthful.

'Well, that's the point. They're bound to offer all sorts of courses. It might lead you to something you've never even thought of.' Johnny took a sip from his bottle of beer. 'Look, you've been doing this job for how long?'

'Too long. Feels like a lifetime.'

'Exactly. Come on, you need to find something you really love doing and now's the time to start doing it. What do you think?' He looked genuinely excited. The fact that he was so invested in her happiness slightly threw her, in a good way. Previous boyfriends had all been far more interested in themselves to worry about a girlfriend's growing existential crisis.

'Fine, I'll have a look online tomorrow, I promise.'

Of course, Flora hadn't looked the next day, or that week, and before long months had gone by and she still hadn't done anything about it. She was ridiculously busy at work, but with every day that passed she felt more nauseous about going in. She and Johnny were still hopping between each other's flats, which suited them both. It seemed too soon to have the 'shall we move in together' chat; it had been barely six months since they'd met.

So no one was more surprised than Flora when she realised she was pregnant. That growing sick feeling in her stomach hadn't been about the job at all, it had been the work of a very tiny human growing inside her. At first she'd put off finding out for sure, not wanting to see it in black and white, or rather in blue lines on a stick. But after a week or so of knowing in her bones that she was almost certainly pregnant she took a test and called Johnny.

'Is everything OK? You sound... a bit weird.' She could picture his face, a frown on his forehead.

'Yes, I'm fine. But I need to talk to you. Like, now.'

'Are you... are we...?'

'Johnny, please can you just come?'

'On my way.'

Twenty minutes later they sat in Flora's flat, looking down at the pregnancy test in front of them.

'Johnny, I'm so sorry...'

'Hang on, what do you mean? I think you'll find I had something to do with this, too. Why are you apologising?'

'I know, I just thought... anyway, whatever. What do we do now?' She looked at him, his eyes still fixed on the thick blue line. He closed them for a second then slowly turned to face her.

'I want you to marry me.'

'What?' Flora stared at him in disbelief. 'Are you *serious*?'

Johnny's blue eyes sparkled. 'Well, I've never proposed before but I'm pretty sure it's not something you ask for fun.' He took her hands in his. 'Flora, I'm sure this might not be quite what you had in mind but I'm being absolutely serious. In fact, I don't think I've ever been so sure of anything in my life. I love you, Flo.'

'I... I...' Flora wasn't sure which was more surprising: finding out she was pregnant or being proposed to. 'Johnny, I don't know what to say. I just didn't think I'd be having a baby quite yet. I thought I'd be in my thirties, not my twenties.'

'But that's the thing. The plan is ours to make together.' He tilted her face to his with his hand under her chin. 'Come on, what do you reckon? Are you up for it?' A wide grin spread across his face, so wide it made his eyes crinkle at the edges.

Flora swallowed hard. 'I'm in.'

'Is that a yes?' He laughed, springing up from the sofa.

'Yes, it's a yes!' Flora stood up to meet him and he picked her up, twirling her around before falling back gently onto the sofa, both of them lost in tears and kisses.

* * *

Telling friends had been a doddle. Informing their parents, on the other hand, had been slightly more painful, at least for Flora. Her parents had met and married when they were young, barely a penny between them, as Kate often liked to remind Flora and her brother, Billy. And even though they were so different – or maybe because they were – the marriage had always been a happy one, as far as Flora knew. She couldn't help but feel she had a lot to live up to.

Her father had been delighted. Kate, on the other hand, had been all smiles but Flora could sense her disappointment. This was not how Kate had imagined this moment *at all*.

'So, where will you live? I mean, you can't bring up a baby in your tiny flat, can you?' Kate asked Flora.

'Well, we'll have to for a while. I'm going to move into John-ny's flat and sell mine. We're thinking of trying to find somewhere with a bit more space, a small garden, perhaps. But not yet.' Flora tried to sound as upbeat as possible, ignoring the look on her mother's face.

'What about work?' Kate probed further.

'Actually, Mum, I've been thinking about changing career anyway...'

'Since when?' Kate's mouth dropped open.

'Darling, we didn't know you were unhappy.' Her father was clearly concerned.

'I'm not. It's just, well, I'm really not exactly loving the advertising business any more so I'm going to explore other options, that's all.'

'And have a baby. And get married. I'm not sure it's the right time to take stock, do you, Robin?' Kate turned to her husband.

'Mum, it's exactly the right time. For me, I mean. Please, just trust me... us,' Flora looked at Johnny, 'to work it out.'

'Of course we will.' Her father looked at her mother. Kate's mouth was open like a goldfish's. He turned back and smiled at them. 'Now, shall we open something to celebrate?'

'That would be great, thank you, Robin.' Johnny looked back at Kate. 'We'll make it work, I promise.'

Kate sighed. 'Well, I certainly hope so.'

'Flora, come and help me choose something from the garage. I'm sure I've got a decent bottle stuffed away in there somewhere.' Her father gestured for her to join him. Grateful for the chance to escape before she said anything she shouldn't to her mother, Flora followed.

Robin put his arm around his daughter as they made their way outside. 'Don't worry about Mum. She'll come round eventually. It's just a bit of a shock, that's all. Two big bits of news at once and we've only just met Johnny. Not that that matters – he's wonderful, Flora. You seem very happy together.'

'Dad, we really are. And I'm sorry it's not quite how you imagined things to happen, but I am *really* happy. Apart from the job, but I guess you can't have everything.'

'So what else do you think you might want to do?'

'Honestly, I haven't a clue. What about this one?' Flora pulled a bottle from wine rack and held it up. 'Ooh... Crémant. This'll do nicely.'

'Darling, I don't even know what that is. Or where it came from. Let me have a look.' He took the bottle from her.

'It's not cold but stick it in the freezer for ten minutes and it'll be fine to toast with. Not that I can go anywhere near it. The smell of wine makes me want to throw up at the moment.'

'That's it! Wine!' His face lit up.

'What do you mean?' Flora was confused.

'Why don't you do a proper wine course? An evening course, perhaps. You've always been interested in what's on the table. I never really know, to be honest. I just like drinking it.' He chuckled, passing her back the bottle. 'Come on, tell me more about this one.'

'Well,' she looked at the label, 'it's from Burgundy, look here... Crémant de Bourgogne.' She pointed at the words. 'So, basically, it's made in the same way as champagne but from a different area. I've no idea how old it is because it's non-vintage, but there's only one way to find out if it's any good...'

'You see? You're a natural!'

'Oh, come on, I went to a wine tasting, like, once. And that was with work. Everyone just got pissed, including me.'

'Yes, but you're interested in it. Always have been, really. Didn't you join the Wine Society at university?'

'Yes, but that's because it was the cheapest way to get four half-glasses of wine on a Thursday night.'

'Well, it's just a thought.' He looked at her, an eyebrow raised.

Later that evening, when they got back to Johnny's flat, Flora curled up on the bed in her pyjamas and opened her laptop. Indeed, it was just a thought but it was a good one. She typed *wine courses near me* into the search bar.

'Hey, Johnny, there's one not far from here I could do, one evening a week, and then there's a test at the end.'

'So you'd get like a proper certificate?' He came in from the bathroom, toothbrush in hand.

'Yes, it's just the most basic certificate, but it's a start and it says it's a great introduction for anyone thinking of making a career out of wine.'

'Sign up before you change your mind. I think it's a brilliant idea. I'll never have to worry about looking like an idiot with the wine list again.'

Flora was so used to the cold blanket of dread covering her on a Sunday night ahead of going back to work, but now she realised that for the first time for years it just wasn't there. In fact, for a moment she was excited at the prospect of what might just lie ahead. Then she caught herself.

'Hang on, Johnny. Am I being completely stupid? I don't mean getting married, obviously. Or having a baby. But throwing in a career change at the same time? *Really?*'

'Look, if you don't do it now you might never do it. There's nothing stopping you. Now go on, put your name down before you change your mind.'

Flora looked back at the screen, the cursor blinking on the page, and typed in her name.

## 3

Mack was not in sight when Flora got to the shop the next day, although the smell of freshly made coffee gave away his presence.

'Good morning, Mack,' Flora called out.

'Hello, Flora. With you in a minute.' He was in the stockroom; at least, that's what they called it. Basically, it was a room at the back, stuffed from floor to ceiling with boxes and wooden crates. Flora had tried to install some sort of stock-rotation system, but with so little room, Mack hadn't seemed to notice.

The shop sat on the high street in a small market town. It occupied a two-storey whitewashed brick building with a green awning hanging over two windows at the front, the name of the shop, Ten Green Bottles, in thick white lettering across it. Inside, the room was narrow but long, with exposed brick walls and old wooden floorboards giving the space a wonderful cellar-type feel. Thick dark wood shelves, built by Mack himself back when he first opened the shop in the early 1980s, were loaded with wines. It looked like a mad sweet shop for grown-ups. In the early days he'd enjoyed roaring trade with a long list of loyal customers, both private and in the restaurant trade, keeping the business hearty and healthy. Mack had even opened a bar at the back of the shop in the tiny courtyard garden for a while. But then the recession hit and, to make matters worse, a supermarket opened up smack bang opposite the shop, on the sunnier side of the street. It wasn't a huge supermarket, more 'express' size, but Mack struggled to compete with their prices.

For years now the shop had limped on, barely covering its costs, but Mack loved his customers and did everything he could to keep them happy. He held monthly wine tastings in the shop, his clients perched on wooden boxes, trying his latest finds from tiny producers in France, Italy, Spain or some remote region further afield that it was unlikely anyone had heard of. He'd always had help in the shop, not least because he needed someone to run the place when he was out making deliveries. But more than that, it was for the company. He'd lived on his own since his wife, Elizabeth, had died, almost ten years ago. They'd been together for over forty years and he'd adored her. The irony was she hadn't even liked wine that much.

Flora remembered Mack mentioning his son, just the once, when she'd asked him one day if he had any children.

'We did. But he died too, sadly.' He'd not offered any more than that, not even a name. Flora sensed from this response that it wasn't something Mack wished to talk about and she'd quickly changed the subject.

'Ah, there you are.' Mack emerged from the back, glasses askew. 'I know I've got some Château Palmer '85 back there somewhere, I just can't for the life of me remember where I put it. Old Mr Peters called yesterday asking if we had any; wants it for a birthday present.'

'Yes, you have, and I think I know exactly where it is. Let me go... I'll just put this stuff down.' Flora shrugged off her coat and went to put her bag on the shelf below the counter.

'No books today?' Mack had got used to Flora carting the heavy tote bag with her everywhere she went.

'Not today, Mack. I've got to the point where I feel like every time I learn one thing, I forget another. So, I'm giving it a break for a bit.' The truth was she knew that she and Mack would need to have a proper talk about the future of the shop, and she was fully expecting to be sent home today with an apology that her job was no longer viable. And as much as that saddened her, the thought of Mack losing his shop broke her heart even more. She'd wanted to talk to Johnny about it before he left for work but he was up and gone by the time she'd woken up that morning.

'Coffee? I've just made it.' Mack poured out two cups and handed one to her.

'Thank you. So, how did yesterday go?'

'At the bank?' Mack took a long sip of his coffee. 'Not great.'

'Oh, Mack, I'm so sorry. What did they say?'

'I can't get another loan, I'm afraid. They said they've done all they can. I'm going to have to sell the lease, possibly the building.'

'But where will you live?' Flora immediately thought of Mack's flat upstairs. It was remarkably similar to the shop, just with books rather than wine lining the walls and piled up in every corner. She couldn't bear the thought of Mack losing his home.

'I'm not sure yet. I hadn't really thought about it. But the shop's going to have to go. I've tried, but it's just not making enough to keep trading. Not by a long way, I'm afraid.'

'I'm so sorry. That's awful. I don't know what to say.' Flora reached across and put her hand gently on his arm. Mack looked at her, his face softening with a smile.

'Honestly, I knew it was coming. Has been for a while, but I had just hoped that we'd have enough business to keep us ticking over. Technically, I should have retired long ago but, to be honest,

I wouldn't know what else to do.' He looked around the shop. 'I built this place, but you know what? It's only bricks. And bottles. All good things, as they say.'

'There must be something we can do, Mack. How about a proper marketing campaign? We could start online wine courses or pop-up tastings? Or, I don't know… how about running a mini wine festival?' Flora was speaking quickly, wishing she'd pushed him harder to consider these ideas long before now. She had tried in the past, but he'd always insisted they were fine as they were.

'You're kind, Flora, but really, it's too late. I've already been to the estate agent's at the bottom of the high street. They're coming to have a look at the place later. I really am so sorry, but let me know if there is anything I can do in terms of a reference for another job. And I'll pay you for another month's work.'

'You don't have to do that, Mack. I know you've done what you can. This must be so very hard for you.' Flora felt desperately sad.

'Thank you. I just wish it didn't have to be this way.' Mack looked at her, his eyes glinting with tears. 'Now, did you say you knew where that bottle of Palmer was? Mr Peters will be here to pick it up soon.'

\* \* \*

'Glass of wine?' Flora grabbed two glasses from the dresser and put them on the table. 'Sorry about the mess.'

'I can't believe you're apologising for the mess. Have you *seen* my house?' Tilda laughed as she picked up the empty beakers from the table. 'Yes, please… Thanks for feeding them today; you didn't have to do that.'

'Pleasure. I owe you anyway.' Flora put the glasses on the table, unscrewed the wine and poured a generous measure into each. From the garden, the squeals of the children reached them as they flipped and flung themselves at each other on the trampoline. 'Please be careful! You've only just finished eating!' Flora called across to them, only to be completely ignored. 'Cheers!' She raised her glass to her friend's.

'Cheers, happy Friday.' Tilda took a long sip. 'God, that's good. What is it?'

'Pinot Gris from New Zealand... a bit like Pinot Grigio but with more meat on its bones. You like?'

'I like. Very much, actually. So, when's the exam?'

'Exams. Plural.' Flora looked at her glass. 'In a couple of months, and that's just the first lot. I've got to do another load of exams next year, too.'

'So, is this like a diploma?'

'Exactly. God knows what I was thinking when I decided to do it.' Flora absent-mindedly swirled her glass as she spoke. 'I think I might have been temporarily deranged.'

'Oh, come on. If you're going to take exams, at least you're doing ones where you get to drink wine.'

'I know, I know. I really shouldn't complain.'

It had all started with that evening course. Flora had turned up thinking that if she just did a few classes it would get it out of her system before going back to her old job and that would be that. Instead, before the end of that first evening, she knew she'd found something she loved. And it wasn't just about whatever wine was in the glass. She fell in love with everything about it, from the people who made the wine, the place it was from, the culture surrounding it, the combination of tradition and innovation, the assault on the senses... all captured in that glass. The whole thing absolutely fascinated her.

Within a few months she'd completed the evening course – gaining her first official wine qualification – and promptly signed up to do the next level before she changed her mind. Shortly after

Pip had been born and when her bosses at work had refused her request for a part-time role, she'd resigned, switching instead to earning a modest income from copywriting through old work contacts. Meanwhile, Johnny was making good money from his job, enough for them to sell his flat, move out of the city and buy a small house in a quiet seaside village on the south coast. It was a small Victorian red-brick house set back from the road, reached by a gravel track, and had – as the estate agent put it – lots of potential. Of course, they'd had grand plans when they'd first arrived, of knocking down walls and creating an open-plan, modern living space. But apart from giving the whole place a lick of paint, the house was still pretty much as it had been when they'd first moved in. Still, as Flora often reminded herself, one spent more time in a house looking out than the other way round. And the views from the inside out were quite spectacular, the small garden backing onto fields with woodland behind. Best of all, the beach was a five-minute walk away, miles of shingle over-looking the Solent and the Isle of Wight beyond that.

As soon as Pip had started nursery Flora had gone back to studying wine part-time from home, gaining a further two certificates along with another baby in between. By now she was itching to get back to something other than churning out copy for advertorials found in the back of magazines. So it was she found herself sitting in Mack's shop one day with her two-year-old son Tom asleep in the buggy, begging him to give her a job.

'But what about this wee fella?' Mack pointed at the boy, cheeks flushed hot with sleep.

'I've got a place for him at nursery starting next term so I'd be free three days a week to come and work for you.'

She'd been so eager, Mack hadn't the heart to say no. A month later, Flora started working in the shop. She'd been able to keep up her studies, signing up for the wine diploma that she was now almost halfway through, and thinking that she just might have bitten off more than she could chew.

'You love doing this stuff really. Your mind would turn to mush without it.' Tilda shrugged, her glass waving in the air.

'I know, you're right. Anyway, how's your work going?' Flora emptied a couple of packets of teddy bear-shaped crisps into a bowl. 'Sorry, it's all I can find.'

'Well, being a doctor's receptionist isn't exactly the most taxing job in the world but at least I know exactly who's on Viagra in this small town.'

Flora's eyes widened. 'Really?'

'Oh, you'd be amazed. They might look old but, my goodness, there are plenty of them still having a lot of fun. Must be all that sea air. And I'm a pro at finding out who's doing what with whom.'

Flora laughed out loud. 'Really? What do you mean?'

'Well, it started when someone came into the surgery claiming he'd no idea where he'd picked up a particular, er, ailment. But a few quick searches and I found pictures of him on Facebook with someone who definitely wasn't his wife. Let's just leave it at that.' Tilda winked at her friend and took another sip of her wine. 'How's the shop?'

Flora sighed. 'Not so good, actually. Mack's got to sell.'

'Seriously? Oh, that's so sad.' Tilda's face fell. 'Why?'

'It's been on the cards for a while but I just thought, you know, he's managed to keep it going all these years, I'm sure he'll think of something. But it turns out trade is just too slow. He's done.'

'What will you do? I mean, do you think it might stay as a wine shop?'

'I've no idea. If he can't make it work – and he's been there forever – then I'm not sure anyone can.'

'Rubbish! It's not enough to just sit there with a shop and

expect people to come to you these days. You've got to go out and find them!' Tilda was adamant.

'I know, I've been through all this with Mack, but he doesn't want to try. It's his shop and, well, he says he's done with it.'

'What about Johnny – can't he help with setting up an online shop or whatever? I mean, he does that kind of thing at work, doesn't he?'

Flora shrugged. Johnny did work in IT but she had never been entirely sure what he did *exactly*. Selling software packages, she knew that much.

'Actually, Johnny doesn't know yet. I only found out this morning and he hasn't picked up my calls all day. I know he's been really busy at work. I even tried his direct number today. He was in meetings for most of the day, apparently.' Flora topped up their glasses. She gave hers another swill, sticking her nose in to savour the aroma, all limes and nectarines.

'Just this, then I must go.' Tilda turned to the open window. 'Kids, five minutes, OK?' They all stopped and turned for a split second before resuming their bouncing. 'Well, whatever happens, here's to Pinot Gris. I think it's my new favourite.'

Flora clinked Tilda's glass. 'You always say that.'

**4**

———————

Mack sat back in his chair, a well-thumbed copy of *Great Expectations* in his hand. He'd picked it up from a stack of books on the side in an attempt to take his mind off the situation, even for just a few moments. But it hadn't worked. He sighed and reached for his glass, taking a long sniff. The smell of old leather and spice filled his nose.

The wine inside was brick red in colour, an Australian Shiraz at least twenty years old. Instantly, the aromas in the glass took him back to the time when he'd arrived in London from Australia looking for work. He'd walked into a pub to ask for a job. The pub was practically empty save for the landlord and a couple of regulars propping up the bar, but before long Mack was running it, turning the place from a beer-soaked boozer into a heaving wine bar serving wines from all over the world. His bestselling wine was an Australian Shiraz, which was something of a novelty back then. Soon one bar became three, then five across the city before he sold the business and 'retired' to the south coast with his wife, Elizabeth, and their young son, Jamie, who'd just turned twelve.

He hadn't intended to open a wine shop but there wasn't one

nearby, so for mainly selfish reasons Ten Green Bottles was opened on the site of an old antiques shop in a listed building at the top of the town. Mack's neighbours included a bakery on one side and a hardware shop on the other.

He had renovated the space, stripping the plaster from the walls, taking them back to the original brickwork and crafting shelves from locally sourced oak. He and Elizabeth had also set about turning the dingy flat upstairs into a home for the three of them. She'd made curtains, cleaned carpets, cleared cupboards and painted furniture, transforming it into something quite charming.

Soon the shelves in the shop were stacked with wines. Now all Mack needed were some customers. But London was very different from this small seaside town; barely a dozen people came through the door in the first few weeks.

'How about we throw a free wine tasting so people can see what you're all about?' Elizabeth suggested. The next day Mack placed an advert in the local paper, Elizabeth ran up some bunting to decorate the courtyard garden and Jamie posted flyers through the door of every shop and house the length of the high street and beyond.

The day of the tasting arrived and Mack had opened fifty different bottles, wines from all over the world, lined up on tables for people to try for themselves. Plates of bruschetta and crudités sat on side tables dotted around the courtyard, assembled by them both early that morning.

The sun shone brightly in a cloudless blue sky above. But still no one came.

'Where *is* everyone? What's wrong with these people? I'm offering them free wine!' Mack was exasperated.

Elizabeth sprang up from her chair. 'If they won't come to us, let's take it to them. Instead of sitting out here at the back where no one can see us, why don't we set up the tables at the front of the shop instead? Jamie, run and get some paper cups from next door. Then we can give them a taste. That'll get them in.'

By the middle of the afternoon the courtyard was rammed. Mack was in his element, pouring wines for people, telling them stories about the winemakers and places the wines had come from. He asked what sort of style they liked and found them new things to try. Elizabeth scribbled orders and took down customers' details in a big black book. Jamie had positioned the old stereo upstairs by the window at the back and as the afternoon went on, the sounds from Mack's jazz record collection floated down across the courtyard.

By the time the last customer left, it was almost dark. 'Thank you, my darling,' Mack called across to Elizabeth as they both cleared plates from tables strewn with empty bottles and dirty glasses. 'If it wasn't for you, I'd still be waiting for people to walk through the door.'

'They just needed a bit of persuading, that's all.' Elizabeth smiled. 'I spoke to quite a few who said they didn't really drink wine. But then they tried something they hadn't tried before and loved it.'

'Exactly! That's the thing... People seem to think it's all crusty clarets and expensive Burgundy. But wine should be for anyone who wants to try it, not just for those with money. I think we're on to something, Elizabeth.'

'Mack, if you can pass on just a drop of your enthusiasm for the stuff then, yes, I think you're on to something.'

'I said *we*, Elizabeth; you and Jamie, too. That was a team effort today. Thank you.'

'Come on, let's get this place tidied up. You need this place shipshape and ready for business on Monday morning. Where's

Jamie? Jamie!' She called up to the window, music still playing softly through it.

Jamie stuck his head out. 'I'm here!'

'Right, you, time for bed. It's getting late and you look exhausted.' Elizabeth playfully shooed him away with her hand.

'But, Mum...'

'Go on, off you go. I'll be up in a minute.' She turned to go inside, balancing plates in both hands. 'Mack, grab the empty boxes and we can make a start on the bottles.'

He watched her as she went inside, wondering what on earth he'd ever done to deserve her.

The sound of the book hitting the floor as it slipped out of his hand woke Mack with a start. He looked across at the clock on the wall, squinting to see it in the low light. It was almost two in the morning. Slowly, the events of the last couple of days came back to him: the meeting with his bank manager, where he'd broken the news to Mack that there was nothing more they could do to help.

The money side had never been his strong point – Elizabeth had done the books when the business had been running at full strength – but he'd always found a way to muddle through until now. This time, though, it really did look like it was time to concede defeat to the realities of running a small independent business on a once-busy, now often-deserted high street. Compounded in no small way by the seemingly endless string of cut-price deals on wine from the supermarket on the other side of the road.

He reached for the picture beside him, of Elizabeth and Jamie, taken years before on the beach not far from there. It had been their favourite spot, a small patch of sand on a pebble beach, tucked between two old wooden groynes. They'd often headed there after the shop had shut in the summer months, with a picnic for their supper. After the obligatory swim – Jamie would insist, no matter how cold the water was – they would wrap themselves in towels and sit on the sand, eating still-warm sausage sandwiches straight from their tightly wrapped tinfoil packet.

Mack looked at the picture, the sounds of the sea in his ears. He missed them both so much. It often physically hurt to think about them but, at the same time, it was the thought of them that had kept him going. Knowing they'd have wanted him to stay, to do what he loved, to try to be happy. Thinking about it, Mack realised the shop had been his crutch for all these years, his reason to get up and get on with the day. It had given him a purpose when, really, there were times when he'd rather have not woken up at all.

'I'm so sorry, you two.' Their faces smiled back at him from the photo. The wind had whipped Elizabeth's hair across her face. Freckles dotted her nose and cheeks. Jamie was looking at his mother, laughing. His hair was thick and wild.

Mack carefully put the picture back, picked up his book from the floor and put it on the small table next to him. Lifting himself out of his chair, he slowly made his way to the kitchen to put his almost empty glass in the sink. Tomorrow he'd have to make a start on a stock count to see what could be sold off.

Flora had kindly offered to help Mack with whatever needed to be done to wrap up the business. She'd clearly been upset by the news but, at the same time, wanted to do whatever she could to help. He had to admit he saw something of himself in her, but it was more than just an interest in wine. It was a desire to make other people get as much joy from it as she did. To tell people about it, share the stories and spread the word on particular producers and wines she loved. He'd watched her at work in the shop. She asked questions, finding out what customers usually liked before making a few suggestions on other wines they might like to try. She remembered customers' names, faces, occasions and what they'd bought the last time they'd been in. And best of all, Mack saw that she understood the real power of wine: to bring people together. To celebrate life.

But as he lifted the last sip of red wine in his glass to his lips, he found he didn't want it. Instead, Mack poured it down the sink.

## 5

Flora lay in bed, eyes wide open and sleep seemingly far away. She could hear Johnny's breath, slow and heavy. The evening had been one of highs and lows. She'd decided to break the news to Johnny that she was out of a job over supper. Baked potatoes were in the oven and a hastily thrown together stew sat warming in a casserole dish on the hob. As she called out from the garden when Johnny got home, Flora could tell from his response that something was up. He appeared at the back door, his tie already off.

'What is it, Johnny?' Flora crossed to stand in front of him.

'Can we sit down? We need to talk.'

'Yes, of course... What's the matter?' Flora's stomach flipped. His eyes were dark, the familiar light behind them gone.

'Daddy!' Pip and Tom appeared in their pyjamas, each hugging a different side of their father.

'Hey, you two.' He ruffled their hair. 'Listen, I've just got to talk to Mummy for a moment.'

'But can you read me a story? Please, Daddy?' Tom looked up at Johnny, his face hopeful.

'Yes, I will. Just give me a few minutes and I'll be in. Go on, go and clean your teeth and get into bed.'

'I've already cleaned my teeth.' Tom showed Johnny his gleaming white milk teeth.

'So you have. Good job. OK, you too, Pip – go and choose a book and read for a bit and I'll be in soon.'

'But I'm nearly nine – can't I watch telly for a bit longer?' Pip looked at Flora. 'Mum, you said I could.'

'Yes, OK, go and watch some telly. We'll be in soon. Just give us a moment.' Flora ushered them towards the stairs.

'Promise?' Pip always required an extra level of reassurance.

'We promise, now go.' Johnny waited until they were out of sight. 'I... I'm so sorry, Flora.'

'What? Johnny, what is it?' Flora grabbed his hands.

'I've been made redundant. I found out yesterday, but I wanted to be sure of the details before I told you. I know you tried to call today but that's why I couldn't take your phone calls. I'm so sorry...'

'Oh God, what happened?'

Johnny lowered his eyes. 'The market just isn't there, I'm afraid. They've had to cut an entire department. Unfortunately, the one that's going is mine.'

'But I thought...'

He looked at her again, tears threatening to fall. 'To be honest, work hasn't been good for a while. I just didn't think the axe would fall quite so soon.'

'But you've been so busy. I thought the company was doing well.'

'We were. And now,' he shrugged, 'obviously, we're not.'

'So... what's the deal? How long have you got?' Flora tried to stop the thoughts flooding her head, urging them to form an orderly queue.

'Well, they've cut me a fair deal, I think. I've been there for quite a long time so the redundancy package isn't bad. I'll get six months' full pay.'

'And what about working your notice?'

'Today was my last day in the office.'

'Wow, that *was* quick. Can you try and get another job in the meantime?'

'Yes, but I can't work for a direct competitor. Which, right at this very moment, is something of a relief. I have to admit, the thought of going back into the same sort of job is just too depressing.'

'So, what are you saying? You don't want to go back into IT?'

'Yes... no...' Johnny looked at her. 'Flora, I don't know. To tell you the truth, being made redundant has made me realise that I really don't love what I do. At all, in fact.'

Flora felt sick. How could she tell him now that she, too, was about to lose her job?

'Daddy...' Tom appeared at the door, book in hand. 'Please can you read me a story now?'

Johnny looked at Flora, briefly wiping at the corner of his eye. 'Let me go and do this and I'll be back.'

'Are you sure? I'll just check the food. Wine?'

'Definitely.'

An hour later they sat at the kitchen table, empty plates and glasses in front of them. Flora had listened as Johnny told her the truth about the last year in his job. About endless meetings, increasingly long hours, the pressure not to be the one in the firing line. And now the whole department had gone anyway. His shoulders were heavy; he looked tired and drawn.

'Why didn't you tell me things were so bad?'

'Because I didn't want to worry you... and because I thought it would be OK in the end. Anyway, you had your hands full with everything going on, the kids. And I know how much you love working in the shop.'

'Actually,' Flora cleared her throat, 'I can't quite believe the timing of this but I've got some bad news on that front, I'm afraid.'

'Oh, no, what? Is Mack OK?'

'Yes, but he's got to close the shop. Trade has been really slow and we just can't compete. The bank said no to a loan, apparently. So he's got to close and he might even have to sell the building.'

Johnny looked even more bereft. 'But that's terrible. Is that why you've been calling me today?'

'Yes, but when you came home it didn't seem quite such a big deal. I mean, my job barely brings in enough to pay for our food, for goodness' sake.'

'Flora, it's not just about the money, it's about a job that you *loved*.' He got up and moved around the table, wrapping his arms around her shoulders.

'Shit, Johnny, what are we going to do? Will we lose the house?'

'Listen, we've got a roof over our heads. We've got two brilliant kids. And I've got six months' salary to tide us over. Things could be worse. A lot worse.'

'And we've got each other.' Flora squeezed his arms tight.

'Yes, my love.' He kissed the side of her cheek. 'We've got each other.'

'So there is one other thing I've got to tell you, and this might just push you over the edge...'

'Go on.'

'My parents are coming for lunch on Sunday.'

'Oh God, really?'

'I can put them off.'

'No, don't. I'll have to tell them sooner or later. I might as well get it over and done with.'

'Billy's coming, too – at least he said he was. I must ring and check. I'll call him tomorrow.'

'Brilliant, it'll be good to see him.' Johnny loved seeing Flora's younger brother. Billy could always be relied upon to liven up proceedings, particularly a Sunday lunch with the in-laws.

'You know they'll ask what we plan to do next.'

'I know, Flo.' Johnny sighed. 'We'll think of something.'

'OK, how about this...?' Flora picked up the bottle on the table, one of her favourite Italian reds, and refilled their glasses. The scent of tar and roses hit her as she lifted the glass to her lips. 'So, if you could do anything now, like change career completely, what would you do?'

Johnny sat back down opposite her, picking up his glass and looking thoughtful. He took a sip, without bothering to sniff, Flora noticed. 'You forgot to smell it first! What have I been telling you all this time? Sipping without sniffing is like looking at a picture with one eye closed. You're missing out on most of the fun.'

'I happen to think the fun part is drinking it, but whatever.' Johnny laughed. 'OK, if it makes you happy.' He lifted his glass and gave it a swirl. Wine went straight down the front of his shirt and he let out a laugh. 'Well, at least I don't need this one for work again anytime soon.'

But Flora was on a roll. 'Gently, Johnny. Swirl it like this...' She held the glass by the stem and moved her hand very slightly, making the wine in the glass move around in a small circular motion. 'Come on, you've done this before.'

Johnny did the same with what was left in his glass.

'Right, now sniff.'

Johnny took a long, loud sniff of his glass. His head shot up. 'Oh, wow, that's amazing. It smells of... what is that?'

'Mack gave it to me today, said to enjoy it before we tackle the stock count next week. It's a Barolo from a small family producer. Earthy but elegant with a whiff of roses, in my humble opinion.'

Johnny took another sip, this time taking a little longer over it. 'That's exactly it. You're good at this.' He grinned at her.

'Why, thank you. Now, as I was saying, if you could do anything, anything at all, what would it be?'

'Well, assuming you don't mean watching films, uninterrupted, whilst sitting on my luxury yacht, I think what I'd really like is to be my own boss. I just don't want to do the big company thing any more.'

'Fine. And say you are your own boss, what does your company do?'

'I don't really know. Except I know I don't want it to be software.' Johnny laughed a little. 'Definitely not software.'

'So...' Flora put her glass down on the table. 'How about we run a wine shop?'

Johnny put his glass down too. 'What, you mean Mack's shop?'

'Well, it's not going to be Mack's shop for much longer. Before we know it it'll probably be another Starbucks or whatever. Unless, that is...'

'We take on the lease?'

'Exactly! What do you think?'

'Well, for starters, I don't know anything about wine.'

'But that's the point: you can leave that bit to me. Your job could be to make sure the shop runs profitably. And with your experience, we can move the business online, too. Come on, Johnny, what have we got to lose? I've been longing to do it for ages, but now we're both out of a job, well, it's the perfect time.'

Johnny picked up his glass again, swirling the wine slowly. 'Hmm, I suppose you're right. We really don't have much to lose, although I'd have to look at Mack's numbers.'

'Actually, I'm not sure they'll help. But his experience will. He's so good at things like running tastings, and once I get my diploma I can start teaching wine courses.'

'I think you're on to something here. Hang on, I'll get the laptop. Let's have a look at what other online wine shops there are. Might pour myself a whisky for this bit. Want one?'

Flora shook her head. 'I'll stick with this.' She raised the half-glass of red in her hand.

Hours later, having filled a notepad with thoughts and ideas, they fell into bed. Johnny was asleep within minutes. Looking across at him, Flora felt terrible for not seeing how unhappy he'd been in his work. He'd always gently pushed her to pursue her wish to make a living through her love of wine. Was she now talking him into doing something just to keep him busy? Then again, he did seem genuinely excited at the prospect of taking a failing business and turning it into something successful – profitable, even.

Flora looked at the clock by the bed, the illuminated numbers telling her she had about four hours until Tom, an early riser even by a six-year-old's standards, would be by their bed asking if it was time for breakfast. An owl hooted in the woods, the sound clear in the quiet night. She closed her eyes and tried to calm her thoughts. Beside her, the numbers on the clock continued to climb.

# 6

Flora stood at the top of a small stepladder holding a string of lights, trying to loop an end over a branch of the birch in the garden.

'Why don't you let me do that?' Johnny called over from the back door. 'It's not even going to be dark when they're here – why do we need lights in the tree?'

'Because I want them up, at least... and anyway, Billy said he'd stay after Mum and Dad have gone so I thought we could sit out here.'

'Honestly, let me do that.'

'Actually, I've just got to finish laying the table. Pip and Tom can help me. Where are they, anyway?'

'Still in their pyjamas, last time I saw them.'

'What? Their grandparents will be here any minute and I don't want them thinking our kids don't get dressed before midday!'

'Well, they don't usually on a Sunday.'

'That's not the point! My mother will never let me forget it.

Right, I'm going to sort them out. Please can you finish doing the table?'

'Before or after I finish putting up the lights?'

'Johnny, please don't. I need your help here.'

He held his hand out to her as she climbed down the ladder. 'Flo, relax. It's only your parents, not a royal visit.'

'God, I know. It's just... I want them to see that we're fine, you know? I mean, they are going to freak out when we tell them about our jobs. Well, Dad probably won't, but Mum definitely will. And it doesn't help that Billy is so bloody sorted they don't have to worry about him at *all*.'

'Flora, stop. We're more than fine. Now, go and do whatever you've got to do and leave this stuff out here to me.' He leaned down to kiss her, slipping his hand under her loose white shirt and around her waist.

'Now you stop!' she laughed, grabbing his hand and removing it firmly. 'Come on, we've got work to do.'

Inside she found her children sitting together on the sofa, glued to the television. 'Hey, you two, go and get dressed, please. Grandpa and Granny Kate will be here soon and I need you looking presentable. Same goes for this room.'

'But, Mum...' Both started their separate protests but Flora had already moved on to the kitchen to finish chopping vegetables. She'd been up early tidying the house and getting things ready; her mother was bringing a pudding and Billy was on cheese duty.

Picking up the phone, she hit Billy's number. Predictably, it went straight to voicemail. She quickly tapped out a message.

Just checking you haven't forgotten lunch at ours today?! x ps don't be late x

Flora watched, waiting for the ticks to turn blue. They stayed grey. If he had forgotten, she'd never forgive him.

* * *

The traffic on the road was sluggish. Kate sighed. 'I don't under-stand why people come and spend the day in the country, then park their cars right by the side of the road to have a picnic.'

'Maybe they're happy with the view from there?' Robin ventured.

She looked at the queue of cars, snaking slowly around the roundabout ahead. 'We'll have to leave not long after we get there at this rate. I'm going to text Flora. She'll be wondering what's happened to us.'

'We're literally ten minutes away. I don't think she'll mind terribly.'

'Honestly, I can't wait to see the children. Hopefully they won't look quite as scruffy as they did the last time we were there. I'm sure Tom had nits; he couldn't stop scratching his head. And Pip could be so pretty but you can barely see her eyes with that long fringe in the way, and she does insist on dressing like a tomboy. It doesn't appear to bother Flora at all. Perhaps you should say something? I mean, she gets so touchy when I try and gently suggest something as simple as a haircut, or perhaps a few new clothes.'

'Darling, I really wouldn't worry about it. You've got to let Flora and Johnny do it their way. The most important thing is that the kids are happy. And they are, they're a delight.'

'Of course they are. I'm not saying they're not. It's just that making an effort doesn't cost much and it makes all the differ-ence. That's all.'

Robin weighed up whether to take Kate to task over this, but decided to engineer the conversation away from a row, given their imminent arrival at their daughter's. 'Well, it'll be good to see Bill, too.'

'Oh, I know, I can't wait. It feels like months since we last saw him.'

'Nearly six months.'

'Has it been that long? It can't have been. Are you sure it's that long?' Kate glanced at Robin.

'Yes, almost. It was just before Christmas, anyway.'

'Goodness, time flies. I'm just thrilled he's got time to pop down to see us all together.'

'Yes, aren't we lucky?' Robin couldn't hide the note of sarcasm in his voice.

'There's no need to be like that, darling. He's very busy, as you know.'

'I'm just saying it's been a while, that's all. And you cut him a lot more slack than you allow Flora.' And just like that the words were out there.

'I'm sorry but that's just not true. I mean, how could you say that?'

'I'm sorry. I didn't mean...' Robin realised his timing was terrible. He needed to get Kate back on side if he wanted to get through the afternoon without her scowling at him every time he spoke. 'He's very busy, I do understand.'

'Yes, he is. His job is very demanding, as you well know. Flora has her hands full too – I'm not saying that what she does isn't equally important – it's just different, that's all.' They turned into the track leading to Flora and Johnny's house.

'Right, come on, darling,' said Robin. 'Let's enjoy our day.'

\* \* \*

Lunch was a jolly affair, despite the empty chair. Billy had finally replied to Flora's message to say he was running late and to start without him. Flora popped up and down, whack-a-mole-like, fetching plates, grabbing glasses, passing dishes around. Johnny offered to help but, in an unspoken trade-off, agreed with a glance between them that he was on hosting duty. He knew Flora was happy as long as he carried on talking to her parents. The children were on their best behaviour, answering questions politely; Flora's promise of hot chocolate topped with marshmallows before bed had worked like a dream.

Robin sat at one end of the table, shaded by the branches of the horse chestnut at the bottom of the garden now in spectacular flower. 'You're going to have plenty of conkers later this year, by the looks of it,' he said, glancing up. 'You must have played conkers at school, Tom?'

Tom looked at his grandfather blankly.

Johnny came to his rescue. 'They banned it at school, apparently.'

'Why on earth would they do that?' Kate was incredulous.

'Too dangerous, they said.' Johnny shrugged to show his solidarity.

Robin looked at Pip and Tom. 'Well, when you come this year I'll show you both how to make a champion conker. I used to be a demon at it in my day.' His blue eyes lit up as he spoke.

'Any news from your brother?' said Kate.

Flora could sense the effort in her mother's voice as Kate tried to sound calm, despite her obvious annoyance at her son's tardiness.

'Yes, he'll be here any minute. I've saved him some food. Kids, why don't you go and wait for him out the front, wave him down?' But before they could get there, a screech of tyres on gravel signalled Billy's arrival. The children squealed and jumped from their seats, racing to greet him.

'I'll just grab his plate.' Flora went inside, hoping to intercept him. She planned to prime him on the job-news front so that he could at least act like it wasn't a total disaster – in fact, maybe a blessing in disguise – even if she didn't quite feel that way about it now she was faced with the prospect of telling her parents.

But Pip and Tom had pulled their uncle from the car, dragging him through the small gate at the side of the house. He walked into the garden, carrying each child like a rugby ball under his arms as they wriggled, helpless with laughter.

'Look what I found!' Billy grinned, blond hair falling into his eyes.

'Put me down!' Pip protested, beating his chest with her fists.

'OK, fine... here you go.' He put them both back on their feet. 'Sorry I'm late, Johnny.' They shook hands warmly. 'Hi, Mum.' He moved to kiss Kate first, ducking down to reach under the brim of her wide straw hat. 'Hey, Dad, how are you?' He kissed his father on the cheek.

'Finally!' Flora came out of the back door, walking towards her brother with her arms outstretched. 'Take your time, why don't you?'

Billy gave her a bear hug. 'I'm so sorry, Flo. Traffic was terrible...'

'You also had a late night, I can tell.' She spoke quietly so their parents wouldn't hear. 'Your eyes are still bloodshot.'

'Oh God, really?' Billy rubbed his eyes with his fists. 'I'll stick my sunglasses on.'

'Good plan. Now go and sit down next to Mum, give Johnny a break. I'll get your food. Hair of the dog?'

'Just water for now, thanks.' He turned back to the table,

sunglasses in place, and took Flora's empty seat. 'So, how is everyone?'

The afternoon wore on gently, the sun dipping down behind the trees on the other side of the garden. They sipped bright, juicy Beaujolais from tumblers and picked at grapes and hunks of cheese (Billy hadn't forgotten to bring some, much to Flora's surprise) from a thick wooden board in the middle of the table. Then came Kate's pudding, bowls of fresh summer berries topped with Barbados cream, a childhood favourite of both Flora and Billy's. She used to make it, bringing it to the table like a giant white cloud in a bowl, every Sunday. They'd then wipe their own bowls clean with their fingers when their mother wasn't looking.

As Flora carried a tray of strong coffees to the table, she caught the tail end of her father's question to Johnny.

'Yes, well, there's been a slight change on that front, Robin.'

Shit, thought Flora. Here we go. She gripped the sides of the tray a little harder.

Johnny shifted in his chair. Kate stopped mid-sentence, turning her attention from her son to Johnny.

'Have you been promoted? Oh, I knew it! Didn't I say so, Robin?'

Flora shot Billy a look; he recognised the plea for backup in her eyes. He threw his sister a gentle nod, noticeable to no one other than her.

Johnny spoke evenly. 'Actually, it's not good news, I'm afraid. I've been made redundant.'

A short silence followed. Then Robin said, 'Oh, my dear fellow, I'm so sorry to hear that.'

'Yes, bit of a shock, to say the least. But still, we have a plan, don't we, Flo?' Johnny looked at Flora across the table. 'Well, Flora came up with the idea and I think it's a pretty good one, given the circumstances.'

Kate adjusted her hat, lifting the brim. She turned to Flora. 'So, what's this great idea of yours, darling?' She smiled at her daughter, her face expectant.

'Um... well.' Flora's cheeks burned. She took a breath. 'Johnny's always wanted to run his own business and I, as you know, love working in the wine shop. So, as fate would have it, it looks like Mack is selling the lease to the shop and we thought we might buy it – we'll put Johnny's redundancy money towards it – and, you know, try and make a go of it as a business.' With some effort, Flora fixed a smile on her face. Her fingers dug into her palms. She looked at Johnny.

'It just seems like a really good opportunity for us to do something we both want to do,' Johnny continued.

'It's a lovely idea but is that really going to be enough to replace your job, Johnny?' Kate turned to Johnny, adjusting her hat so she could see him.

'I think it sounds like a great idea.' Billy reached for a chunk of cheese, winking at his sister across the table.

Flora picked up her glass. 'Thank you. I think it could be something really exciting, actually. The shop used to do great business years ago, according to Mack, but then what with the supermarket opposite and the fact that he's never moved the business online, it's been struggling for a while.'

Johnny grabbed the figurative baton from Flora. 'But now I've got some time, we can put together proper plans. We're going to talk to Mack about it next week, see what he thinks. If we can make it work, we're hoping he doesn't have to sell the building so he can continue to live above the shop.'

'Does that mean we get a family discount?' Billy looked hopefully at his brother-in-law.

'I'll see if I can work it into the plan. But knowing your consumption...'

'Fair enough,' Billy laughed.

Robin raised his glass. 'Well, I'm delighted for you both. I think you make a great team. To Flora and Johnny's wine shop...'

Billy clinked his father's glass enthusiastically. 'Me, too – here's to it.'

Kate kept her hands in her lap. 'Well, if you manage to make a living out of a hobby then good for you.'

Flora looked like she was about to say something but Johnny cut in, catching her eye as he raised his glass to meet the others. 'Thanks, Kate, we'll do our best.'

# 7

---

'I mean, why does she do that? Why can't she just be happy for us? Or actually, it's not even that... Why sound like she's kind of hoping something goes wrong?'

The sun threw dappled patches of light across the bright green grass. Kate and Robin had been gone for less than ten minutes and Flora was letting rip as the three of them sat around the table. Pip and Tom sat side by side under the tree, their mouths and tongues matching the vibrant blue colour of their ice pops.

'You know what she's like. I honestly don't think she means to, but she just can't help herself.' Billy knew his mother didn't really deserve defending but he didn't want to fuel Flora's fury any further.

Johnny topped up Flora's glass with the last of the red wine. 'I think she just wants what's best for you, Flo. I mean, I can understand her horror at the thought of me not having a "proper" job...'

'But this might just *be* a proper job and she's writing it off before we've even started! She doesn't even really know what you did beforehand, let's be honest about it.'

Billy put his hand on his sister's shoulder. 'Look, she has no idea what I do really either. She works on top-line information only, as we know. And anyway, what you're about to do is really exciting! I'm kind of jealous...' Billy looked across at Pip and Tom. 'Hey, where's mine, you little toerags?' He gestured at their lollies.

'I'll get you one, Uncle Billy. What colour would you like?' Tom was already on his feet, delighted to be of service.

'Hmm, I think I want my mouth to look as revolting as yours does so I'd better go for blue too.'

'Be right back!' Tom shot off towards the kitchen.

'Don't drip yours on the floor inside!' Flora shouted after him. 'Well, that's kind of you to say, Billy. But it might be a non-starter if Mack says no. Then we're back to square one.'

'Well, I've got a good feeling about it.' Billy clapped his hands.

'Me, too,' said Johnny, pushing his doubts back down for now. 'Anyway, how's your work going?'

'Fine. Busy, actually. It's been a tough year but buildings still need building. Looks like I might be off to work for another company soon, though.'

'Headhunted *again*?' Johnny laughed.

Billy looked slightly embarrassed. 'Yeah, I guess.' He ran his hand through his hair. 'But I'm not really sure about it. It's more money, but it would mean staying in London and I'd hoped to move out of the city at some point. Maybe move nearer to the coast.'

'Near us? Oh, please do, Billy. God, we'd love that! Babysitting on tap...' Flora laughed. 'Ooh, how's...?' Flora waved her arms around her head, willing the name to come back to her.

'Ruby?' Billy volunteered, putting Flora out of her misery.

'Yes, Ruby! Exactly, Ruby... What happened?' Flora had

learned from experience not to grow fond of Billy's girlfriends, given the fairly high turnover, but she'd really liked the sound of Ruby.

'You don't want to know.' Billy shook his head.

'Oh, I think we do, Billy.' Johnny nudged his brother-in-law playfully.

Billy looked sheepish. 'She ended it. I was a bit gutted, to be honest with you. But I just wasn't...' He trailed off.

'What? But we didn't even get to meet her! And she sounded so lovely! God, you're annoying sometimes.'

'I know, I'm sorry. I'm just not very good at...'

'Being a grown-up? Oh, come on, Billy, you're going to have to be one sooner or later.' She threw a grape at him across the table.

'Now who's being childish?' said Billy, dodging it neatly. 'I know, I know. I've been an idiot. But I'm meeting her next week; she's agreed to one drink.' He picked up another grape from the table, returning fire on his sister.

'Well then, try not to fuck it up.' Flora laughed, catching the grape and popping it in her mouth.

\* \* \*

As children they'd been peas in a pod, born barely eighteen months apart. They'd grown up in the house where their parents still lived, a rambling old farmhouse set back from the banks of the Beaulieu River. Of course, there had been the usual sibling fights, usually over disputed toy ownership or what to watch on television, but mostly, they'd had each other's backs. Flora, being the eldest, was in charge but Billy was usually happy enough going along with whatever activities his elder sister had planned for them. Even if that did mean dressing him up in their mother's old clothes and painting his face thick with make-up pinched from her dressing table in order to perform plays that Flora had written (and usually insisted on starring in).

They spent much of their childhood summers on bikes or building dens in the garden, taking food rations so they could stay out all day. Flora would make sandwiches, carefully wrapping them in paper and putting them in a tin. Billy's job was stealing as many biscuits as he could without being caught. He was particularly good at it. Sometimes they'd sneak down to the river that flowed beyond the garden, and fish or swim in the cool waters when the tide was in, even though they'd been strictly forbidden to do so without an adult around. When the tide was out, they'd race around on the mudflats, covered in thick dark grey mud from head to foot and sliding into the water to wash it off.

When Flora was ten years old and Billy almost nine, his pride and joy had been his BMX bike. Flora would look up from her book from time to time as Billy tried to perfect his jumps and bunny hops. Once, when she hadn't looked up at the right time, Billy had let out a long squeal of pain. She had run over to him, lying on the floor having come off his bike, to see his arm lying at a strange angle. Leaving their bikes, she'd practically carried him home as fast as she possibly could, then waited whilst their mother had taken him to hospital. He'd returned home hours later with his arm in a cast. 'Broken in two places!' he'd said, pleased as punch. It became quite the talking point, Billy's story of the jump. It grew more dramatic with every retelling.

Flora persuaded Billy to paint the cast, covering it in green paint they'd found in the garage. Kate was horrified, ordering them to wash it off. When they tried, the plaster disintegrated, falling off in chunks into the sink. Back to the hospital they went, to get a new cast put on. They still managed to swim in the river that summer, Billy holding his arm aloft so as not to get the cast wet. Together, they were a real team.

When Flora hit her teens she lost interest in her little brother for a short while, finding him simply too annoying. But that didn't last long; he was far too much fun for Flora not to want to be around him. By the time they were in their late teens, they shared friends and stolen booze and cigarettes alike. When Flora left home to go to university, Billy missed her dreadfully. The house seemed so quiet without her and he felt quite lost, noticing for the first time how much he and Flora had been one unit, his parents another.

The following year Billy joined Flora in the city as soon as he got a job. They lived about a mile apart, meeting up pretty much every week in the pub at the end of Flora's road for a catch-up over a few drinks, sometimes with friends, sometimes just the two of them. They tag-teamed when it came to calling home, each covering for the other if their mother complained about a lack of communication from either side.

When Flora went to meet him after telling him about Johnny's proposal and their impending parenthood, Billy had been ecstatic. 'But don't you think it's a bit quick? I mean, we've haven't been together for that long.' Flora knew her brother would be honest.

'That's because the previous ones weren't the right ones. But if this feels right then do it. He's so good to you, Flora. He clearly adores you. And he's definitely different from the rest of your ex-boyfriends. God, some of them were dire.' Billy rolled his eyes dramatically, then grinned at her.

'You make it sound like there was an army before Johnny! There weren't that many.'

Billy opened the packet of crisps between them, one of four. He could never buy just one packet. 'Look, he's just... he seizes opportunities. And I think that sort of freaks you out because you like things to happen, well...'

'What are you trying to say? I can be spontaneous if I want to be! I mean, I'm having a baby! That wasn't part of the plan, not yet anyway.' Flora laughed.

'Come on, Flo, you know what I mean. Just don't overthink it. But for the record, I think he's brilliant. And I think he's kind of perfect for you.' Billy picked up his now empty glass and pointed at hers. 'Time for another lime and soda?'

Every other month Flora and Billy always made the trip home together to see their parents for Sunday lunch. Flora loved those journeys. They'd always stop at the same service station before they'd even left London, usually both a little hung-over, loading up on drinks and snacks in an attempt to feel better before they reached their parents' house about two hours' drive away. Kate would make a great fuss of them coming, only to make them feel they were putting her out almost as soon as they got there.

And even though Flora was now the host, officially a grown-up with children of her own, she still couldn't bring herself to confront her mother about her behaviour. Instead, when they were together they all reverted to their assigned roles – Billy the kid, Robin gently reassuring – whilst Kate peppered the conversation with digs wrapped in conversational tissue paper at Flora. At least, that's how it felt.

'I'm so sorry but I'm going to have to make a move.' Billy leaned back in his chair, stretching his arms above his head. The children sat on either side of him in their pyjamas, sipping hot chocolate. They'd talked into the early evening, discussing ideas for the wine shop. Flora sat with her notebook in front of her. Tomorrow she would talk to Mack about their ideas, and see what he had to say.

'Please don't go, Uncle Billy!' Tom pleaded.

'Come on the trampoline with us!' Pip begged her uncle, hoping he could execute the backwards somersault he'd managed the last time he'd been down to see them.

'I really don't think I can.' Billy patted his stomach. 'I'm still stuffed. Sorry, Pip – next time, I promise.' Billy held up his little finger to Pip. 'Pinkie promise, isn't that what you always say?'

'Pinkie promise.' Pip hooked her little finger round Billy's, shaking it and nodding her head earnestly.

'Well, we're just pleased you made it, Bill.' Johnny stood up, picking up a few empty plates as he did.

'I know, for a minute I thought you might bail on us,' said Flora.

'Never!' Billy grinned at his sister.

'OK, well, listen, we'll do this again soon. And next time, maybe you might want to bring a friend...?' Flora couldn't help herself.

'I think we all know that's not going to happen.' Billy stood up, his tall frame towering over his big sister. He hugged her, lifting her up from the floor. 'Thank you, Flo.'

'Not so late next time, please.'

'Yes, ma'am.' Billy bowed his head, solemnly. He turned to his brother-in-law. 'Thanks, Johnny... and let me know what happens with the shop. I can help if you need to do some kind of refit... with any contacts you might need.'

'Thanks, Billy. That would be great. We'll let you know.'

As they stood on the front step of their house, waving him off, Johnny put his arm around Flora. They watched his car disappear in a cloud of dust. 'You miss him, don't you?'

'I really do. It was so lovely to see him. I just wish we saw more of him.'

'He'd bug you if he was here all the time. That's what little brothers do.' Johnny laughed gently.

'I guess. Still, I miss him.'

Johnny tightened his arms around her shoulders. 'Come on, you get them into bed, I'll clear up. Then we've got a business plan to write.'

'Now? Really?'

'Not the whole thing, just enough for you to take Mack through tomorrow, so he knows we've really thought about it. We need him to see we're really serious about this.'

'Thank you.'

'What for?'

'Seizing opportunities.'

'What do you mean?'

'Just that.' She rose up on her toes to kiss him, then turned to go inside, smiling as she left.

## 8

Mack woke to the sound of the phone ringing downstairs. He reached for his watch by the side of the bed. It was just past nine o'clock in the morning. Slowly, he made his way downstairs, the shop still in darkness. The phone stopped ringing just as he got there but soon started again.

'Hello?' His voice was gruff with sleep.

'Mack? It's Flora. I know you said not to come in today but I wondered if I could. I need to talk to you about something.'

Mack looked across from behind the counter to the front door. The sign on the back of the door hung in its usual place, the word 'OPEN' facing him.

'Yes, Flora, of course.' Mack was pleased to hear her voice. He still felt terrible about having to let her go. 'I'm not intending to open today, actually. Thought I'd use the day to tidy up a bit. The estate agents want to come and have a look around.'

'Well, about that... Can you put them off until I've been in? I need to talk to you about an idea I've had.'

Mack switched the light on behind him. 'Um, yes, I suppose so. I'll give them a call now.'

'Great. I'll be with you in about half an hour.'

'I'll get the coffee on, then. See you shortly.' He put down the phone and looked around the shop, feeling surrounded by the presence of people and places as much as bottles. He made his way back upstairs, a tiny spark of hope in his heart.

By the time Mack was dressed and downstairs, Flora was already at the door. He went to unlock it, instinctively reaching to flip the shop sign over, stopping himself at the last minute.

'Morning, Mack.' Flora was smiling from ear to ear. 'I'm sorry again to call so early but I just wanted to get here before you did anything.'

'Coffee?' Mack headed back towards the pot, two empty cups on a tray ready for them.

'Ooh, lovely. Yes, please. Listen, I've got a proposition for you.'

'Go on.' He poured the coffee and handed Flora a steaming cup.

'Thank you.' She put it straight back down, unable to stop herself. 'OK, I have good news and bad news. I'll start with the bad. Johnny's been made redundant...'

'Oh dear, I am sorry to hear—'

Flora cut Mack off. 'No, it's fine, honestly. He got a fairly good redundancy package; he's been there for, God, I can't remember how many years. Anyway, the point is, what he'd really like to do is run his own business, and so we thought, if you're happy to, we could perhaps take over the lease of the shop. Obviously, you could still live above – if that works for you, if you wanted to, of course – and we hope you would still want to be involved in the business. But we wouldn't want you to feel like you had to, you know? It would be totally up to you how much or little you do.' Flora looked at him, hopefully. 'So, what do you think? I mean, take your time, you don't have to...'

Mack took a sip of his coffee and put his cup on the counter, turning his face away from Flora.

'Mack, I'm sorry, I didn't mean to bulldoze you. Johnny did say perhaps we should wait a bit, ask you more formally. If so, please ignore everything I've just said.'

'Flora...' Mack turned his head to face her. The tears in his eyes were barely perceptible but Flora knew him well enough to spot them. 'Are you sure you and Johnny want to take this on? I mean, it's not going to make you very much by way of income...'

'We both *really* want to do something we love. Johnny's going to – if you say yes, that is – draw up a proper business plan, take it to the bank so we can afford to do it properly. We'd plan to move some of the business online, all that kind of stuff. And if it doesn't work, it doesn't work. But we're willing to give it a go. What do you think?' She held her breath.

'I think that's just about the most wonderful thing I've heard for a long time.' Mack's face broke into a wide smile. 'But are you sure you really want an old man like me around?'

'Mack, we wouldn't be here if it weren't for you. So yes, we really do want an old man like you around, as much as you want to be.' Flora laughed, relieved. 'Now, shall I turn that sign on the door over?'

Mack raised his cup to hers. 'We should be doing this with wine really, but yes, turn the sign over.'

She moved towards the door.

'And, Flora? Thank you.'

'Fingers crossed.' Flora smiled back at him, then flipped the sign over.

* * *

'So, what did he say?' Tilda sat on the swing next to Flora. They'd gone straight to the playing fields after school pickup in the hope the children might run off some energy.

'Well, it's not a done deal, by any means. We've still got to secure a business loan, but Mack's keen and that's the most important thing, I guess.'

'Flora, that's fantastic news. I mean, your own wine shop!'

'Well, it won't technically be ours but it's as near as we're going to get to having one for the time being. So yes, we're over the moon. Johnny seems genuinely excited about it.'

'Well, you're going to have some sort of launch party *obviously*.' Tilda loved a party, throwing them on the flimsiest of excuses. Her children's parties were as much for the adults as they were for the kids. 'Let me help you organise it?'

'That's a great idea, but we've got masses to do before we get to that, not least sort the stock out. Mack's carrying stuff he's had for years and we definitely need to get some more affordable wines in if we're going to compete with the supermarket over the road. But at least the shop is in fairly good nick. We'll have to have a clear-out, freshen it up and build a few more shelves so we don't have piles of boxes all over the floor. Maybe get a tasting bench...'

'I don't know what you're talking about, but I like the sound of it.'

'Sound of what?' Another voice called across to them.

'Susie! You made it... but where are the kids?' Flora jumped up from her swing to offer it to her friend.

Susie gestured to her car. 'I've given them my phone. I need ten minutes without fielding questions from small people.' She rolled her eyes.

They'd first met Susie a few years before, standing at the school gates. She was terrifyingly immaculate, as were each of her four children, but she was also terrific fun. Before long Flora and Tilda had been invited over to Susie's house one evening for drinks. Of course, they'd both jumped at the invitation because, more than anything, they had wanted to see what the inside of their new friend's house – tall and imposing with its pale stone Georgian front – was like.

Susie was funny, whip-smart and – as Flora and Tilda found out that evening – married to a fairly unpleasant man. Her husband, Julian, appeared in the kitchen at one point to ask when dinner would be ready. He barely acknowledged them sitting around the kitchen table. Susie jumped up. 'Julian, this is Tilda... and this is Flora. They've got kids at school, too.' Susie's face lit up with a hopeful smile. 'We're just having a quick glass before dinner.'

'Yes, hi!' Tilda raised her glass. 'We won't be long.' She laughed, a little too loudly judging by the look on Julian's face.

'Yeah, hi.' He glanced across at them briefly before opening the fridge. He looked inside. 'We're almost out of beer.' He took a bottle from the fridge door and left the room.

'Sorry, I meant to get some today. I'll go tomorrow...' Susie called after him, but he was gone before she could finish her sentence. An awkward silence followed. 'He's not normally... He's a bit stressed at work at the moment.' Susie looked mortified.

'Don't you apologise...' Flora wanted to ask if he was always so rude. Also, why didn't he buy his own beer if he was so worried about running out? Instead, she bit her tongue.

'God, don't you worry. Pete's a nightmare when he comes back from work. Honestly, he can barely string a sentence together.' Tilda felt bad giving her husband such bad press when, actually, while he was a bit annoying sometimes, he was hardly a nightmare.

After that night the three of them barely spoke about Julian again, other than the odd passing reference. If ever Flora or Tilda brought his name up in the hope of encouraging their friend to talk about him a bit more, Susie would quickly steer the conversation away to some other topic.

Now, taking the vacated seat on the swing next to Tilda, Susie began to gently swing back and forth, her feet on the floor. 'So, how was your weekend?'

'Eventful, actually.' Flora laughed. She brought Susie up to speed on Johnny's redundancy, on her near redundancy and the plans to take over the shop. Susie listened intently.

'And the best thing is,' Tilda grinned at Susie, 'that we get to help organise the launch party, and get free wine.'

'Oh, now that is exciting.' Susie's eyes lit up.

'Hang on, we're not there yet!' Flora didn't dare tempt fate. 'And I don't think I ever said *free* wine.'

'Look, you worry about getting the shop ready, leave the party to us,' said Tilda. 'We'll get all the mums in from school...'

'We could start a monthly wine club! Oh my gosh, that would be so fun.' Susie practically whooped at the thought.

'That sounds a little too serious for me. I'd rather just be able to come along and drink it,' said Tilda, laughing.

'Well, no, it wouldn't have to be like *super* serious, would it, Flo?' Susie turned to Flora.

'No, of course not. It could be more like a monthly wine social, you know? More like an open-pour event so you can... Hang on, stop!' Flora held up her hands. 'I honestly don't want to get ahead of myself. It might not happen and then, well, I'll probably have to give up wine altogether and do something else.'

'Thank goodness Johnny is a glass-half-full person.' Tilda threw her friend a look.

'I know, sorry. I can't help it. I just don't want to jinx anything.

OK, fine. You two start thinking of ideas. But don't get carried away, deal?'

Susie and Tilda exchanged solemn looks then nodded at Flora, before bursting out laughing.

* * *

Later that night Flora lay on the sofa, feet up on Johnny's lap and a thick wine textbook lying open flat on her stomach. Johnny's gaze moved between the television and his laptop, balanced on the arm of the sofa, his glasses perched on the end of his nose.

'How's it looking?' Flora could see a spreadsheet on the screen in front of him.

'Hmm?' Johnny continued tapping at the keyboard.

'That. How's it looking?'

'Well, I need to get a look at the current books but I'll go and see Mack tomorrow. It might take me a week or so but, with a bit of luck, if I can sort them into some sort of order I can get in to see the bank next week. Then we'll know if it's a goer or not.'

'What do you reckon our chances are? I mean, fifty-fifty? Or less?'

'I think we've got a pretty good chance.' He rubbed her foot through her thick fluffy socks with one hand. 'We'll just have to wait and see. We'll need to make an offer, agree our terms, factor in business rates... but if it comes together we might just have a new business on our hands next month.' He closed his laptop.

After the meeting at the bank, they tried to forget about the prospective business on which their future depended for a few weeks, but Flora's heart jumped every time she heard the clatter of the letterbox. In the meantime, she and Mack continued running the shop, avoiding the subject for fear of having to face the reality that it simply might not happen. As each day passed without news, so her hopes faded a little more.

Then, three weeks to the day that Johnny had gone to the bank, a letter arrived confirming them as the named leaseholders on the building.

Flora and Johnny went straight to the shop to tell Mack the good news and then Flora messaged Billy, who was predictably over the moon for them. Later that day a huge bunch of flowers arrived for them, along with a box of brightly coloured, beautifully decorated cupcakes spelling out the name of the shop. When Flora messaged to say thank you, Billy confessed the cakes had been Ruby's idea. Flora replied, saying she was thrilled to hear they were back together even if Ruby was clearly too good for him, and that he shouldn't do anything to piss her off ever again. He promised to do his best, signing off with two kisses and a winking face emoji.

# 9

Kate sat at one end of the kitchen table, buttering a piece of toast. At the other end Robin slowly turned the pages of the newspaper spread out in front of him. Light flooded into the large kitchen. Outside, beyond the French doors, lay a sweeping lawn bordered by flower beds filled with tulips in full bloom. A gap in the hedge gave way to a glimpse of the river that ran along the bottom.

'Are you listening to this?' Kate reached across to the portable radio on the table.

'Not really. Turn it off if you like.' Robin didn't look up from his paper.

'Pass the marmalade, please, darling.' Kate gestured with her hand.

'Hmm?' Still Robin didn't look up.

'Marmalade, please. I can't reach from here.'

'Yes, sorry, darling.' Robin stood up from his chair, reaching for the jar and opening it for her.

'Thank you.' Kate took it. 'So, what did Flora say when she called yesterday?'

'Well, she just wanted to fill us in on the shop. Such good news, don't you think?'

'Well, yes, absolutely. I'm just not sure exactly what's happening because obviously she spoke to you about it and not me.'

'That's only because I happened to answer the phone, darling.' Robin looked up at Kate. 'I did tell you what she said.'

'Oh, I know. I'm not... It's just... she never seems to want to speak to me.'

'You were at the other end of the garden. You could have called her back.' Robin returned to his paper, sensing a small confrontation coming over the horizon.

'I just think she doesn't really want to talk to me. At least not like she talks to you.'

'Kate, she was calling to tell us her news. How could she know who was going to answer?' Robin tried to alter the course of the conversation before it was too late to avoid a row. 'She asked if you could go and see her in the shop. She wanted your advice on something. To do with the décor, I assume.'

Kate had, for many years, worked at a glossy interiors magazine.

'Interior decoration, darling, not décor.' Kate took a small bite of her toast, the sound of the crunch as brittle as her words.

'Sorry, you know that's what I meant. Anyway, she said that they plan to give the place a good clean, spruce it up a bit. Then the idea is to have a launch party a few weeks after that for customers and friends to, you know, spread the word.'

Kate finished chewing, hand to her mouth. 'Are we invited?'

'Of course! She said she'd confirm the date as soon as possible. You can ask her when you call her back.' He closed the paper and folded it in half, placing it neatly on the table. 'Well, I'd better get going.'

'Where are you off to?' Kate sounded surprised.

'I did tell you, darling. I'm helping Mick with the boat this morning.' Mick was their neighbour, and had been for years. Robin and Mick always had some sort of project on the go but this particular one – restoring an abandoned old wooden boat – had gone on far longer than most. 'The sooner we get it done, the sooner we can go fishing.'

Kate forced a smile. 'Yes, I remember now. Well, I'd better get on anyway. Lots on.'

Robin kissed her on her head as he walked behind her. 'Right, I'll see you later. I've got lunch.' He raised a Tupperware box as he left the room.

Kate was left at the table. The dog, a long-haired dachshund, sat at her feet looking up at her hopefully. 'Are you interested in what I'm doing today, Monty?' She stroked his head. 'No one else seems to be.' Monty tentatively lifted his paws onto her lap. 'Oh, come on, then, up you come.' She scooped him up and he settled into her lap. Then she reached for her phone and dialled her daughter's number.

* * *

Flora stood in the middle of the shop, surrounded by boxes. Mack was at the counter with a pile of large hard-backed note-books in front of him and behind him sat Johnny, perched on the stairs, balancing his laptop on his knees.

'Right, I've started moving the stocktake to here,' Johnny pointed at the screen, 'and I think we need to sort out what we're going to put into the bin-end sale if we're going to make room for some new stuff.'

'Which is all over here...' Flora pointed to a stack of boxes behind her. 'Mack, if I get this lot set up, shall we taste through them together later this week?'

'Yes, good idea.' Mack turned to Johnny. 'Where are we moving the fine wine range to?'

'Over there, along the back wall, I thought. Less chance of it getting nicked if it's there where we can see it.'

'Fair enough.' Mack guessed Johnny would have spotted the small hole in the fine wine accounts, but if he thought it had anything to do with Mack, Johnny had obviously decided to keep it to himself. 'And do you want to keep it merchandised by country? Or should we do it by price?'

'I think stick to country. At least then you have more of a chance to get customers to trade up and spend a bit more, don't you think?' Johnny looked at them both.

'Definitely.' Flora nodded. 'OK, so I'm thinking we have New World stuff down this side,' she pointed at the wall furthest away from the counter, 'and Old World either side of the counter. Then spirits behind. What do you think?'

The phone rang. Mack picked it up. 'Hello, Ten Green Bottles...'

'I'm going to start moving this lot,' Flora whispered to Johnny, putting her hand on the pile of boxes in front of her.

'Yes, of course Mrs... Kate, of course... very kind.' Mack held the phone out to Flora. 'It's your mother.'

Flora carefully picked her way across the floor and took the phone. 'Mum, hi... I spoke to Dad, did you get my message? I just wondered if you could pop by the shop today. We're just rearranging stuff but we need to make it look good on a shoestring. I thought you might have some good ideas... You will? Brilliant.' Flora gave a thumbs up to Johnny and Mack. 'Yes, any time before three – I've got to leave to get the kids by then... Great. Thanks, see you in a bit. Bye.'

'What time is she coming?' Johnny asked.

'She said she'd leave straight away so she should be here in half an hour or so.'

'Mack, you're in for a treat.' Johnny raised an eyebrow at the other man.

'Hey, that's my mother you're talking about.' Flora looked at Johnny in mock disapproval. 'She's not that bad, Mack, honestly. Just a bit, well...'

'I'm only joking, you know that. She's lovely really, Mack, just a little, um... challenging sometimes. Maybe?' Johnny looked at Flora.

'Yeah, I guess. She means well but,' Flora sighed, 'she's got this slight "poor me" thing going on. And *everything* is about her.' Flora caught herself. 'God, I'm so sorry, Mack. I'm sure the last thing you want to know about is my slightly complicated relationship with my mother.' She laughed a little. 'I love her really.'

'Oh, no, don't you worry. I'm sure you do,' said Mack, nodding sagely. 'Right, let's get these wines off the shelves.'

'No, Johnny and I can do that. You take down the point-of-sale cards...'

Just then the door opened. Mack looked up to see a tall, dark-haired woman smiling at him. 'I'm sorry but we're not open yet.'

'Oh, no, I'm not here to buy wine. I just thought you might want an extra pair of hands.'

'Susie! What are you doing here?' Flora went to give her friend a hug.

'Well, I thought the least I could do was come and help you, given that it's very much in my interest that you're open for business as soon as possible.' She laughed, pulling her long hair into a ponytail. 'Hi, Johnny.'

'Mack, this is my friend Susie. She lives just at the top of the high street.' Flora grinned. 'This is really kind of you but, honestly, you really don't have to—'

'I want to, seriously. Gets me out of the house.' She winked at Flora.

'That's brilliant, thank you.' Johnny came over, handing her a coffee cup. 'You'll need this before we get going.'

Before long the shop floor was covered in bottles and Flora, Johnny and Susie were wiping the empty shelves. Mack was busy setting more bottles up on a long table in the room at the back of the shop, ready to be tasted. The doorbell went again and there stood Kate, hair piled up on her head, sporting a leopard-print tabard.

'Mum! What on earth are you wearing?' Flora burst out laughing.

'I've just bought it in the hardware store next door, along with this.' Her mother gestured to the mop and bucket in hand. 'What do you think?' Kate did a half-twirl and a curtsy for the crowd.

'You look ridiculous. But thank you.' Flora got up and went to kiss her mother. 'We really appreciate it.'

'Hi, Kate!' Johnny waved from the back of the shop, still on his knees beside the shelves.

'Hello, darling, how are you?' Kate turned to Susie. 'I don't believe we've met, I'm Kate, Flora's mum.' Kate extended her hand.

'I'm Susie, very nice to meet you. Gosh, you look so alike.'

'Do we really? Flora won't like that, will you, darling?' Kate laughed, looking at her daughter.

'It's a great compliment, Mum.' Flora managed a smile despite her mother's response annoying her. Not because she didn't think they looked alike – they undoubtedly did – but the inference that Flora wouldn't like it irritated her. Every. Single. Time.

'Anyway, I thought I might as well come and make myself as

useful as possible.' She looked towards the back of the shop. 'So where is the famous Mack?'

'He'll be through in a minute. He's just out the back.' Flora took the mop and bucket from her mother.

'So what were you thinking in terms of the space?' Kate glanced about the shop. 'The exposed brick is beautiful and the shelves...' she touched the nearest one, built by Mack all those years ago, '... lovely. But you could brighten the space up by giving the ceiling a fresh coat of paint.' Kate looked over to the counter. 'And you could top that with something like copper to give it a slightly more up-to-date look.' She peered over the counter at the stairs. 'And a runner on those stairs wouldn't go amiss.'

'Good idea, but we've got the tiniest of budgets to do this place up so...' Flora glanced at Johnny.

'Don't worry, darling,' said Kate. 'I can sort that out. Leave the paint to me, too. Not the actual painting, obviously. But I can get the right colour for you, a lightish grey, I think. I'll have a look.'

'Thanks, Mum, that would be amazing. And what about an area with a tasting table, given we've not got much space?'

'Well, let's see. You could...' Kate stepped carefully across the floor towards the back of the shop, '... have a bench along this wall, one that folds down so you can put it up when you're not using it. And a table that comes down from this wall,' she pointed, 'topped to match the counter.'

'Like Flora said, we're on a tight budget.' Johnny stood up.

'Leave that with me, too, Johnny.' Kate threw him a smile. He knew her well enough to know she was on a mission and the best course of action, for now, was to let her get on with it. They could argue over numbers later.

'Thank you, Kate, that's great.'

'So this must be your mother, Flora!' Mack appeared from the back of the shop. 'Pleased to meet you.'

Kate shook Mack's proffered hand. 'And you're Mack!' She laughed, gesturing to her tabard. 'Do excuse the get-up.'

'Not at all, it's very kind of you to come and help. And I'm sure you don't need me to tell you, but your daughter and son-in-law have both been wonderful. I really thought it was the end of the wine road for me but these two absolutely refused to give up.'

'Well, I'm not sure they had much choice, to be honest,' replied Kate.

Flora shot Johnny a look and he gently shook his head. She rolled her eyes before turning back to Kate.

'OK, Mum, that's enough chit-chat.' She handed her a cloth. 'We've got work to do. Just mind the bottles.'

## 10

'Can you please not eat those straight from the packet?' Johnny took the cereal box from Pip, passing her a bowl. 'Sit down and pour them properly, please.'

'Are you taking us to school today?' Tom spoke through a mouthful of cereal, his face hopeful.

'Yes, Tom, my turn today... and it's a big day for your mother. She's got one of her wine exams today.'

Flora rushed into the room, bags already over her shoulder. She looked terrified. Johnny put his arms on her shoulders. 'Hey, how are you feel—'

'Have you got everything ready for school? Did you finish your homework, Pip? Tom, have you got your—' Flora stopped, turning her attention to whatever she was rummaging for in her handbag.

'Relax, they're here.' Johnny grabbed the keys from the side and handed them to Flora. 'We're on it, seriously. You go, you don't want to miss your train. What time will you be back?'

Flora kissed him briefly on the lips. 'Hopefully around six, unless I decide to drown my sorrows somewhere.'

'Come on, you know you're as prepared for this as you possibly could be. You've done loads of studying.'

'Yes, but it's the last tasting paper today, and I feel like I've totally forgotten what anything smells like, let alone what it tastes like. And what if they put really random wines in?'

'In which case, go with whatever comes into your head first, you know, gut feel. It's your best bet.'

'How come you're suddenly the expert?' Flora managed a laugh.

'I'm not. But I know you. Just don't overthink things. Go with your instincts and you'll be fine. Better than fine, you'll be brilliant. Now, go.' He kissed her again.

Flora kissed both the children then headed for the door. 'Thank you. See you later!'

'Bye, Mum!' chorused the children. The front door thumped shut behind her.

'OK, let's get going. Ten minutes and counting. Off you go and brush your teeth when you've finished. I'll be back in a minute.' Johnny stepped into the back garden, mug of tea in hand. He looked up at the trees at the back, now thick with bright green leaves against a light blue sky. The sun was already warm on his face. He took a last slug of his tea, the liquid now lukewarm.

A robin flew down in front of him and landed not far from his feet. He watched the bird hop across the lawn. 'What do you think? Do you reckon she'll be OK? I reckon she'll ace it.' He sighed, closed his eyes. 'Now, if we can just make the shop work...'

Johnny had spent the last few weeks honing the business plan, negotiating terms with suppliers both new and old, sorting out the accounts and setting up a shiny new website. The newly laid-out shop was looking good, freshly painted, and the copper-topped counter and tasting table were the smartest finishing touches. If – and it was a big if – they could take the business from a small neighbourhood wine shop to one that also operated profitably online, sold to restaurants and other businesses wholesale and ran wine courses Johnny felt they were on to something that might just allow them to earn a decent living. At least, that was the plan. The last thing he wanted to do was put Flora under pressure, but the truth was there was a lot riding on her gaining her diploma.

* * *

Flora took another long sniff of the liquid inside the glass in front of her and looked at what she'd written. Taking a furtive glance around, she thought everyone appeared far more comfortable than she felt. One candidate sat back in his chair, casually tapping his pen on the table. Another went along the row of wines in front of her, sniffing each one furiously, smiling as she scribbled down her notes. It took Flora all her willpower not to cross out everything she'd written and bolt for the door.

You know this is Fino sherry, she told herself. You've tasted this a hundred times before. That unmistakable tang, the searing acidity that whips across the taste buds quite unlike anything else...

Flora forced herself to put her pen down and move along to the next drink. Picking it up, she tilted the glass and looked at the wine. Closing her eyes, she stuck her nose in the top of it and inhaled deeply. Booze-soaked nuts and raisin aromas hit her immediately, so powerful she felt slightly intoxicated. 'Light tawny red fading to brick at the rim,' she wrote. Tawny port, final answer, she thought as she continued with the tasting note, describing its aromas and palate before assessing the wine's overall quality in detail.

She glanced at her watch. Twenty minutes left and she still

had another flight to go. It was going to be tight, but if she could just keep her focus…

By the time the invigilator called time, Flora felt like she was burning up. Whether through panic or just because the exam room was unbelievably stuffy, she couldn't quite tell. Either way, relief flooded through her. As they left the room other students talked excitedly, comparing verbal notes on the wines. She heard snippets, enough to make her doubt every word she'd written. Given most of her tutorials had been completed online she didn't really know anyone else on the course, but the last thing she wanted now was a 'What did you think wine number six was?' kind of conversation.

Five papers down, one assessment to go. And that didn't have to be handed in for a while yet. Flora hitched her bag onto her shoulder, popped a piece of chewing gum into her tannin-coated mouth, took a deep breath and headed out of the building. As she waited to cross the road, staring mindlessly at the red light, she saw someone waving at her from the other side of the road.

'Billy!' She crossed over to meet him, giving him a great hug when she got there. 'What on earth are you doing here?'

'I asked Johnny what time you finished and thought you might like a quick drink before you head back. I'm working not far from here at the moment. Don't worry, he said not to rush back; said he'll sort the kids out. And I know a great pub just round the corner.' Billy grinned.

'Actually, I really need a gin and tonic after all that tasting, but I'm driving at the other end, so I'd better stick to tea.'

'Well, I'm gasping. Come on.'

They sat at a small table in the corner of the pub, all dark wood and old paintings. Billy returned from the bar with a tray holding a pint, a pot of tea and four different-flavoured bags of crisps.

'So, how did it go?' He put the pot and empty cup and saucer in front of her. 'Sorry, they only had these.' He pointed to the tiny carton of milk on the table.

'No, honestly, that's perfect. Thank you.' Flora reached for the tea. 'It went OK, I think. But you never really know, do you?'

Billy laughed, remembering his own exam performance. When it came to studying for exams, he had always left everything to the last minute, somehow scraping through by the skin of his teeth. 'You'll be fine, you know you will. I don't think you've ever failed an exam in your life. Well, apart from your driving test. How many times?' He laughed, knowing how much this annoyed her.

'Oh, shut up, it was just bad luck!'

'Three times?'

'Actually, I passed third time. All the best people do.' She shot him a look.

'Whatever.' He chuckled, then took a noisy sip from his pint.

'Anyway, how's it all going with Ruby? Is it back on?'

'Yeah, I think so. I do really like her, actually. She's… gorgeous.' He grinned.

'God only knows what she sees in you,' Flora teased.

'Well, clearly it's my sparkling personality and devastating good looks.' He gestured to his face.

'Yeah, right.' She laughed.

They sat and exchanged news, Billy asking about the children, Flora about his plans for the summer in the hope she might get him to commit to coming to stay for a few days at some point. They talked about their parents, including the obligatory moan about their mother whilst agreeing they wouldn't have her any other way. It was all part and parcel of family life, however old you were.

Flora glanced at her watch. 'Oh my God, I didn't realise it was so late! I've got to go or I'll miss my train and I don't want to be on the later one: it'll be so crowded.'

Billy drained his pint. 'Go on, go!' He shooed her away.

Flora hugged him and thanked him for the tea. 'Just what I needed, thank you.'

'Next time, it'll be a gin and tonic.'

'Definitely. Doubles.'

'Of course.' He waved her off and Flora ran all the way to the station.

She made the train with a minute to spare but managed to find a seat. Plonking herself down, she rested her head against the glass window and settled in. She scrolled through her phone. Five new messages in her group chat with Susie and Tilda – both wishing her luck along with a couple of random GIFs involving people drinking enormous glasses of wine, together with a couple from Johnny telling her he was thinking of her and asking how it went. She tapped out her responses and sent one to her parents, letting them know she'd got the last exam out of the way.

She put her phone in her pocket and picked up the paper in front of her, the words a blur. Her eyes ached. The sound of a ping had her reaching back into her pocket. Looking at the screen she saw a message from Billy.

Good to see you, sis. Bet you smashed it. See you at the party next week xx

She smiled to herself, her thoughts turning to the shop. At least now she had a bit of time to focus on getting the launch organised. An email had gone out to the few current customers Mack had email addresses for, as well as to friends and family. Suppliers old and new had generously donated a few bottles each to the opening so that customers could try different wines. If the weather continued as it was, they'd be able to use the courtyard at the back, too, which would provide a bit more space.

She checked her emails before opening the Instagram page Johnny had set up for the shop, now populated with before and after pictures of the shop makeover. There were bottles, wine-makers and even pictures of her, Mack and Johnny. She felt guilty for not having helped more with this side of things, but Johnny had been insistent ('You've got exams and, anyway, you never post anything on Instagram. And you hate Facebook'). She wouldn't have known where to start but he'd made it look fantastic.

Her job, he'd told her, was to pass her diploma. Then she could start teaching wine courses from the shop, bringing in an additional income stream. She felt her stomach flip at the thought of getting her results, even though it was months away still.

The train rattled slowly through the suburbs. Flora distracted herself by peeking into the passing gardens and extensions stuck on the back of houses like enormous concrete barnacles. The train picked up speed as it headed to the coast and, as it did, so her worries about the exam began to fade. No good worrying about something you can't change, as her mother was in the habit of reminding her on a regular basis.

Again, her phone pinged. Flora picked it up and looked at the screen. A message on the 'Family' group chat from her mother:

Hi Darling, well done! We've got everything crossed for you. Xxx

Flora started typing.

Thanks Mum, I'm just glad it's all done for now. See you at the party next week. Did you get the email about it from Johnny?

Flora waited for a reply. She could just imagine her mother asking her father about the email. 'Did we get an email, Robin? I didn't see it... Can you have a look? Print it off?'

The guard's voice interrupted her train of thought, announcing the next station. It was the one before her usual stop, but that morning Flora had decided to go from a different station. The car park there was bigger than at her usual one and she hadn't wanted to risk not being able to get a parking spot. She reached for her bag, folded the paper in half and tucked it inside. Standing by the door as they pulled into the station, Flora realised she was feeling something she hadn't felt for a while. Taking a second to register it, she was stunned to notice that the tight knot that had been in her stomach, seemingly for months, just wasn't there any more. Relief, that's what it was. At last.

Stepping onto the platform, she joined the snake of people climbing the stairs, placing one foot in front of the other, head down. When she got to the top, she saw a familiar figure walking a few steps in front of her. It was her father. She went to call out, but something stopped her. He turned to speak to the person next to him, a woman she didn't recognise. Flora slowed down, watching as the woman turned her head to his, lifting her face. He kissed her cheek, saying something that made her laugh. She put her hand gently to his face and smiled again before they both started walking in opposite directions across the car park.

Flora stood rooted to the spot, people passing either side of her. Trying to make sense of what she'd just witnessed, she racked her brains. Who could this woman possibly be? Perhaps it was an old friend he'd bumped into on the train, she told herself. But then what was he doing on the train in the first place?

Flora's legs felt weak. She knew, deep down, that what she'd seen wasn't a goodbye kiss between friends. It was one between lovers.

## 11

'Here you go...' Susie held out two paper cups, bubbles threatening to escape over the sides. She'd instigated a trip to the beach after school, determined to make the most of the warm spell, and she and Tilda were wanting to toast Flora finishing her exams. 'Here's to you, Flo.'

They raised their paper cups in unison.

'Thank you, but you really shouldn't have. Technically, I haven't quite finished them and I'm sure we shouldn't be doing this until I actually pass this damn diploma.' Flora laughed.

'Nonsense, just getting this far is a real achievement in itself and we're going to bloody well celebrate it. Talking of which...' Tilda shifted back on the blanket they'd laid on the pebbles, '... I've been thinking about the party again. We could do a raffle to raise money for a local charity, get people's email addresses so you can add them to your database, Flora. Also, if you do a raffle after everyone's had a few glasses, you'll sell loads of tickets.' Tilda took another long sip from her cup.

'Ooh, good idea.' Flora sat up, lifting her sunglasses as she did so. 'Hey, Pip! Try and persuade Tom to come in with you!' Pip threw an enthusiastic thumbs up back to her mother from where she stood in the water, now up to her knees. Tom was at the water's edge, crouching down to examine stones in the sand. 'And what about doing some sort of actual wine tasting? Or do you think that's too formal?'

'I think you just need to get a good crowd in and let people know you'll be doing wine courses and talks, that kind of thing, in future.' Susie passed a packet of opened crisps. 'Take them away from me, someone, please, before I eat the lot of them.'

Tilda took the packet. 'I think Susie's right. You want this to be about showing off the shop, get people trying a few wines. Make sure they sign up for the newsletter, you know? And, Susie, you do not need to worry about eating too many crisps. For heaven's sake, there's nothing of you – which is very annoying – and sadly cannot be said for me.' Tilda grinned, shoving another handful in her mouth as she did so.

Flora took a sip, then another. Flavours of citrus and just-crushed biscuits filled her mouth. 'God, this is delicious. Did you bring it, Susie?'

'Yep, I nicked it from Jules' wine rack. It is rather nice, isn't it?'

'Pass me the bottle...' Flora reached across, turning it to look at the label. 'Bloody hell, Susie, this is a really good champagne.'

'Oh, shit, is it?' Susie grimaced.

'What is it?' Tilda took the bottle from Flora to take a closer look.

'It's a Blanc de Blancs. Vintage, as well. And this producer is really good. I mean it goes for about £120 a pop.'

There was an awkward silence.

'Well, it is bloody delicious. Even if I did think we were drinking Prosecco.' Tilda laughed throatily. 'Sorry, Flo, totally wasted on me.'

'No, it's not, you said it yourself! You knew it was better than your average. But, Susie, will he mind?'

'Oh, don't worry. I'll replace it before he's even noticed. He doesn't even really drink. It's only there so he can impress people when they come round...' Susie tailed off.

'Suse, is everything OK?' Tilda spoke softly.

Susie looked out towards the children, now splashing in the surf as the waves broke gently on the shore. 'It will be.' She turned back to her friends. 'I can't talk about it yet. But I will, one day, I promise.' She tried a small smile.

Flora reached her arm across to take Susie's hand. 'Ready when you are.'

'Absolutely.' Tilda topped up Susie's cup. 'Here, you'd better have this.'

Susie dropped her head, took in a deep breath and looked up at the clear blue sky above them. 'I know it doesn't have to be like this. I just don't know how to get out of it.' Fat tears fell from the corners of her eyes, rolling slowly down her face.

'Is there anything we can do? I mean...' Flora stopped herself, not wanting to push her friend too hard.

'Honestly, it's fine. Well, it's not fine, but... we're just two people who don't really like each other any more. And we haven't for a very long time. I just need to find the right moment to do something about it.' She wiped her eyes with the back of her hand. 'I know he could make life difficult if he wanted to.'

'Are the children OK? I mean, do they know?' Tilda glanced across at them, doing a quick headcount as she did.

'I don't think so. They might have picked up on something, I suppose. To be honest, there's no real communication, but then there hasn't been for such a long time, I'm not sure they know any different.' Susie picked up a pebble, turning it slowly in her hand.

'I guess I just need to hang on in there for a bit longer, until the kids are a bit older perhaps.'

'But if you're unhappy...' Tilda ventured.

Susie turned to Tilda, shaking her head. 'It's not that simple. But I promise I'm fine; the children are good. Honestly, if I need help, I *will* ask.'

'Well, we're here whenever you need us. Aren't we?' Flora looked at Tilda.

'Absolutely. And anytime you need us to polish off another bottle of his very expensive champagne you just let us know.' Tilda raised her glass and an eyebrow.

'Thank you.' Susie couldn't help but laugh. 'I'll keep that in mind.'

Having bribed the children out of the water with the promise of biscuits, they left them wrapped in towels on the rug and walked together down to the edge of the water to wriggle their toes in the shallows, the movement of the water constantly shifting the sand beneath their feet. Susie tossed the pebble she held in her hand into the sea. Together they watched the ripples it left behind as it sank to the floor.

* * *

When they had made their way home, Flora walked into the house, following the trail of wet towels and swimming costumes dropped by the children, like a line of soggy breadcrumbs leading to their whereabouts. Picking them up as she went, she headed to the kitchen. Johnny sat at the table, the top of it covered with paper.

'How was it?' He smiled up at her.

'Glorious, actually. Susie sweetly brought – well, stole – a bottle of very lovely champagne to toast finishing my exams. And the kids all went in the sea.' She dropped the towels by the washing machine. 'How was your day?'

'Well, I think we've done as much as we can. This...' he gestured at the papers surrounding him, 'is my best guess at how we can maximise sales from the range we've got. We haven't got much to go on, given that Mack didn't have an online shop before now – God knows how he's managed to keep it going for so long without it – but having gone through the last few years' transactions I reckon we've got a small number of loyal customers with a pretty high spend.' Johnny tapped at the keyboard as he spoke. 'What we need to do is work on getting more engaged new customers, ones who'll be willing to spend a bit more. Basically, we're always going to have some customers who, I reckon, want nothing more than a cheap bottle of Pinot Grigio in their fridge door or a cheap bottle of Spanish red on the side in the kitchen. And that's fine; we've got wines for them. But if we're going to grow the business, we need to focus on building up this middle bit,' he pointed at a coloured pyramid on the screen, 'and in time, move them into our loyal customer group.' He reached for a piece of paper, holding it out to Flora. 'See this?'

She took it and tried to figure out what she was looking at. 'Give me a clue.'

'Projections. On the left is what will happen if we carry on as we are. We've got six months before our cash flow dries up. But on the right...' Johnny pointed to a column of numbers, '... is what could happen if we really work at it. I mean, we won't be retiring anytime soon, but it does mean we'll be making more than enough for the shop to wash its face and some left over to invest and grow the business. Perhaps eventually open a café at the back of the shop and roll out the events side.' He looked up at her.

Flora took a deep breath. 'Are we completely mad, doing this?' She couldn't help but voice her doubts out loud.

Johnny stared back at the screen. 'Possibly, yes. But, what do they say? You never know if you don't try. And I'm all for giving it a go.' He looked up at her, his eyebrows raised, a smile on his lips. 'How about you?'

She slid herself between the table and his chair, sitting on his lap facing him, arms wrapped around his neck. 'Count me in.' She kissed him.

'Ew, really?' Pip walked into the kitchen, a book in her hand.

'I am allowed to kiss him, you know.' Flora climbed off Johnny's lap.

'I know but still, gross.' Pip pulled a face.

'Hey, Pip, I hear the beach was good fun.' Johnny started collecting up the papers.

'Yeah, it was good. Water was cold but Tilda gave us a whole packet of Jammie Dodgers to share.' Pip picked up an apple from the fruit bowl on the table and wandered off again.

'Ooh, that reminds me.' Flora went to the cupboard, taking out a packet of pasta and a tin of chopped tomatoes. 'I did have a thought at the beach. How about we get some proper music for the party? You know, a small band or something?'

'I think a band might be pushing it. We haven't really got the budget for that.' Johnny shut the laptop.

'I could ask Billy if he knows of anyone. He usually does, when it comes to this kind of thing. It was just a thought…'

'Good idea, if he knows of any DJs – not expensive ones – that would be amazing.'

'Great, I'll message him in a mo.' She called down the hall. 'Can you clean yourselves up, please? Food in fifteen!' She put on a pan of water.

Just then the phone rang. Flora knew it would be her mother, because she was the only person to call on the landline. She saw the familiar number on the screen. 'Hi, Mum, how are you?'

'It's Dad, actually. How are you?'

'Dad! I'm fine, is everything OK?' Flora instantly felt panic in her chest.

'Yes, all fine, darling. Your mother asked me to call to see if there was anything else we can do to help with the party next week. I know you're very organised but if there's anything, you will let us know, won't you?'

Flora closed her eyes. She hadn't told Johnny what she'd seen at the station. She knew he'd try to reassure her there was probably a perfectly innocent explanation. But she knew what she'd seen, and it hadn't looked innocent at all. In fact, it had looked loaded, as if there was a whole history and a whole story that she didn't know about. Part of her didn't even want to know; wished she had been just a few more steps behind so she hadn't seen her father at all.

But the fact was she had seen him. And she knew that at some point she would have to ask him about it. She'd have to know the truth eventually but she wasn't ready yet.

Tom came into the kitchen. 'How long till we eat?'

Flora took the phone from her ear. 'Not long. Didn't you hear me call? Go and wash your hands.' She shooed him out of the kitchen. Putting the phone back to her ear, she tried to think of something to say.

'Are you OK?' Her father sounded completely normal.

*What were you doing with that woman? Why did you look so comfortable with her? How could you do that to Mum?* Flora wanted to shout at him. But the words wouldn't come out.

'Yes, all fine, thanks, Dad. I think we're pretty sorted, actually. If anything, please can you just make sure you're not too late? I know Mum's late for everything, but I think we'll do a little speech early on and I'd love for you to be there for that.'

'Of course, we'll be there. Looking forward to it. See you then.'

'Thanks, Dad, see you then. Bye.'

She put down the phone. Pouring the pasta into the now boiling water, she wondered if she'd ever pluck up the courage to ask. Or was it easier just not knowing and hoping that, over time, it would get easier to ignore? Having set the timer on the oven, she kicked off her shoes and walked barefoot into the garden. Deep down, Flora knew, like a stone in a shoe, what she'd seen would be impossible to ignore for long.

## 12

The morning sun found its way through a small gap between the bottom of the blind and the windowsill, falling on Kate's face. She opened her eyes slowly, stretched her legs, before swinging them round and down to the floor, feeling for her slippers. She crossed the bedroom quietly, picking up the silk dressing gown draped across the small chair in the corner as she passed.

She padded downstairs, Monty trotting close behind her. Robin didn't approve of Monty sleeping in their bedroom but had long given up arguing over it. Kate looked at him, the dog's big brown eyes peering up at her expectantly. 'Come on then, my little sausage.' Opening the French doors, Kate followed Monty out into the garden. Dew still covered the grass, and the birds were already busy at the feeders.

The tulips in the borders had started to shed their petals like fat confetti onto the lawn. Before long the irises, Kate's favourite, would start to come through. She adored this time of year in the garden, so full of promise. Sweeping her gaze across the lawn, she breathed in the cool morning air. She glimpsed the river below as it snaked past, the angle of the moored boats giving away the direction of the tide. Looking behind, back up to the house, her eyes settled on the upstairs window, her and Robin's bedroom. She wished she could sleep as deeply as her husband, but she'd woken early, as usual. She had been thinking about Flora's launch party – worrying about it – although she didn't really know why. Picking a few flowers on her way, Kate wandered back up to the house. She put the stems in a jar, popped them on the side and started laying the table ready for breakfast.

She pottered a while, emptied the dishwasher, finished washing the pots leftover from the night before. Finally sitting at the table, she tried to distract herself with the crossword from the previous day's paper. But she couldn't concentrate. What had started as a fleeting thought when she woke up was now filling her mind. She tried to push it out, summoning other things to fill its place. But no matter how much she tried, she knew it wasn't the party worrying her. Kate closed her eyes, gently shaking her head as if to rid it of the thoughts now flooding in. She threw her head back and opened her eyes again, determined not to let the tears fall. Monty's front paws appeared on her knee. She scooped him up.

'Am I a fool, Monty?' she whispered to him. He looked at her briefly before settling down onto her lap. 'Perhaps I am. But he'll never leave me. So really, who's the fool?'

They both sighed heavily. She gently stroked his soft head, waiting for the uninvited thoughts to leave her mind so she could get on with her day.

\* \* \*

'Tea?' Ruby stood wearing Billy's shirt from last night, her voice a little too perky for his liking at this time in the morning. But given that it had taken quite the effort to win her back round after their temporary split, he knew he was lucky to have her there at all.

Billy pushed his palms into his eyes, rubbing them, desperately trying to wake himself up. He sat up, reaching for the mug of steaming tea. 'I could get used to this.'

'Don't push your luck, sunshine. Your turn next time.' She slipped back under the covers, nestling into him.

'Hey, careful!' He laughed, putting the mug back down on the table.

'Do you really have to go to that meeting?' Ruby ran her hand across his chest, kissing his skin softly.

'Yes, very annoyingly I do. And I'm not going to be back here until at least nine tonight, which means I'm going to have to miss Flora and Johnny's launch party.'

Ruby sat up, hair falling across her face, her eyes wide. 'You have told them, right? Please tell me you have.'

He grimaced.

'Oh, Billy, no! That's really, really rubbish. Why can't you move the meeting? Or just say no, you can't go at such short notice? Flora's going to be so disappointed, not to mention bloody furious, you didn't tell her before. And as for your mother...' Ruby reached for her cup of tea.

'God, I know. But the client brought it forward from next week and now it's a site visit too. I really can't get out of it. I've got to be there. It's the biggest project I've got on at the moment.'

'Well, call Flora this morning and tell her. You must.'

'I know, I know. I will, promise. And Mum. But – and I'm not saying this gets me off the hook – I have organised a surprise for the party, even if I can't be there. Well, not a total surprise, but Flora asked if I knew anyone who might be able to sort out some music. So I've called in a favour from a couple of mates, brilliant DJs. They mix jazz, reggae, you name it... Last time I saw them they finished their set with a reggae version of "Wish You Were Here".'

'Sounds bloody awful, if you ask me.' Ruby blew gently on her tea before taking a sip.

'It sounds better than it, well, sounds. Honestly, they're perfect for this kind of thing.' Billy put his mug down on the table beside him. 'Now, the good news is I don't have to leave for another hour...' He grinned at her and slowly slipped below the covers.

'Billy, no, come on, I've got to get to work.' She laughed, wriggling underneath him. Resisting Billy was never easy. Ruby resigned herself to being late for work. Again.

\* \* \*

Mack poured himself another coffee and carried it outside to the small courtyard at the back of the shop. The air outside was cool, the sun yet to reach it. He took a seat in the corner, the smell of the young lavender plants hanging gently around him. With Kate's help, Flora and Johnny had transformed the flower beds that ran around three sides, clearing them of weeds, filling them with fresh earth and planting them up. Kate had produced a huge antique outdoor mirror from a reclamation yard and it hung on the back wall, reflecting light back into the space.

He looked up at the window above, remembering with a jolt how his own son would sit on the windowsill, watching the grown-ups below. Changing the records so that the music wouldn't stop and, more importantly, the party wouldn't end. Which in turn meant he could stay up that little bit longer. The familiar stab of love and pain filled Mack's chest. How he wished Elizabeth would appear at the back door, gently chiding him to get a move on, finish his coffee and get the shop opened up.

The last few weeks had taken their toll on him. Not just the physical demands of sorting out the shop, but emotionally, too. Of course, he was relieved not to be carrying the business on his own any more, but there was also a sense of it moving on without him. As much as Johnny and Flora insisted his involvement was invaluable, he couldn't bear the thought that they might just feel sorry for him. And though he knew it was time to slow down – the ache in his bones after shifting so many boxes reminding him of that with every move he made – he didn't know what he would do without the shop. It had been his companion for so many years; a constant when those he'd loved had gone. His alibi when he hadn't wanted to engage with the world outside the walls of it.

Now, a brand-new sea-green awning hung in place over the front of the shop. The new window display consisted of wooden boxes painted in bright colours and piled high with various bottles perched on the top (Kate's idea; Flora had been dubious at first, but they all had to admit it looked fantastic).

Inside, the mix of Mack's original wooden shelves with the new tasting table, copper-topped counter and thoughtfully positioned, warm spotlighting (all Johnny's work) had transformed the space. Mack had got so used to climbing over boxes, he hadn't registered the fact that they stopped customers actually being able to get to some of the shelves. But he loved how it looked now. He just wished Elizabeth was here to see it, and he knew she'd have loved it too.

A loud banging on the door brought him out of his reverie. Making his way towards it, he saw a smiling face at the window, waving. It was Colin, all in green. In his arms was an enormous Tupperware box.

Mack unlocked the door. 'Colin! Come in. What are you doing here so early? We're not open yet.'

'Morning, Mack. I know, my sincere apologies for not giving you warning but I wanted you to be able to smell these whilst they're still warm.' Colin nodded his head towards the box, putting it down on the counter. 'Oh, my word, look at this! It looks fantastic in here, Mack!' Colin took in the spruced-up surroundings. 'I love this...' He tapped the new counter-top, then looked around again. 'And look at the tasting table, so clever!'

'Well, thank you, Colin. Flora and Johnny—'

'And who did these?' Colin peered down at the cards on the shelf near him, started reading. '"If you like Sauvignon Blanc, you'll love this crisp, fresh English white wine from a wonderful producer in Devon, made from the Bacchus grape..." Oh, that is very good – did Flora write these?'

'Yes, she did. It must have taken her hours. She's done them so beautifully... Would you like a coffee, Colin?'

'No, no, not stopping. I just wanted to drop these off, as I said.'

'Ah, yes... what's in there?' Mack peered at the box.

Colin lifted the lid with a flourish. 'My much-loved, though I say so myself, home-made Parmesan biscuits. Thought they might go down nicely tonight at the party. I'll need the box back but I hope there'll be enough for everyone to have one or two. How many are you expecting?'

'They look absolutely delicious, thank you. You really didn't need to do that, you know.'

'Oh, come now, it's the least I could do, after all these years you've kept my glass topped up.' Colin put the lid back on the box, clearly delighted with the praise. 'I thought they'd go a treat with our drinks tonight. I assumed you'd be serving something sparkling?'

'Yes, of course, thank you. I think we're about fifty people so plenty enough for a good party.'

'I'd say so. Well, I am very much looking forward to it. I'll leave you to it now, but do let me know if there's anything I can do to help later. I'd be so happy to.'

'I think Johnny and Flora have got everything well under control, but thank you. Just come along and enjoy the celebration, try some new wines. And you're very welcome to bring a friend.'

'No, it'll just be me.' Colin headed for the door. 'It looks wonderful in here, Mack. It really does.'

'Thank you, Colin. Yes, see you later.'

Mack waited until Colin was out of sight, then opened the box and popped a still-warm biscuit in his mouth, letting it melt a little on his tongue. They'd work a treat with the Crémant de Bourgogne he'd picked to be served that night.

'Ooh, have I missed breakfast?' Flora came through the door, catching Mack still finishing off his mouthful.

'That was Colin...'

'Yes, I just passed him. He's very excited about tonight.'

'He just brought these in, he made them himself.' Mack pointed to the box.

Flora lifted the lid slightly and inhaled deeply, the smell making her mouth water. 'Oh, my word, those look amazing. May I?' She took a bite of one, catching the crumbs with her free hand. 'Absolutely delicious...' She nodded her head in appreciation whilst finishing her mouthful. Then she reached into one of the bags she was carrying over her shoulder and pulled out a handful of brightly coloured tissue paper. 'Look what I've got for the garden.'

'What on earth are those?' Mack squinted at them.

'Paper lanterns. I'm going to tie them to strings of lights. It's going to look so gorgeous, Mack.'

'I know you will make it just so, Flora.' Mack picked up the box. 'Right, I'm going to take these upstairs before I eat any more of them. Then shall we make a start on setting up what we're tasting tonight?'

'Good plan.' Flora beamed at him. 'Honestly, Mack, I can't quite believe this is really happening.' Just then her phone pinged in her pocket. She pulled it out and glanced at the screen, reading the first few words of a message from Billy. 'Oh, no...' Her shoulders sank.

'Everything OK?' asked Mack.

'It's my brother, he can't make it tonight.'

'Oh, that is a shame. I was looking forward to meeting him. He sounds like quite a character.' Mack laughed.

'Yes, he is. But also really annoying sometimes, especially when he doesn't show up at the last minute.' Flora rolled her eyes. 'Never mind, his loss. I'll give him a call – and a piece of my mind – later. Come on, we've got lots to do and no time to waste.'

## 13

The first guests were by the door on the dot of 7 p.m. The evening air was warm, the sky clear despite the forecast predicting otherwise. As people arrived and moved through the shop they cooed over the fresh interior, peering at bottles on the shelves, before spilling out into the courtyard.

Flora and Johnny worked the room with perfectly chilled bottles of Crémant in each hand, topping up glasses as they moved through the increasingly noisy crowd. Mack stood at one end of the tasting table, pouring wines for a rapt audience.

Upstairs Pip and Tom sat by the window, watching the grown-ups moving underneath strings of lights and paper lanterns Flora had hung below.

'Here you are, darlings!' Kate appeared at the top of the stairs.

'Hi, Granny!' they chorused.

She came to join them at the window. 'Doesn't it look lovely from here? Although this place could do with a tidy up.' Kate glanced back around Mack's sitting room, noting the piles of books and papers, the dark walls and furniture giving the place a heaviness that made her feel quite claustrophobic. 'How on earth does he live in this mess? It could be wonderful with a bit of TLC...'

'Can we come downstairs for a bit? Please, Granny?' Tom looked up hopefully, deploying his best puppy-dog eyes.

'Darling, I think Mummy wants you both to stay up here. It's not for long.'

Pip fixed Kate with a pleading look. 'Please, Granny? Just for a few minutes...'

'OK, but just for a bit. I don't want you getting me into trouble. Perhaps if you do something useful, like pass some food around, your mother won't mind.'

Just then the sounds of a piano, bass and trumpet floated up from the courtyard. Pip ran back to the window, peering down.

'Listen! There's music! Come on...' Pip grabbed Kate's hand and together they headed downstairs, Tom close behind.

They moved through the crowd in the shop and out into the courtyard. Flora stood by the DJs where they'd set up against the back wall.

Clocking the children, Flora saw her mother was with them. 'Hey, what are you two doing down here? I said you could watch a film upstairs.' She looked at them, their eyes shining with excitement. 'OK, you can stay down here just for a bit, then back upstairs.' She ruffled the tops of their heads then turned to her mother, giving her a disapproving look.

'I said they could come down for a little while, then I'll take them back up, I promise.'

'It's fine, I just didn't want them getting in people's way. And a wine shop isn't the ideal place for a couple of kids to hang out, Mum.'

'I know, I'm sorry... Who are these guys? They're great!' Behind the decks the DJs worked away, overlaying the music with their own percussion instruments.

'Take a guess who sent them.' Flora spoke in Kate's ear over the music.

'Billy?' Kate looked around for him.

'He's not coming, Mum. Something came up, apparently. He messaged this morning. A work meeting up north – he couldn't get out of it.'

'Oh, that's so disappointing.' Kate's face fell, then recovered as she held her glass out when someone passed with a bottle.

'Oh, Mum, this is Colin. You must meet him.' Flora put her hand out to stop him, resplendent in yellow. 'Colin, this is my mother, Kate.'

Colin did a little bow. 'It's an honour to meet you, Kate. You must be very proud of your lovely daughter. She and Johnny really did come to the rescue with the shop.'

'Yes, we are very proud. Aren't we, darling?' Kate looked at Flora, smiling.

Flora remembered her mother's reaction when she'd first mentioned the shop, but she resisted the urge to remind her. 'Yes, hopefully this is just the start of something good.' She smiled back then gestured to the bottle in Colin's hand. 'You don't have to do that, you're a guest.'

'I'm very happy keeping people topped up, Flora. It's so nice to see everyone. And I'm telling them all to join the mailing list.'

'You are brilliant, thank you.' Flora turned back to her mother. 'Colin's a regular, Mum. He's been buying wine from Mack for years.'

'Since he first opened, in fact.' Colin topped up his own glass. 'I remember when he first moved here and he brought all these new wines nobody had ever heard of. We all thought he was quite mad.'

'Well, this is lovely, whatever it is.' Kate raised her glass, taking a sip.

'Oh, look, there's Tilda.' Flora called out and waved. 'I'm just going to go and say hello. She's brought a few of the other mums from school, too. Back in a minute.'

'Hey, you!' Tilda called out, glass in hand. 'Look how beautiful you've made it out here! It looks amazing!'

'Ah, thank you.' Flora squeezed her friend's hand then turned to the others. 'Have you all got drinks? Good. Mack's opening some bottles at the new tasting table and there's plenty to eat, but be quick, it's going fast.' Flora pointed to the counter covered with plates of cheese, smoked salmon-topped blinis and bowls of olives.

'Sorry I'm late!' A clearly flustered Susie appeared by Flora's side.

'You're really not late, and I'm so happy you're here. Let me get you a glass of something. Is Julian with you?'

'No, he said he had to work, but he might come later. I'm sorry...'

'Really, don't worry. It's much more important that you're here. I'll get you some fizz, don't move.' Flora glanced around as she crossed the room to see if she could see her father. No sign.

Just then, Johnny appeared at her side. 'Hey, I was just thinking we should probably say a few words now that most people are here, what do you think?'

Flora nodded. 'Good idea. Shall we get Mack, too?'

'He'd rather I spoke. I did ask him but he's very happy to leave it to us.'

'Then let's do it. Just a quick welcome and thank you. I'll give this to Susie and go and ask them to stop the music for a moment.'

Flora made her way back out to the courtyard. Her father was standing in the corner.

'Hey, Dad, I didn't see you come in. What do you think?'

'It looks fantastic, Flora. You've both done a brilliant job.' He raised his glass to hers. 'Music's a bit loud, though? Sorry to sound like an old man.' He smiled apologetically.

She leaned towards him, speaking into his ear. 'I'm about to ask them to turn it down anyway. We're going to say a few words to thank everyone for coming. But I need to ask you something before you leave.' Flora swallowed hard. She knew it wasn't the best time but given it might be the only one for a while when she'd be able to get him on his own, she'd resolved to ask her father this evening about what she'd seen.

Robin looked at her. 'What is it, Flora? Is everything all right?'

'I don't know, Dad. I was hoping you'd tell me before I had to ask, actually...'

'Flora, what are you talking about?' If he knew what she was getting at, he wasn't showing it.

'Hi, Robin!' Tilda appeared at Robin's side, cheeks flushed with Crémant.

'Hello, Tilda. How are you?' Robin smiled warmly.

Flora looked at her father. 'Before you go, OK?' She looked back at Tilda. 'If you'd like to go inside, Johnny's going to say a few words.'

'Be right there.' Tilda held out her glass as Colin passed.

* * *

'... And last but not least, we'd like to thank Mack for not only running the best wine shop in town – OK, the only wine shop in town...' Flora winked at Mack and the crowd laughed, 'but for having faith in us and our plan for Ten Green Bottles. Johnny and I couldn't wish for a better person to guide us through our next adventure. To Mack!' Flora raised her glass to him.

'To Mack!' The crowd echoed his name, raising their glasses

high too, then whooping and cheering.

'Now, everyone, please make sure your glass is full. You're welcome to stay a while. And for God's sake make Johnny happy by giving him your email address before you leave!' Flora pointed Johnny out in the crowd.

Soon the noise of chatter resumed and the party – and wine – was in full flow. Kate and Colin sat on the wall outside, deep in discussion about interior design. Tilda and Susie perched on the opposite wall, an open bottle of wine between them. The children, having managed to successfully avoid detection, stood behind the decks, Tom banging a cymbal, Pip hitting a cowbell whenever one of the DJs gave them the nod.

'Mack, are you OK staying on the till for a bit?' Flora asked, conscious that he'd been on his feet for much of the day.

'I'm very happy, Flora. Nothing like sending a good wine home with a happy customer.' He winked at her, seeming genuinely happy.

'As long as you're sure... Would you mind if I just go and catch my father? I can see him by the door.'

'Of course, go.' He shooed her away.

Flora slipped behind Mack and caught Robin just as he was putting on his coat. 'You're not leaving Mum here, are you?'

'No, I'm just going to get the car. I had to park further down the high street earlier but I said I'd pick your mother up outside in ten minutes.'

'Dad, does Mum know?'

'Of course she knows, I've just told her.'

'I don't mean that, Dad.' Flora looked around, then back at her father. 'Does she know about the other woman? The one I saw you with at the station the other day. Does she know about that?' Flora felt her neck and cheeks redden. She clenched her fists. 'I'm sorry, I know this isn't exactly the best time to bring this up, but I haven't been able to stop thinking about it and I just need to know. Because...' Flora took a breath, 'you need to stop it and if you don't, Dad, I'll tell her what I saw.'

Her father's look of surprise was almost immediately replaced by one of guilt. 'Flora, I...' He cleared his throat. 'Yes, I think she does know.' Robin lowered his eyes for a brief moment before meeting her gaze again. 'It's complicated, Flora.'

'Really? Because actually it's very simple, I think. You're married. And that means you shouldn't be with another woman at the station. I was there, Dad, I saw it. And I feel sick that I know and Mum doesn't. It's not fair...'

'But, darling—'

'I haven't finished, Dad. I notice you're not denying you're having a relationship with this woman, and you need to stop it. Right now. I'm sorry I saw what I saw, but I did and there's nothing I can do to unsee it. Please tell me you'll stop seeing her, whoever she is.' Flora felt a tear on her cheek, quickly wiping it away.

Robin stood, now looking at the floor again. He spoke softly. 'Flora, I'm so sorry—'

'Is everything OK?' Johnny appeared at Flora's side. 'Flora?' He looked at Robin. 'What's going on?'

Flora fixed Robin with a gimlet stare.

'I was just going to get the car, Johnny. Thank you so much. What a wonderful party.' Robin put on his coat. 'Flora, I'll talk to you tomorrow.' The door closed quietly behind him.

'Flo, what was that all about?'

'I'll tell you later. Let's get this party finished and this place cleared up.' She managed a smile.

'Sure?'

'Sure.' She kissed him briefly, needing to feel his skin on hers. 'Time to get this lot out.'

## 14

The last of the guests stood in small groups in the courtyard, laughter still in the air. Tilda and Susie collected empty glasses, sloshing leftovers into an ice bucket on the counter as they went.

'No sign of Julian, then?' Tilda looked around the room.

'Nope, he didn't make it, but he had told me he probably wouldn't. Surprise, surprise...' Susie sighed, draining the wine in the glass in her hand. 'Pete here?'

'Yes, he's outside, being cornered by that Year 4 mum. Or more accurately, her tits.' Tilda rolled her eyes.

'Doesn't that annoy you?' Susie peered outside, catching the Year 4 mum in question as she employed her very best hair toss followed by a killer pout aimed directly at Pete. In turn, Pete swayed slightly before dropping his wine glass on the floor.

'God no, Pete wouldn't actually do anything. If she tried, he'd run a mile.'

'How can you be so sure?' Susie suddenly realised how that sounded. 'I mean, I know he wouldn't because he's got you, for goodness' sake. But doesn't that make you feel jealous?'

'Of course! I'd kill for those tits!' Tilda laughed heartily at her own joke.

'Tilda, that's not what I meant.' Susie plonked a few more empty glasses on the counter.

'I know, Susie, sorry... It's just that Pete and I, well, we trust each other. Because if you don't trust each other, then, man...' Tilda shook her head gently, 'marriage is going to be one very long, painful journey.'

'But how do you get there? I mean, to a place where you can trust them completely?'

'Shit, Susie, I don't know. I'm hardly an expert, I'm afraid. I've only done it once.' She grinned at her friend.

'I mean, you seem to just assume it's all going to be OK. How do you do that?'

'Because I'd rather that than anything else. I'd rather have Pete than not and, I don't know, maybe it won't last forever but I love him, and if that means trusting him when he's face to face with much bigger tits than mine then that's what I have to do.'

'God, I wish I could be so... I don't know...' Susie looked at her friend.

'Drunk?' Tilda held up an empty glass.

Susie laughed, then shook her head. 'No, thank you. Actually, I think I'd better get home. I didn't realise it was so late.'

'You go. We can stay and help here.' Tilda looked over at Pete. 'I think it's time I went and retrieved him.' She rolled her eyes at Susie. 'What *is* it about boys and boobs? See you tomorrow.' Kissing her friend on the cheek, Tilda turned and headed for the courtyard.

* * *

Mack, Flora and Johnny sat around the tasting table, a small glass of dark amber liquid in front of each of them.

'What on earth is this?' Johnny sniffed at the glass. 'Smells like burnt toffee... in a good way.'

Mack picked up his glass and took a sniff, closing his eyes. 'It's 1976 Terrantez Madeira, aged in American oak casks for twenty-one years.' He took a slow sip and was instantly transported to the small hillside vineyard on the island he'd once visited with Elizabeth many years ago. He could almost see her standing in front of him, straw hat on her head, smiling right at him. 'I opened it yesterday to give it a bit of time to recover. I'd been saving it for a special occasion and this definitely qualifies.' He looked at Flora. 'What do you think?'

Flora lifted the glass to her nose, swirling the liquid gently around. She, too, took a long sniff. 'Oh, my goodness...' she opened her eyes, '... that's insane, Mack.'

'Isn't it?' He smiled at her, then stuck his nose back in the glass.

Flora took a sip, letting the liquid roll around her tongue, taking in the tiniest bit of air to get as much flavour out of it as she could.

Johnny watched them both, amused and amazed at how this drink could seemingly transport both Mack and Flora to another vinous place. Finally, after various noises of appreciation, Flora declared it heavenly.

'And if you try it with a bit of cheese, this one especially...' Mack picked up a piece of crumbling blue cheese and popped it into his mouth.

'Ooh, good idea.' Flora did the same.

'So, what makes this so special, Mack?' Johnny reached for a piece of cheese too.

'Well, Madeira is a funny thing. Basically, back in the seventeenth century, the wine from the island of Madeira was transported on ships in barrels to the tropics and, actually, people realised the wine tasted better once cooked by the sun. Nowadays, most Madeiras are artificially heated up and aged, but the finest ones are still stowed away in casks in the eaves of lodges on the island and heated naturally over years by the sun. Like this one...'

'Hence the baked flavours?' Johnny looked more closely at his glass.

'Exactly. Do you like it?' Mack looked from his glass to Johnny.

'It's one of the most extraordinary things I've ever tasted in my life.' Johnny raised his glass to Mack.

Flora joined him. 'Thank you, Mack. What a treat. You didn't have to open this just for us.'

'I didn't. I opened it for me, too.' Mack smiled, then looked back at the bottle. 'Good wine always tastes better when you drink it with good friends.'

'Well, thank you.' Flora raised her glass to his. 'I'm very glad you did although I'm relieved I didn't get this in the exam. I would have been stuffed.' Flora took another sniff.

Johnny looked at his watch. 'I'm sorry to break up the party but our taxi will be here in about ten minutes. I'll come and pick up the car tomorrow morning.'

Flora looked around the shop. 'Well, if you're happy, Mack, I think we've done as much tidying up as we can now. We're all set for our first proper day tomorrow.' She crossed her fingers.

'Absolutely, you two get going. I'll see you in the morning, Flora.' Mack picked up the bottle. 'Here, take this home with you. I'd rather you finished it off over the next few days. It's not going to keep.'

'Really?' Flora took it lovingly from Mack. 'Thank you so much. That's very kind of you.'

Just then, her phone sounded from inside her bag.

Rummaging to find it, she pulled it out and punched in her passcode. 'Message from Billy. He says he hopes we liked the DJs...' she scanned the message, '... and he's sorry he couldn't make it, but it was murder on the motorway, apparently.' She dropped her phone back into her bag. 'I'll reply on the way home.'

'Thanks again, Mack. See you tomorrow. I'll just go and get the kids from upstairs.' Johnny picked up Flora's coat from the back of her chair as he passed and held it out to her.

Just then, the sound of breaking glass pierced the air.

Flora spun round. 'What the hell was that?'

On the floor, just in front of the wall of fine wine at the back, lay a broken bottle. Red wine seeped out slowly, spreading fan-like across the floor.

Before Mack could get up, Johnny had crossed the room, checking the shelves to make sure nothing else was about to fall.

Flora joined him. 'How on earth did that happen?'

'What was it?' Mack called across.

Carefully, Flora picked up the biggest bit of glass, the label still intact. 'Volnay '82 from... I can't make out the domaine.'

'Don't worry, I know which one that was.' Mack tried to make light of the accident but he was clearly shaken. 'Someone must have picked it up off the shelf to have a look and not put it back properly. It was a bit past its best, if I'm honest, so we don't need to worry too much. Come on, you get going. I can clear this up.'

Flora turned to Mack. 'Absolutely not. I'll go and grab the bucket and mop and find something to put the glass into. It won't take a minute. Johnny, you go and get the kids and, Mack, pour yourself another glass of this.' Flora put the Madeira bottle back down in front of Mack.

'If you say so, Flora.' Mack smiled and poured a small measure into his glass.

## 15

Stephen stood a little away from the rest of the group, drawing heavily on the cigarette held between his thumb and forefinger. The others were climbing into the car, laughing at some joke Stephen clearly wasn't in on.

'Come on, what are you waiting for?' his friend Joe called.

It was supposed to have been a one-off, but borrowing a car from the garage where Stephen worked had somehow become a bit of a regular occurrence. This was their fifth outing, and the plan was always the same. Stephen would collect a car, pick up the group of friends and from there they'd drive to the old airfield outside of town, taking it in turns to perform screeching dough-nuts, and racing up and down the runway. Stephen would then return the car, clean it up if necessary, and leave it in the hope his boss would be none the wiser. He'd wanted to put a stop to it after the first time but somehow he hadn't quite found the courage to say no. Not to Joe, anyway. Joe could be very persuasive. And besides, Stephen didn't want to lose face. Or lose friends, for that matter, even if he knew deep down they were only spending time with him because of the cars.

'Yeah, I'm coming.' Stephen threw the end of his cigarette on the ground and climbed into the passenger side.

'Strap in, lads, we're going for a ride.' Joe revved the engine. The car was a rather unimpressive family saloon but the thrill of it being stolen more than made up for that, as far as Joe was concerned.

Stephen looked across at Joe, wanting desperately to ask if he was sober enough to drive, but instead he clenched his fists and stared ahead. The windscreen was spotless – Stephen had cleaned it himself earlier that day – and as he remembered his boss thanking him for a good day's work, a wave of nausea washed over him.

This really would be the last time, he told himself, as the boys headed out of town in the stolen car.

* * *

Denise Hirst stood in her kitchen, watching the kettle boil. The sound of it grew louder and louder, seemingly magnified by the silence blanketing the room. She glanced at the clock on the wall. It was late, much later than usual. Normally Stephen would come through the door whilst she was still on the sofa, feet up, watching something pleasingly familiar and benign on the television.

She made herself a cup of tea, stirring it slowly, watching the surface of the liquid as she did so. Maybe one more text message wouldn't hurt.

Sitting back down at the table underneath the window, she reached over to move the bottom corner of the curtain to see if there was any sign. But the street outside was quiet, not a soul to be seen. Picking up her phone, she squinted at the screen before typing out another short message. She put the phone back down, picked up her steaming cup and took another quick look outside.

Being the mother of a teenager was never going to be easy, but she'd assumed there would have been a point where he'd start to make slightly more sensible choices.

Her son was nearly nineteen and still living at home. It was just the two of them, and had been since Stephen's father had left her just after Stephen's second birthday. Not that that had ever worried Denise; in fact, had Stephen's father stayed she was sure life would have been a whole lot more complicated.

They'd met when she was just eighteen and, within a year, she was pregnant. They'd talked about getting married – at least, he had – but the pregnancy had been something of a surprise to Denise and she just wasn't ready to marry him. So they'd stayed together, getting themselves a small flat on one of the 'better' council estates, and for a while life had been good. When Denise gave birth to Stephen, she'd never been happier.

Then everything changed. Stephen's father lost his job at the local engineering factory and, after months of fruitless job-hunting, turned back to old habits. He'd managed to hide his very toxic relationship with alcohol from her before they met, but now within a few months the bottle was the most important thing in his life, and with it came a vicious temper. Mercifully, days away from his wife and son became nights away too, until one day he just didn't come home at all.

Denise had spent the first few years after he left hoping he might walk back through the door a changed man, but over time she and Stephen became an increasingly tight unit of two. Stephen had no memory of his father, or so Denise assumed, so she removed almost every trace of him from the flat. The only memento she allowed to stay was one photograph of the three of them together, taken by Denise's mother years ago. The picture was one of pure happiness, Denise looking down adoringly at her beautiful baby boy, Stephen's father smiling at her. She kept it in a drawer beside her bed, face down, every now and again permitting herself a moment to look at it and remember them as a family of three. But it was never long before the more familiar memories of hiding her bruises flooded her mind, along with a crushing sense of shame.

Instead, Denise had long ago decided it was safer to rewrite history, for Stephen's sake. She'd told him his parents had decided to separate because they weren't getting on and that his father had taken a job abroad. She lied about him sending money back each month for the two of them, not wanting Stephen to know that she worked twice as many jobs to make up for the shortfall.

When Stephen started school, his natural shyness held him back from making friends easily. He was always on his own; Denise didn't remember him ever bringing a friend back after school. Desperately worried for her son, she moved him to another school in the hope that he might settle. But he didn't and before long the bullying started. Stephen withdrew into himself more than ever before, and as much as Denise tried to gently persuade him to find hobbies or play football with the other local children, Stephen barely left his room.

Then, in his last year of secondary school, he met Joe, an older boy on the estate. Joe seemed to take Stephen under his wing and before long Stephen was out with his 'friends' almost every evening, but Denise feared they were up to no good. She knew she had to give Stephen some space, but every time she tried to talk to him about what he was doing, Stephen shut her out.

'They're my friends, Mum. You don't know them! Why do you always think the worst of them?' he'd shout.

'Because I'm your mother and it's my job to worry about you.'

'Well, what else am I going to do, Mum? Sit here with you, watching mindless crap on the telly?' The arguments invariably ended with Stephen leaving, slamming the door behind him, and taking Denise's heart and happiness with him.

Getting a job at the local garage had been, she'd hoped, just the kind of change Stephen had needed. Determined not to have to go back to school, he got himself a position as an apprentice and, much to Denise's relief, seemed to have found something he genuinely enjoyed. He worked hard, spending long hours at the garage and he clearly loved the company of those he worked with, talking about them occasionally with his mother when they ate together in the evenings. For a while, she felt that things were at last settling down to something nearer normal.

But then the trouble started again. Stephen heading out late at night, not getting back until the early hours, Denise lying in bed wide awake, or sitting by the window with a cup of tea, waiting for him to return. She asked him who he was with, what he was doing, but his responses were non-committal at best.

Denise rinsed her empty cup and put it upside down on the draining board. She pulled the cord around the middle of her dressing gown a little tighter and headed to her bed, leaving the hall light on behind her.

* * *

Joe hit the dashboard. 'Drop us up here. You're OK to take the car back, aren't you, Stevie-boy?' The two others laughed in the back.

Stephen was now driving; the roads were empty. 'Yeah, no problem.' Actually, he was relieved. The sooner they got out, the sooner he could get the car back. And this was, he told himself, absolutely the last time he was going to let this happen. If he was found out, he'd lose his job and he *really* didn't want that.

He pulled over in a lay-by and they got out of the car, slamming the doors behind them. It was barely a mile back to the garage so Stephen turned down the music, tightened his grip on the steering wheel, and set off towards the industrial estate.

Just then, his phone vibrated in his pocket with a message. He reached for it, shifting in his seat. Pulling the phone out, he glanced at the screen. Three missed calls and a message from his mum. His stomach lurched. He felt guilty for causing her to worry but he felt angry, too: why did she treat him like a baby?

Stephen threw the phone onto the passenger seat, looking back up at the empty road ahead. One last quick blast before returning it the garage wouldn't hurt, would it? And besides, this was the last time he was going to borrow a car so he might as well make the most of it. It wasn't like he needed Joe any more. He'd made new friends at the garage and, unlike Joe, they didn't expect him to steal cars for fun.

The light of the street lamps bathed the road ahead in a soft orange glow. He turned the music up again and put his foot down.

\* \* \*

Billy had tried to get away earlier but the client had insisted on treating him to dinner after the meeting. He'd felt bad enough missing the launch party at the shop, but then he'd had to call Ruby and tell her not to wait up; he knew he wouldn't be back until well after midnight.

'Seriously, Bill, why don't you just crash up there for the night? You must be knackered...' Ruby hated the thought of him not coming home but she didn't like the idea of him driving so late either.

'It's fine, honestly. I'd rather head back tonight. Then I'll come and stay at yours and see you tomorrow, OK? We'll do something together tomorrow night.'

'All right... but drive carefully.' Ruby sighed. 'Love you.'

'Love you, too. See you tomorrow.'

Thankfully, the roads were pretty quiet and he was making good progress, listening to his favourite playlist. A bank of bright yellow flashing lights came into view, an illuminated sign telling him the motorway was shut just ahead. Billy sighed with frustration as he turned off, following the diversion signs, taking him into the outskirts of a town he didn't know.

He carried on along unfamiliar roads, through sets of traffic lights and past deserted business parks. The map in front of him on the dashboard shifted continuously in an attempt to send him back to the motorway. Clearly, it hadn't got the diversion memo.

Billy wasn't sure if he was even heading in the right direction – his senses told him he wasn't – but he had no choice but to follow the yellow signs for now.

Despite dinner earlier that evening, his stomach was rumbling. Seeing a garage up ahead after yet another set of traffic lights, he realised he was starving and his thoughts turned instantly to an urge for drinks and snacks. Billy could almost taste the sweet tang of his beloved energy drink, the one his sister always turned her nose up at. 'I don't know how you can drink that stuff,' she'd say, screwing up her face. Given that he was on his own, he thought he might even go for a packet of prawn cocktail-flavoured crisps.

Billy waited for the lights up ahead to turn green, wondering why they all seemed to stay on red for so long in this town. Just then, a song came on that reminded him of Ruby. Listening to the opening bars made him smile, thinking of how she loved to dance to it, limbs flying, a big smile plastered across her face.

The lights changed from red to green. Billy glanced in the rear-view mirror, then moved off. He could see the garage in the corner of his eye, the light of the forecourt bright against the dark sky. What he didn't see, let alone hear, was the car coming from his right, until it was too late.

* * *

Stephen had been surfing the green wave ever since he'd dropped the others off and, as he looked at the empty road ahead, saw no reason why he couldn't make this one too. Putting his foot down, he gripped the wheel. He saw the lights change to red but by then he'd committed to crossing the junction. He pushed his foot further to the floor.

The car came from the left, almost as if in slow motion. Stephen watched it rush towards him before a loud bang seemed to run through his entire body. Then it fell quiet. He opened his eyes, his ears ringing. An airbag pushed at his front, seemingly holding him in place. He couldn't see through the shattered glass of the windscreen or windows.

As Stephen pieced his thoughts together he tried to move but his body just wouldn't respond. Closing his eyes again, a low moaning noise started to come from somewhere. It took him a moment to realise he was making it. He thought of the other car, tried to move his body again.

He heard voices, a man asking him if he was OK. Stephen nodded slowly. 'Don't move; stay there for a second. An ambulance is on its way.' The man spoke to him through the shattered window. Smoke slowly curled up from the front of the car. Stephen tried to speak but the words wouldn't come out.

'It's OK,' the man said. Stephen wanted to believe him but the look on his face suggested that was far from the truth. 'When will they be here?' Stephen heard him say to someone behind him. The man looked back at Stephen. 'The ambulance will be here any minute. Just keep still for now, all right? We'll get you out of there as soon as we can.'

'What about...?' Stephen heard him ask someone standing behind him, a woman.

'It doesn't look good,' she replied. Her words would haunt him for the rest of his life.

## 16

The sound of her mobile phone ringing slowly dragged Flora from her dreams back to reality. She picked it up to see who could be calling this early and she saw it was her father. The time on her screen was 05:14. Flora's chest tightened.

'Dad, what's happening?'

'Flora, is Johnny there? Is he awake?'

Flora reached across and gently shook Johnny's shoulder. 'Yes, he's here. What's happened? Please, you're scaring me.'

'Flora, Billy's been in a car accident. A serious one. He's at the hospital now and we think you should come as soon as you can.'

Flora could hear the words, but it was as if they were far away, not quite real. She shook Johnny again.

'Flora, what's going on?' Johnny sat up beside her.

'It's Billy, he's been in a car accident. I...' Flora stared at Johnny, unable to make any more words come out of her mouth so he gently took the phone from her.

'Robin? It's Johnny – what's happened?' Johnny nodded, saying 'OK' over and over. Then: 'We'll be there as soon as we can.'

He put the phone down and took Flora's face in his hands. 'Put some clothes on. I'll call someone to see if we can get the kids sorted.'

'Tilda, call Tilda. She'll come.' Flora felt her fingers tingling. She tried to move them, but they were stiff, as if they didn't belong to her. 'Johnny, what did Dad say? Is Billy all right?'

'They're at the hospital now. Billy's being operated on. Let's just get there. Come on, put these on.' Johnny held out Flora's jeans and a jumper grabbed from the pile of clothes at the end of the bed.

She tried to pull them on, but her fingers were trembling too much and she couldn't make them stop. 'Johnny, I can't...'

He moved round to her side of the bed and helped her into her clothes. 'Flo, you're breathing really quickly; try and slow it down a bit. Put your jumper on, I'll go and call Tilda.'

'Is he going... is Billy going to be all right?'

'Your dad didn't say. Now come on, let's just get to the hospital. Put these on.' He pushed her feet into her trainers.

'Johnny, what if—'

'Flora, let's just get there.'

Johnny sat Flora at the kitchen table as he scribbled a note on the pad on the dresser, waiting for Tilda to arrive. Flora tried to make sense of what she'd been told but nothing seemed real. She was shocked to realise that what she felt most was furious. She was so angry at Billy. Angry that he'd been driving too fast, angry that he'd been out too late. How could he have been so stupid?

Tilda swept in, gave Flora a tight hug and nodded at Johnny. 'You go. I'll sort out the kids when they wake up.'

'Thanks so much, I've written down details of where we are on here. I'll call when we know more.' Johnny put his hand on Flora's shoulder. 'Come on, Flo.'

They drove through the cold grey light and soon joined the

early morning traffic on the motorway, red tail lights slowly snaking their way towards the city. Johnny looked across at Flora in the passenger seat, her hands in a tight bunch in her lap. He so wanted to tell her everything was going to be all right, but the truth was he had an awful feeling that might not be true. Something in Robin's voice had told him the situation was far more serious than that.

Flora looked at the people in their cars. She envied them, simply going to work, going about their lives as normal while hers was collapsing. Her fingers were still trembling.

'It's not too far, just another half an hour or so.' Johnny glanced at her again. The colour had literally drained from her face.

Half an hour later Flora was still staring at her hands, her voice barely audible. 'I can't feel them.'

'Not long now, darling. We just have to park. Try not to think about it until we get to see your parents.'

On arrival at the hospital, Johnny went to the reception desk and before long a nurse was showing them through a set of double doors to a small waiting room off to one side. Flora's parents sat side by side on green plastic-coated chairs, holding hands. They both looked up, their eyes red-rimmed.

'How is he?' Johnny asked, putting his arm round Flora as he did.

Robin shook his head slowly. 'I'm so sorry, Flora. They did everything they could.'

Flora put her hands over her ears, trying to stop the words becoming real.

Kate sat motionless in her seat, staring at the floor.

'Oh God, Dad. No, please don't...' Flora looked at her father, willing him to change his story. This was not what was supposed to happen. Billy always pulled through. All through his life, whatever scrapes he'd been in, he'd always walked away in one piece. She closed her eyes, furious with her brother for not walking away from this one.

Johnny took her in his arms. 'I'm so sorry, Flora.' Her ears started ringing. She felt her limbs lighten, as if suddenly not part of her. Everything felt fragmented yet horrifyingly real. And as much as she wanted it to stop, she knew she couldn't change what was happening.

Flora was only vaguely aware of various doctors coming and talking to them in the small waiting room, gently explaining how they'd tried to save Billy. But the damage done in the crash was too traumatic for his body to bear and, in the end, there was nothing more they could have done. She looked around at her family sitting in that waiting room, her parents and Johnny, and thought: everyone seems so still. And there was no sound. Just stunned silence.

* * *

When there was nothing more the doctors could say, they left the hospital together and walked across a bridge towards a church on the other side of the river from the hospital. Not that they'd ever been a churchgoing family – Easter and Christmas visits to their local village one when the children were younger was about the extent of it – but it had been Kate's suggestion, and no one was going to argue.

As they walked along the pavement in the morning sunlight, Flora wanted to stop the people passing her, tell them about her brother. Tell them that he'd died in a car crash. Tell them that he was far too young to be gone. And it was hideous and unfair, and she hated that life was carrying on outside on the street as if nothing had happened.

They filed into the church after Kate, taking in the vast, silent space in front of them, the stillness in stark contrast to the noise of the outside world. Flora headed to a pew at the back and took a seat, Johnny next to her. He squeezed her hand. She felt the physical gesture but as much as she tried to sink into her body to find a feeling, she couldn't feel a thing.

'Johnny, why am I not crying?' Her seemingly cold reaction frightened her.

'Darling, you're in shock.' He looked at Flora, his eyes red-rimmed. 'And you're exhausted. Let's get home and you can get some rest. I'll talk to your father now, see if there's anything more we can do before we go.' Johnny kissed her hand and slipped out of the pew.

Flora slowly raised her head, her eyes drawn to the light streaming through the enormous stained-glass window at the front of the church, the sun lighting up the bright blues and deep reds from behind. She looked to the walls on either side, covered in plaques and memorials. Declarations of love and devotion to people she'd never know, their memories reduced to stone. This was how she felt, like stone. Suddenly, she wanted to sleep. To close her eyes, curl up on the seat and drift off to a place where Billy was still very much alive, waiting for her.

\* \* \*

'Darling, time to go.' Kate gently placed a hand on Flora's shoulder.

Flora opened her eyes, the smell of wood and polish and the sight of the flagstone floor signalling unfamiliar territory. She sat up, putting the heel of her hands to her eyes. 'Oh, Mum...'

Kate looked at Flora. She went to say something, then closed her mouth again before standing up and walking towards the door through which they'd come in.

Flora looked around for Johnny, seeing him talking to her father just outside. She stood up and went slowly towards them.

Stepping out into the sunlight again felt like rejoining a world Flora wasn't ready for.

'Right, Flo. We're going to head home. Your parents are, too. There's nothing more we can do here for now, but your parents will let us know what... happens next.' Johnny tried to make this sound normal, even though the words were anything but, and were the last thing Flora wanted to hear.

Her father appeared beside Johnny. 'I think we all need to get some rest. We can get together again tomorrow.' Robin gently kissed his daughter on the cheek.

'Where's Mum?' Flora looked around for her.

'She's just gone ahead to the car. She said to say goodbye.'

'We'll come over first thing tomorrow, then?' said Johnny.

'Yes, do. Take care, you two.' Robin hugged his daughter, then Johnny.

In the car on the way home, Flora lay with her cheek on the cold window. The journey they'd taken just hours earlier that day felt like a lifetime ago. How she wished she could go back to the day before. Perhaps if she'd really insisted on Billy coming to the party, he wouldn't have gone on that work trip. Or if she'd called him when he was on the road he might have slowed down (she always told him off for driving too fast) and then he would have been just a few more cars behind. More thoughts flooded her head: 'if only', 'I wish', 'why didn't he...?' She screwed her eyes up, willing the thoughts to stop. But still they kept coming.

'You OK?'

'I'm fine.' She'd never been so far from fine in her life and yet this seemed like the easiest thing to say. She knew she should perhaps be asking questions about the accident, about who the other driver was, about what was going to happen to him. But the truth was she didn't care. It seemed pointless knowing anything about it because it didn't make any difference, as far as she was concerned. Most of all, saying next to nothing meant she didn't have to say what she was really feeling, an emptiness so deep it terrified her.

* * *

The next few days passed in a fog. Flora spent much of it at her parents' house, and together, round the table, they planned a small family-only funeral. The shock of losing Billy so suddenly had left them reeling, and organising this seemed, for all of them, the only thing that mattered. Music was chosen, Flora asked to read from one of their favourite childhood poems and Kate insisted on picking flowers from the garden for the small chapel. Johnny kept their whisky glasses topped up and took care of the children.

The day before the funeral, as they sat around the table, Robin brought up the subject of the police report after the accident.

'Dad, I'm sorry but I don't want to know. I don't want to know his name, or anything about him.' Flora put her hand up to stop him talking. 'I don't expect you to understand but, honestly, I don't want anything about it in my head, at all.'

Kate looked at Robin. 'It's fine, darling,' she said gently. 'If she doesn't want to know, that's up to her. We can talk about it later.'

Silence fell again. Flora thought of Ruby. They'd never even met, but Billy had clearly been far fonder of her than he'd let on. 'What about Ruby? How is she? Do we know?' Flora felt terrible; she'd barely given her a thought until now.

Robin cleared his throat. 'Well, obviously we've never met her but I told the police about her when we were at the hospital. They were going to get in touch and tell her what happened.'

'Can I contact her? I want to see if she's OK, let her know we're thinking of her... or something.' Flora thought of the poor girl, sure she would be in pieces, too.

'Yes, of course. I asked the police to give her our contact details so she can reach us if she wants to. I thought it was better that way. I'm sure she'll want to come to the memorial service. I'll let you know when she gets in touch.'

The funeral was held at a small crematorium, a boxy, ugly building just outside the nearest town from Flora's parents' house. The rain hadn't stopped all morning, but when they pulled up at the allotted time that afternoon, the clouds had lifted, replaced with a pale blue sky. Together with their local vicar, a man who'd known Billy all his life, they got through the short service as best they could. Flora squeezed Johnny's hand throughout, feeling as if she was there in body only. It was the saddest day of her life.

Billy's memorial service took place a few weeks later on a bright, sunny day. After the intense, sombre experience of the crematorium, this felt more like a celebration of his life, the church packed with Billy's numerous friends. Songs were sung with gusto, the contributions of friends bringing ripples of laughter with some of the stories. The eulogy, read by Robin, brought both gentle laughter and silent tears to many in the assembled crowd. It was as if a surprise party was being thrown, only for the guest of honour not to show up.

At the drinks in the church hall afterwards, Flora greeted people with a smile. She listened whilst they told her their memories of Billy, how sorry they were for her loss, doing her best to make them feel at ease, knowing they in turn were doing their best to make her feel better. Flora had contacted Ruby just before the funeral, a tearful phone call she'd never forget. Ruby had said she didn't feel it was right to come to the funeral but she did come to the memorial service with her parents. With her blond hair drawn off her pale face, Ruby clearly looked shattered by what had happened.

'I'm so sorry.' It was all Flora could think of to say.

'I'm so sorry, too.' They'd hugged each other tightly, Ruby's eyes filling with tears. 'Can we keep in touch?' she asked shyly.

'I'd love that,' Flora replied. And she meant it.

His friends started to drift on to the village pub once the drinks in the church hall were finished, trying to drag Flora and Johnny with them. But she knew that she needed to stay with her parents, particularly her mother, who by this stage looked utterly exhausted, despite the smile Kate had stuck firmly on her face.

'Mum, do you want me to run you back?' Flora gently squeezed her mother's arm as one of Billy's friends commiserated with her on his way out.

'I'm not leaving until the last person has gone,' Kate said quietly.

Looking into her mother's eyes, Flora could see the pain. She felt her heart break all over again.

* * *

In the weeks that followed, to all appearances Flora started to function more normally again. But really, she felt permanently underwater, seeing shapes and hearing sounds but unable to connect with any of them.

She spent most of her days at home, as instructed by Johnny, taking time out to get some rest. She was barely sleeping at night, too busy fighting to keep the darkest of thoughts out of her head. Subsequently, she was exhausted during the day, unable to focus. Sometimes she'd wake up, forgetting that anything had changed at all. Then, within seconds, it all came back to her and the same feeling washed over her, draining colour from the room.

The children had taken the news as expected, confused at first, then visibly sad. Pip wrote a long letter to Billy, telling him how much she'd miss him, and Tom drew a picture. They hung them on the tree in the garden until one day they weren't there any more, taken by the wind. They asked the occasional question about his death and Johnny calmly explained it was an accident, sudden and shocking, but that the important thing was to remember all the happy memories they had of their uncle, rather than think about the way he had died.

One morning, whilst Johnny stirred porridge for the children at the stove, Flora walked into the kitchen wrapped in her dressing gown, took a seat at the table and suggested it might be time for her to go back to work.

Johnny turned to face her, noticing the dark circles under his wife's eyes. 'Are you sure? I mean, take as much time as you need. Mack and I can manage for now.'

'I want to, Johnny. I need to do something other than sit here, trying not to think about things I don't want to think about. I want to be busy.'

Johnny was reluctant but Flora insisted, and so, later that day, she joined him in the shop.

Mack greeted her with a warm smile. 'It's good to see you back, Flora.'

'Thank you, Mack.' She walked towards the counter, stopping at a gap on the shelves. There, where the bottle of Volnay once stood, sat a single dried white rose in an empty jam jar. She looked back at him.

'I put it there the day after the accident. I've been thinking of you all. I'm so sorry, Flora.' Mack looked at her over his glasses.

She managed a smile, worried the tears that threatened to fall might never stop. Blinking them away, she nodded her thanks, picked the rose out of the jar and made her way into the courtyard.

Johnny went to follow.

'Leave her for a moment.' Mack's words took Johnny by surprise.

'But—'

'Believe me, it'll do her no harm.'

'You've been here before, haven't you?'

'Well, I didn't lose a sibling, but my son died when he was very young.'

'I did know that. I'm sorry if this is bringing back difficult memories.'

'Ah, it was a long time ago, but I do remember feeling, well, very lost for a while. Here but not here, if you know what I mean.'

'I do, as it happens,' said Johnny, softly.

'And it's hard for you because you've got to grieve and keep everyone afloat. But if anyone can do that, Johnny, it's you. Flora is very lucky to have you.'

'I don't know about that...'

'She is. She will get through this, but it's the only way to do it, I'm afraid. To go through it – you can't go round it.' Mack looked at Johnny, his eyes sad. 'I think I've said enough. I don't mean to interfere.'

'Not at all, Mack. I can't tell you how much I appreciate it. Seeing her like this, it's just so awful to watch. And to not be able to make her feel better...'

'But you will be helping, more than you know. Now,' Mack lowered his glasses and peered at the screen in front of him, 'can you take a look at today's orders? Make sure I've not missed anything? Then I can take the van out later.'

'Sure. Thank you.'

Mack nodded. 'My pleasure. I'm just going to go and make some fresh coffee.' Slowly, he made his way up the stairs.

Johnny peered out into the courtyard where Flora sat perched on the wall, eyes closed with her face to the sun. He noticed her hands were in her lap, her fingers holding the rose. Then she leaned down and picked up a small white feather from the ground, holding it between thumb and finger. She looked at it, a faint smile on her face, before letting it go and watching it float gently back down.

## 17

Robin walked slowly over to Kate's bedside, putting the cup of hot tea down carefully on top of her book on the table.

She waited until he'd gone before opening her eyes. In all the years they'd been married, she'd always been the first up, even back when Robin used to catch an early train to London for work. She'd have tea and toast ready for him on the table, the crossword half-done so that she could ask him about the ones she was stuck on before he left, see if he had any bright ideas. Now, for the first time in her life, she just couldn't bring herself to get out of bed, preferring to stay in the half-dark of their bedroom. There she could just lie and lie and think of nothing.

In the weeks since Billy's memorial service, friends had called by, but Kate hadn't wanted to see anyone. Flowers had been left on the doorstep with handwritten notes, all shown to Kate by Robin. Food arrived – endless quiches and lasagnes, pots of home-made jam and bottles of wine – but as much as he tried gently to persuade her that she might like a walk in the garden or down along the river, or to see a friend for a short while, she just shook her head.

Robin had tried again, unsuccessfully, the evening before, to suggest something they might do that day. Now, returning downstairs, he went back into the kitchen to answer the ringing phone. It was Flora.

'I was worried. Mum didn't answer her mobile.'

'She's still in bed, actually.'

'Really?' Flora checked her watch. It was after eleven.

'I'm not really sure what to do.' Robin spoke quietly, not wanting Kate to hear him talking about her. He looked out at the garden, the trees now bare, the flowers in the beds mostly gone.

'Oh, Dad, I'm sorry not to be there to help.' Flora felt guilty even saying the words. The truth was she couldn't face seeing her mother like this and was relieved not to be there, having to deal with it.

'It's OK, darling. I'm sure she'll start to feel better soon.'

'Has she seen anyone?'

'Not a soul. She refuses. And given how many friends she has, there has been quite the procession of people to the house. I've never made so many cups of tea.'

'Oh, Dad, I wish I could come and help. But I just can't... I've got the kids. And work.' Another pang of guilt.

'I know, don't apologise. Life does go on but your mother's not ready yet. She doesn't want to talk about it. All I can do is be here for her, I think.'

'I'll come over at the weekend, bring Pip and Tom.'

'I'll tell her. I think she'd love that. I'm sure she won't say no to her grandchildren. How are they?'

'Amazing, really. They still ask lots of questions and I find that quite hard. About the accident, I mean. I want to talk about Billy, but not about the accident.'

'And you, Flora, how are you? How's Johnny?'

'We're OK, really, Dad. Johnny has been amazing, doing most

of the school runs. I'm back at the shop, though. I needed to do something. Sitting at home was doing me no good at all. I'm better off keeping busy.'

'Quite.' Robin looked at the pile of unopened letters to Kate on the table. 'Right, I'd better go. I'll take up some toast, see if I can persuade her at least to get dressed today, perhaps come out for a bit of fresh air later.'

'Dad, before you go...'

Robin's heart sank. The conversation they'd had at the party all those weeks ago had been left where it was, neither daring to bring it back up again at a time of such devastation. 'Yes, darling?'

'I just want to say, what we talked about at the party, I'm sorry if I put you on the spot. Can we just pretend it didn't happen?'

'It's forgotten.'

'Good.' Flora wasn't quite sure what he meant by that, whether the subject was closed or whether the affair was over, but for now it was enough.

'Fine, so see you at the weekend? Saturday? I'll bring lunch.'

'Lovely, see you then. Bye.'

Robin put the phone back in its cradle. Monty sat at his feet, looking up at him. 'Right, shall we see if we can get her to eat something?' Monty wagged his tail. 'You'd better come with me. Maybe you can persuade her.'

Kate heard them coming up the stairs. She pulled the covers up higher, almost covering her head. Slowly, Robin opened the door, pushing it with his elbow. He walked carefully across the bedroom, placing a tray with some toast and marmalade on his side of the bed.

'Darling, would you like something to eat?' He gently stroked the top of her head, her curls escaping across the pillow.

'I'm not hungry.' Her voice was muffled.

'Please have something, Kate. You haven't really eaten properly for days.'

'I'm said I'm not hungry.'

Robin noticed the untouched cup of tea on her bedside table. He quietly sighed. 'Well, I'll just leave it here, then. It's there if you want it.'

'Thank you.'

'But, Kate, please talk to me. I want to help but I don't know what to do.'

'There's nothing you can do. He's gone and that's it.'

Robin closed his eyes. 'I know. I miss him too.' He tried to keep his voice even.

'Please just go away, Robin. You can't help.'

He stood for a moment, unsure what to do. He so wanted to be able to make her feel better, make her see that life had to go on. She turned her back to him. He sighed quietly, then left the room.

A few days later Kate sat in the waiting room at her doctor's surgery. Robin sat beside her, flicking through an out-of-date car magazine.

'I really don't think I need to do this.'

'It was Flora's suggestion. She told me she'd gone to her doctor for something to help her sleep and it really helped. She thought it might help you too.'

'Did she? Well, I'm sleeping fine, actually. It's the living part I'm having trouble with.'

'Kate, please don't say that.' Robin looked at her. 'Let's see what Dr Harris says.'

As it turned out, Dr Harris asked lots of questions. She asked

Kate if she was able to talk to her family or to a friend about how she was feeling. Kate had said that, no, she couldn't talk to her husband because everything felt broken. Their family, their marriage, everything. And once Kate started talking, she couldn't stop. About how angry she was at Billy's death.

How angry she was at Robin for, she suspected, being in love with someone else. And especially how the latter made her feel so guilty, the fact that she was even thinking about her husband's infidelity when she'd just lost a son.

Dr Harris listened intently, gently, then wrote down a number. 'Kate, you need to talk to someone. Properly, I mean. Give them a call. It's a local counselling service. I think it'll really help. If it doesn't, come back and see me again and we can go from there. And in the meantime, these will help you with your sleep and with your mood.' She handed Kate a prescription.

Robin quickly stood up from his chair when he saw Kate walk back through the doors.

'What did she say?'

Kate looked at him, his face so familiar. She noticed how tired he looked, realising she hadn't really seen him, not properly, for weeks.

'I've got something to get me over the bump.' Kate held up the prescription. She decided not to tell him about the counselling suggestion for now.

'Ah, right. That sounds like a good idea. Well, let's get home, shall we?'

They walked out of the surgery to the car side by side, yet in all their years of marriage Kate had never felt they were so far apart. No matter what life had thrown at them before, they'd weathered it as a team. More than that, they'd always brought the best out in each other. But now everything felt different.

They drove home in silence bar the quiet classical music on

the radio. Robin attempted to engage Kate in conversation but each time she cut him off with a one-word answer.

The sky was steel grey, the light flat. Robin tried hard not to, but he couldn't help but think of Ally. It had been weeks since he'd spoken to her. They'd met at a work function years ago and had managed to conduct their affair without anyone knowing, or so he had assumed. Robin still had the excuse of travelling to London for the occasional meeting, where they would see each other, mostly for lunch and a short walk in the park before returning to her flat for a time before Robin headed home.

Things had got more complicated when Ally had decided to move out of London, retiring from her City job. She sat on various boards of museums and foundations, which meant she still had an excuse to be in town, but she wasn't there as often as she'd once been.

Still, they'd continued to see each other when they could, always meeting in town and travelling back together to the station near her home. He loved Kate, too, but Ally was so different from Kate. They talked endlessly. She made no demands. And, of course, the sex was better.

But since Billy's death, he'd not been able to bring himself to call her. And she hadn't been in touch – why would she? She'd always left it to Robin to make contact. Sadly, he realised what he missed most was having someone to talk to. Kate seemed to be disappearing before his eyes, moving further and further away.

The thought of Billy made him ache for a time when they'd all been together, before the children had grown up and moved away, when they were happy as a family of four. He missed that terribly now.

Robin looked across at Kate, lost in her own thoughts as she stared out of the window. How he wished he could reach across, touch her face, but the gap felt too wide.

She'd always loved him unconditionally and he, in turn, had been foolish. He'd put the greatest love he'd ever known at risk for purely selfish reasons. Seeing her now, and with everything that had happened, he knew it was up to him to help bring Kate back to life.

## 18

Mack had opened the shop as usual and was just sorting through the deliveries in the back room when Johnny walked in.

'Morning, Mack.'

'Morning. I'll be out in a minute,' he called back.

'No rush. I'll just go through the numbers and have a look at what's come in.' He helped himself to a cup of predictably strong coffee on his way past the counter, then took up his usual post, perched at the tasting table with his laptop open before the shop got busy with customers. Trade had picked up lately but Johnny didn't want to push Flora too hard. She seemed to be getting back into some sort of routine, but he was conscious that it would take time.

'How's Flora doing?' asked Mack, as if reading his mind.

'Good, thanks. She seems much better. I mean, she's still not sleeping brilliantly. And I know she's emotionally pretty exhausted but she's keen to try and keep busy. Having said that, she's not coming in today. She's meeting up with her friends for a long walk on the beach this morning, so I told her not to worry about coming in if she didn't want to.'

'Ah, right. Well, one day at a time. How are the orders looking? Do I need to get the van?'

'Yes, you do, I'm glad to say. But I'll do the run today, Mack. I need you to do something else for me whilst I'm out.'

'What's that?'

'Write down which wines to try if we're going to Venice.'

'When are you going to Venice?'

'Well, if it's all right with you I thought I'd take Flora out for a long weekend next month, before we get really busy in the shop in the run-up to Christmas. She went there with her parents and Billy when she was much younger. She used to talk about it sometimes; she obviously loved it. Apparently, Robin insisted on driving them across Europe in their old Morris Traveller to visit the only place where you can't have cars. Anyway, I thought she might like a change of scene and I reckon Venice can provide that. Also thought it might be nice for her to go to somewhere that she once went with Billy.'

'Well, that is...' Mack left it there.

'What? You don't sound convinced. Not a good idea?'

'Definitely your call, Johnny. It's just that... don't expect too much. Not yet, anyway.'

'Understood. Absolutely no expectations. I just thought she might like it. We've never been together, and it's not too far so we can do it over a long weekend.'

'You're a good man, Johnny. I'll make a list whilst you're out.' Mack smiled but his heart sank a little, knowing they had a long road ahead.

* * *

The three friends walked along the stony beach, the clatter of pebbles beneath their feet. Waves gently rolled in on the rising tide, a soothing soundtrack to their conversation.

Tilda and Susie had been a near-constant source of support for Flora since Billy's death. Susie had supplied endless meals for the freezer, Tilda had taken it upon herself to message Flora every single day with something to try to make her smile, from cat GIFs to crude jokes. And between them they'd taken the kids off Flora and Johnny's hands for various trips to the park at least a couple of times a week. Flora didn't know what she would have done without them.

But the thing she really missed was talking about Billy. Of course, it wasn't their fault – they hadn't really known him. In fact, Susie had never even met him. Flora looked down at her feet, watching the pebbles shift as her feet sank into the ground with every step.

'... And then, you won't believe what she said.' Tilda's voice took on a dramatic edge.

'What?' cried Susie.

'She said, and I quote, "That's ridiculous. Ivo would never bite anyone."'

'But he's the original biter!' Susie rolled her eyes.

'Exactly.' Tilda shrugged. 'I mean, *I* always assume my kids are guilty unless proven innocent.' She laughed.

Flora laughed too, a beat behind the others. She knew they were trying to distract her with the small stuff, and she loved them for it. But however much she tried to be fully present, she just couldn't quite get there.

Tilda broke the brief silence. 'Hey, Flo, how's the shop going?'

'Good, I think. Trade is picking up now. I should be working today but Johnny told me to have the day off.'

Susie squeezed Flora's arm. 'You should. After this why don't you go home and put your feet up with a good book? I'd do anything to have an excuse to have a day off... Oh God, I'm sorry. That's really insensitive, isn't it?'

'It's fine, really.' Flora smiled gently at her worried friend. 'Please don't think you're saying the wrong thing, ever. I honestly don't know what I would have done without you two. You've both been so amazing. I mean, Johnny has too, of course, but I can't expect him to fix everything. And as for my parents...' Flora let out a small laugh.

'What's happened?' Tilda had always thought of Flora's parents as the perfect happily married older couple. She knew things had been tough for them recently but that was to be expected.

'Well, nothing really. But that's the point. They don't really talk about it. About Billy. Or to each other, for that matter, about anything. I've started to find excuses not to visit or put them off coming to see us because – and I feel terrible for saying this – I just can't face it. It makes me so sad. Mum has just shut Dad out. And just before... I saw something I really wish I hadn't seen.'

Tilda and Susie both looked at Flora.

'What?' whispered Tilda.

'I saw my father at the station. He was with someone and it wasn't my mother.'

'Really?' Tilda's eyes practically popped out of her head. 'But your father seems like the last person on earth who'd ever be unfaithful!'

Flora shrugged. 'I thought so too. I tried to tell myself it wasn't anything but I know what I saw. They definitely weren't just friends.'

'Oh, no, Flora, I'm so sorry. Have you asked him about it? It could have been perfectly innocent?' Susie gently put her hand on Flora's shoulder.

'Well, he knows I saw him, but I haven't really talked to him about it properly. I'm too terrified of the fallout. I mean, it would absolutely crush Mum if she knew. She couldn't deal with that on top of everything else.'

Susie felt her stomach tighten. Julian had always assumed she didn't know about his affair, but the truth was she'd always known. 'Are you sure it's still going on? It might change now, given what's happened.' Susie hoped this didn't sound too brutal.

'I just need to think about it – what to do, I mean. I'd hoped I could try to forget it, but I can't even bring myself to talk to him properly. It's like he's making me keep a dreadful secret. If Billy were here...' Flora looked out towards the horizon. She felt completely hollowed out.

'Have you told Johnny?' asked Tilda.

'No, I've just sort of buried it for now. I can't even... Anyway, I think Johnny's planning something. For me, I mean. Like a surprise. The last thing he needs is to worry about my parents, too.'

'Really? What's the surprise?' said Susie.

'I think he's planning a long weekend away.'

'Ooh, how lovely. Any idea where?' Tilda sounded genuinely excited on Flora's behalf.

But Flora didn't really feel anything, neither excited nor bothered. Just totally indifferent.

'Venice, I think. I saw his laptop open on the kitchen table last week. I went there years ago with my parents. I remember it so well. It was the Venice Biennale, not that we knew that when we turned up. The whole place was packed, flags everywhere, great art installations sticking out of the Grand Canal. All quite bonkers, but amazing to see. Johnny's obviously already done a 360-degree virtual walking tour of the city according to the

YouTube video he was watching when I came into the kitchen yesterday. He's nothing if not thorough in his research.'

'Oh, you have to love him for that. How thoughtful!' Susie grinned.

'I know, it's a lovely thing to do but I can't help feel... well, just not as happy about the idea as I should, really.'

Tilda stopped and turned to her friend. 'Listen, Flo. You've been through the most awful time. And we can't even begin to imagine how you must be feeling, but maybe a little bit of time away, in a beautiful place... it might just be a nice change?'

'I know, I don't mean to sound ungrateful. It's just that I feel... I don't know, really. He's going to take me all that way and I'm still going to feel like this. I'm sorry, I sound horribly depressing, don't I? I promise I won't always be like this.' Flora managed a smile for her friends.

'I bloody well hope not.' Tilda threw her arms around her. 'But in the meantime, you be however you need to be. We're not going anywhere, are we, Suse?'

'No, we are not.' Susie smiled at Flora. 'No rush, Flo.'

'Thank you. I really love you two.'

'Love you, too. Right, who wants a hot chocolate?' Tilda pulled a flask from her basket. 'It might have a tiny bit of rum in it, just so you know.'

'Tilda, it's not even eleven o'clock.' Susie laughed.

'I know, but our friend here is grieving so mid-morning drinking is totally acceptable.' Tilda plonked herself down on the pebbles. 'Who's first?'

'Seriously, though, Venice. I'm so jealous.' Susie sighed.

'Well, I don't know for sure. He hasn't mentioned anything yet.'

'Let us know when he does. We can look after the kids

between us, if that helps?' Tilda looked at Susie, who nodded back quickly in agreement.

'Definitely, we can work something out.' Susie took the proffered cup of hot chocolate from Tilda, the soothing, slightly boozy smell hitting her nose before she'd even taken a sip.

'Thank you. I'll let you know if he says anything.'

The three friends looked out at the sea, watching the small white horses on the waves riding into shore. The wind had picked up a little, carrying a chill with it. Curling her fingers around the cup, Flora closed her eyes for a brief moment and let herself think about her brother. She recalled his face, his smiling eyes, slightly lopsided grin and that mop of hair.

She was scared of forgetting what he looked like, what he sounded like, even of forgetting his smell. What if it all started to fade from her memory? She had plenty of pictures of him around the house, including favourites she'd put into frames not long after he died. But it was his physical presence she was starting to forget and that scared her. She wanted to cling to every last part of him she possibly could. She wanted to fill a memory bank with everything he'd said and done, the sound of his laugh, the way he walked.

It felt like time was taking the memory of Billy away from her and Flora couldn't bear the thought of losing him again.

# 19

'How was your day?' Johnny came into the kitchen, laptop under his arm.

Flora stood by the oven, stirring a huge pot of bolognese. 'Good, thank you. I saw the girls this morning. We had a gorgeous walk on the beach. It was cold, though. The kids are clearing up their rooms – at least that's what I asked them to do. How was the shop?'

'It was a pretty good day, actually. I've decided I'm going to start getting out there to drum up new on-trade customers. We've always relied on Mack and his contacts until now, but I need to go and knock on some restaurant doors to see if we can get in to see them properly, show them some wines. But I'll need you or Mack to come and lead the tasting bit. That's way beyond my capabilities.'

'Oh, come on, you're getting good at this stuff. It might be time for you to do a wine course next.' Flora laughed gently.

'You must be joking. I saw what those exams did to you.' He smiled back at her, reaching for an empty wine glass. 'What's open?'

'Actually, this is lovely.' She held up her glass. 'Xinomavro.'

'Zino-what?' Johnny looked at the red wine, taking a sniff of her glass.

'Xinomavro, it's a Greek red grape variety. And it's got something of the Nebbiolo about it.'

'The Barolo grape?' Johnny couldn't help but look quite pleased with himself.

'Exactly.' Flora nodded in approval. 'So it should, in theory, work with this.' She pointed at the pan on the stove.

Johnny took a sip. 'Oh, that is good. Might have to have one myself.'

Flora swirled her glass, sniffed and took a sip. 'Earthy, but not too heavy. Good, isn't it?'

'Don't drink it all. I'll just go and say hello to the kids, then I'll be straight back. I've got something to tell you, actually. Something good, hopefully.'

'Can't wait.' Flora's heart dropped a little. 'I'll pour you a glass.'

As soon as he'd left the room, she put her hands to her face and took a deep breath. Her phone rang. It was her mother.

'Hi, Mum.'

'Hello, darling, how are you?'

'I'm fine, you?'

'Well, I wouldn't describe it as fine, but you know. Whatever.'

'You're right, Mum, I'm not exactly fine either, but you know what I mean. I don't really know what else to say.'

'How about angry? Or sad? Just something other than fine might be more meaningful. I heard you went to the doctor, got something to help you sleep?'

Flora stirred the pot slowly, took a breath before answering her mother. She could hear from Kate's voice she was in the mood for a confrontation. 'Mum, please. I'm not trying to belittle... I'm not... It's just that I think,' she paused, 'I feel differently from you. Of course, I'm sad but I'm not angry any more. I don't think I've got the energy to feel angry.'

'Well, I *am* angry, as it happens.' Kate's voice was flat. 'Angry that Billy isn't here. And I'm really fucking angry that someone drove a car into his and that they *are* still here. They got to live. Billy didn't.'

'Mum, can we not... Please can we talk about this when we're together? I can't do this on the phone.' Flora's head began to fill with thoughts she didn't want in there. The sound of cars, the flash of blue lights.

'I know you don't like talking about it, Flora. But soon there will be a trial and perhaps then you'll understand.'

'Mum, I can't possibly ever know or understand how you feel. I haven't lost a son. No one should ever have to go through that, I know that much. It must be the absolute worst feeling in the world. I can't imagine what I'd do if anything happened to my two. But,' she swallowed hard, 'I lost a brother and that hurts too.'

Kate was quiet for a moment. Her voice softened. 'I'm sorry, darling, but that's how I feel. I'm not saying it's any easier for you...'

'Mum, I just—'

'Let me finish, please, Flora. I'm just saying I feel angry, that's all. And I'd like to be able to say so.'

'OK, Mum. I know. And that's totally fine.'

'Will you please stop using the word "fine", Flora. None of this is fine!'

By now Flora's heart was pounding. She wanted to scream at the top of her voice, wanted to yell that it was so far from fine. But all she could manage was: 'I'm sorry, Mum.'

'No, I'm sorry. I shouldn't be taking it out on you. But...' Kate sighed heavily, '... your father is, well, he doesn't say much, and

I'm left feeling like I'm going mad. The world carries on and I want everyone to stop and know how bad it is that Billy's not here any more. And it wasn't even his fault.'

Flora could hear from her mother's voice that she'd started crying. Johnny walked back into the kitchen, clocking from the look on Flora's face that the conversation was complicated.

'Look, I've got to go. I'm sorry but the kids need feeding and Johnny's just got back.'

'Of course, yes. You're busy. Ring me when you have time.'

'Mum, please don't sound like that. Now I feel bad.'

'No, you go. Bye, darling.' The line went dead.

'Well, that didn't sound brilliant.' Johnny picked up his glass from the table.

'No, it really wasn't.' Flora sat down. 'It was terrible, actually.'

'What happened?'

'It's like, I don't know...' Flora was quiet for a moment. 'The most terrible thing has happened but because we're all dealing with it in different ways, we can't talk about it. Like we're just not able to find a way to talk about it. About anything, really. I literally don't know what to say.'

'What do you mean?' Johnny placed a hand on Flora's.

'Well, Mum feels really angry about what happened while I can't even bring myself to think about the accident. I want to remember the good stuff before I forget it and I'm just left with the bad. But Mum's stuck on that bit. She keeps talking about the court case coming up. And I don't even want to think about it, any of it. Maybe I'm not ready to deal with it. Perhaps I won't ever be... but,' Flora shrugged, 'definitely not yet.'

Johnny thought about it for a moment. 'Listen, I know it feels like things will never be better, but I promise you they will. It just takes time.' He stroked her hair, his fingers moving to her cheek to wipe away the tears slowly falling down her face. 'In fact, I've got an idea, something that might just help.'

Flora looked at him. 'What?'

He took both her hands in his. 'I've been thinking we should go away for a few days, just us. Have a change of scene, spend some time together without having to worry about the kids, the shop. Or your parents. I love them but, you know... I just think you could do with a small break. So, how about we go to Venice for a couple of days? Good idea?'

She looked up and smiled at him. 'That would be lovely, thank you.'

'Are you sure? You don't look very sure.'

'No, I am, really. I'm sorry... that would be amazing.' She forced an even bigger smile onto her face.

'You went there with Billy when you were younger, didn't you? I thought it might help, you know, to be somewhere that might remind you of him in a good way.'

'That's really thoughtful, thank you.'

'Great, I'll sort it out and we'll go as soon as possible.'

'Tilda and Susie can have... I mean, I'm sure they can help with the kids if it's just for a couple of nights.'

'Perfect. I'll talk to Mack about dates and we can work it out from there. Honestly, I think you'll love it.'

Flora kept the smile on her face but hated herself for not feeling more grateful.

\* \* \*

'Seriously, there's such a lot we've got to fit in.' Johnny pointed at a map on his laptop, Mack behind him with a small glass of wine in his hand. 'There's St Mark's Square, the museums, the Rialto markets... It's going to be a bit of a squeeze but we should be able to just about do it in two days, well, one and a half, if we have a plan.'

'Which, no doubt, Johnny, you will have.' Mack laughed, raising his glass.

'Absolutely, Mack. You know me.' Johnny raised his coffee cup back.

'Where will you stay?'

'I've found a small hotel, just off the Grand Canal but a bit behind the main drag. Nothing fancy but it ticks all the boxes.'

'Sounds perfect. I know you'll want to see all the big sights, but you must make time to just wander through the streets of the Cannaregio area to the north and sit a while with a glass of something whilst you watch the world – or rather, the local neighbourhood – go by.'

'Definitely. You'll have to show me where to go on the map.'

'Goodness, it was a while ago. I went there with Elizabeth, before Jamie was born. We spent the days just walking about. We even went to the Lido and out to Murano, you know, the place with the glass? She loved it. I still have some of those glasses somewhere. We never used them; Elizabeth was too worried we'd break them.' Mack made a mental note to try to find them, take them out of their box and use them from now on.

'So, if it's OK with you, we'd like to try and fit it in before Christmas. Before it gets really busy, that is. I've got some cover lined up: Flora's friend Susie is keen to come and help in the shop during the day. She doesn't know much about wine but is great with people and really keen to help.'

'Fine with me, just let me know when suits you.' Mack put down his glass and peered closer at the map. 'It's this bit here,' he pointed at an area on the map, 'full of little bars and restaurants where the locals go, not just tourists.' Mack shoved his glasses further up his nose. 'I remember one particular wine bar where we drank one of the most delicious glasses of Soave I've ever had. It was so subtle but so pure. I'll have a look through my old wine notebooks, see if I can find the name of the place. If I do, you must promise me you'll go.'

'Based on that wine recommendation alone, I promise,' Johnny laughed. 'Right, I'd better get on with the stocktake.'

'Ah, yes, don't let me keep you from your spreadsheets.'

'You may laugh, Mack, but without those spreadsheets...'

'I know, I'm teasing. You know I'd be lost without you both.' Mack turned to go up the stairs. 'Actually, there's another place I've just remembered. I can't think what it's called but there's a heart-shaped stone, red brick, somewhere in the streets just off St Mark's Square. Legend has it that if you and your loved one both touch the stone at the same time you'll stay together forever. I remember Elizabeth was adamant that we find it.'

'And did you?'

'I'm not sure we ever did.' Mack shook his head, a smile spreading across his face. 'I think we got sidetracked.'

'I'll add it to the list, Mack.'

## 20

---

Kate looked out across the garden. Robin sat at the other end of the table from her, finishing off the crossword she had started earlier that day, a pot of tea between them.

'I really must go and sort out those flower beds, but it's so miserable out there I just can't face it at the moment.'

'Kate, there's no hurry. You don't need to do anything, not right now, anyway.'

'Well, I'm sick of sitting here waiting to feel better.'

Robin put down his pen and went to stand behind her, putting his hands on her shoulders. 'My darling, I'm so sorry. I wish I could make you feel better, I really do.'

Kate let out a small laugh. 'Well, no one can ever make me feel better. This pain is never going to go away! Billy's never coming back!' She put her head in her hands. Every time she thought she couldn't cry any more, along came more tears. Sometimes she felt as if they'd never stop.

Robin sat beside her. 'Please, Kate. I know it's awful. I wish with every bone in my body this wasn't happening. But there's nothing we can do to change what's happened. All we can do is try and come to terms with it. And remember that in all of this, what's important is that our beautiful boy was here with us for all that time. Think of the happy times we had with him, not just the pain of him not being here any more.'

'Oh, for God's sake, Robin, how can you make it all sound so simple? It's not like there's a tap for my feelings. I can't turn them from sad to happy just like that!'

'Darling, I understand. I miss him terribly. But we still have to live our lives; we still have our family to think about. We can't forget Flora, Johnny and the children... they all need us, too.'

'There you go, putting Flora ahead of me. As usual.' Kate looked up at Robin, her eyes red, tears soaking her face.

'Oh, Kate, please don't say that. It's not about putting anyone before anyone else. All I'm saying is—'

'All you're saying is "move on", "pull yourself together".' Kate spat the words out.

'I'm really not, Kate. I promise, that's not what I meant at all.' Robin dropped his head onto his chest, closing his eyes. He gently let out a long, slow breath. Opening his eyes, he saw Monty looking hopefully from him to the French windows on to the garden. 'You want to go out?' Monty wagged his tail and skittered to the window. 'Come on, then.' He opened the doors, turning back to Kate. 'Fancy a walk down to the end of the garden with me? It's not raining any more, at least.'

'No, you go. I'm fine here.' She thought of Flora, their conversation the last time they spoke. 'They'll be in Venice by now.'

Robin looked at the clock on the wall. 'When did they land?'

'About an hour ago, I think.'

'Lucky things, let's hope it gives them a real break.' Robin sighed. 'Do you remember when we went, all those years ago?'

'Mostly the drive.' Kate rolled her eyes.

'Oh, come on, you loved it once we got there. Do you remember the children racing through St Mark's Square, chasing the pigeons through the puddles?' He thought of Billy tearing ahead, shrieking with delight as the pigeons took flight, only to land again just a few feet away.

Kate couldn't help but smile at the memory. She looked up at Robin. She'd loved this man for so long and yet she noticed a different feeling when they were together now. Something was starting to build in the pit of her stomach, like a small fire burning. She wasn't quite ready to think about what it might mean, but she knew it was there. And it was only a matter of time before she'd have to decide whether to let it burn or put it out once and for all.

* * *

The blue-green waters of the Venice lagoon parted under the bow of the water taxi as it sped towards the city. Flora sat at the back, reclining on the seat with her coat wrapped around her, her scarf trailing behind her in the wind, sunglasses firmly in place.

Johnny stood up, taking in the sight of the floating city in front of them. The late afternoon sun cast a pale orange glow across the sky, the outline of towers and domes sitting above the horizon, the sturdy Ponte della Libertà on their right. The driver pointed out various landmarks to Johnny who tried, in broken Italian, to exclaim his joy at seeing it all for the first time.

As the city drew nearer, the taxi slowed and soon, they were gliding along the Grand Canal. Flora looked up at the tall, flat-fronted buildings sitting on either side, many storeys high. Boats passed them on either side, empty gondolas floating lazily at the edges tethered by posts that looked like candy canes.

Before long they had docked at a pontoon and as Johnny waved off their water-taxi driver, Flora took in the scene around her. The fading light brought a melancholy air to the city.

They made their way down a narrow passage towards a small white stone bridge. 'This is it,' said Johnny. Flora noted the slight note of triumph in his voice.

She followed him through an ornate iron gate into a courtyard filled with shrubs in heavy, weathered stone pots. Two large columns stood either side of the glass front door of the hotel, a balcony above. The building was relatively modest compared with those lining the Grand Canal yet still had that unmistakable air of faded glamour about it. Flora loved it on sight.

The receptionist greeted them like old friends, whizzing them through the formality of signing various forms. She placed their room key on the desk. 'Room fourteen on the third floor, second door on the right as you come out of the lift. Would you like me to make a restaurant booking for you this evening anywhere?' she asked, her bright red nails hovering over her keyboard, her short dark hair lacquered neatly into place.

'Well, we thought we'd start with a drink at Harry's Bar and take it from there.' Johnny looked at Flora. 'Don't you think?'

'Sounds good.' Flora smiled.

The receptionist screwed up her nose. 'Is *very* expensive there. Twenty euros for a Bellini the size of your thumb.' She held up hers by way of demonstrating her point.

'Yes, but it's got to be done, don't you think?' Johnny gave a little shrug.

'Well...' She shrugged back. 'Whatever you think... but just in case, head over the bridge towards Dorsoduro and you'll find nice places there, too.'

'Thank you, good to know.' Johnny nodded enthusiastically, picking up their bags. 'Right, see you later.'

Standing in the small lift, Flora hit the button for their floor.

'You OK, Flo? You're very quiet.'

'I'm good, just a bit tired, I think.'

'We can have a rest before we head out, if you like. How about a hot bath?'

'Actually, I'd love that.'

He unlocked the door to their room. Johnny hit the light switch, throwing a stark white light across the room. The double bed, with its imposing wooden headboard, was draped with a deep red cover reaching the floor. Matching floor-to-ceiling curtains hung heavily in front of the windows, an old dressing table between them and a chest of drawers on the wall opposite the bed.

Johnny put his head around the door of the bathroom on the other side of the bed. He looked back at Flora. 'Massive bath,' he called back. 'I'll run you one now.'

Flora went to the window on the right of the dressing table, drawing back the curtain. The light was fading fast, the sun now long gone, replaced with an inky blue sky. She looked out at the crumbling pale orange wall of the building on the other side of the narrow canal, so close she felt if she stretched across, she could touch it.

Flora looked back at the bed. Here she was, in the most romantic city in the world, with the man she loved more than anyone. And yet, all she wanted to do was climb under that thick blanket, close her eyes and sleep. Her heart felt heavy; in the pit of her stomach lay a low, dull ache. Much as she'd hoped she might have left that feeling behind, even if only temporarily, it seemed she had carried it with her to Venice like unwanted hand baggage. She gently lowered herself down to sit on the edge of the bed.

'It's nearly ready.' Johnny crossed the room to her. 'No rush.'

She stood and kissed him gently. 'Thank you.'

Soon after, Flora lay in the bath, wishing the piping hot water would soak the sadness from her bones.

## 21

About an hour later they left the hotel, crossed the small bridge and headed into a maze of narrow alleys, the light from street lamps thrown onto the cobbles beneath their feet. This hidden part of the city felt still, peaceful. They passed under porticos, over more small bridges and down a long street where, at the end, Flora caught a glimpse of the Grand Canal. Turning right, they walked under the arches and into the empty space of the Rialto fish market. Wooden poles poked up like giant toothpicks on either side of the canal, numerous small boats tethered to them.

'Do you know where we're going?' Flora asked, noticing Johnny look at his phone, then up, then at his phone again.

'No, but this does.' He tapped the screen. 'It's this way, over the Rialto Bridge.' He pointed ahead. 'We're crossing there.'

Flora looked up to see the bright white stone of the bridge, lined with archways and seemingly lit from within. They walked across it, the shutters down on most of the shops on either side. She stopped halfway to take in the view, first one way, then the other. The canal reflected back the light from the buildings at the water's edge, small waves making it dance on the surface.

On they went, down streets and along alleys, across squares with enormous churches suddenly seeming to appear from nowhere, past ornate gateways on to courtyards, hinting at the hidden splendour behind the façades. The air was cool on Flora's face. She pulled her scarf a little tighter around her neck and shoved her hands deeper into her pockets.

'Want to walk through St Mark's Square before or after we've had an extortionate Bellini?'

'After, definitely.' Flora smiled.

Arriving at a small wooden door at the end of the narrow street, Johnny pushed it open and waited for Flora to go in first. She walked in, clocking the bar along one side, the dark wood, the waiters in crisp white jackets moving between tables. It was much smaller than she'd imagined. Six bar stools, each topped with a soft padded seat covered in worn light-brown leather ran along the length of the bar, an array of spirit and vermouth bottles lining the shelves behind.

Johnny moved towards one of the small empty tables beneath a window on the far side. They sat and waited, taking in the room and the people in it, a mix of tourists – their selfie-taking an instant giveaway – and locals, talking happily with their companions.

A passing waiter nodded at Johnny and a moment later returned with a small bowl of bright green olives, placing them on the pristine white tablecloth. He looked at Johnny, said nothing.

'Er, *due* Bellinis, please?' He held up two fingers, just in case.

'Of course,' replied the waiter, his accent impeccable.

'I mean, practically fluent,' said Johnny, grinning at Flora once the waiter had moved away.

'Uncanny.' She smiled back. The bar felt cosy, the atmosphere warm. She'd imagined something far grander, given its reputation but, actually, it was perfect.

'So, what do you think so far?' Johnny popped an olive in his mouth.

'Rubbish!'

His face fell.

'No, it's a joke. I was being like the two old guys in the box at the theatre in *The Muppets*. You know?' She pulled a face and put on a voice. 'Rubbish!' She could tell by his face he had no idea what she was talking about, even with a second attempt. 'Sorry, forget it.' A short silence fell between them. Flora grabbed Johnny's hand. 'Look, I know I'm probably as much fun as a poke in the eye at the moment and I really hope you don't think I'm being ungrateful. I'm honestly not.' She looked around. 'This is amazing. I can't believe we're here. I just can't seem to, you know...' Flora's nose wrinkled.

Johnny squeezed her hand back. 'I know. Well, in actual fact, I don't know because I didn't lose a brother and I can't imagine how that feels but...' He stopped when the waiter appeared by their side, holding a silver tray. With swift movements he placed a small plain cylindrical glass in front of each of them, both filled almost to the top with the most beautiful light peach-coloured drink Flora had ever seen.

Flora picked up her glass, the smell of fresh peach hitting her before she could even get her nose to it. She put it back down on the table. 'Johnny, you don't have to say...'

'No, Flora. I'm just trying to say that whatever you're feeling, I might not feel it, too, but I see it.' There was another small pause, their eyes locked. 'That's all.'

She looked at the table, at their hands intertwined. 'Thank you,' she whispered.

'Now, are you just going to look at that Bellini or are you going to have a sip?'

'Given the price, I'm going to sip it slowly, that's for sure.' Flora laughed a little, raising the glass to her lips. She took a small sip, letting the flavours fill her mouth before swallowing. The bubbles sat briefly on her tongue, leaving fresh white-peach flavours on the taste buds. She swallowed and waited a second. 'Oh my God, that is absolutely delicious!' Her eyes were wide, her nose already in the glass to get another whiff of the aromas. 'Go on, have a sip.' She looked at him expectantly.

Johnny raised his glass and took a sip, a third of it gone in one go. He swallowed and looked at Flora. 'Well, I think that was about ten euros worth but you're right, it is absolutely delicious.'

'I didn't have you down as a Bellini kind of guy.' She laughed again.

The waiter came back to the table with a small plate of croquettes. He put them down, his face still expressionless.

'Did you order those when I wasn't noticing?' Johnny whispered.

'No, but whatever happens, you're not sending them back. They smell amazing.' Flora reached for one. 'Ooh, hot.'

'You know, Hemingway used to come here, apparently.'

'I'm not sure there's a bar left in any city he didn't go to. Isn't there another famous one near here he went to? I'm sure I read that somewhere.'

'Yes, near St Mark's Square. We'll pass it on the way back. What about food? Shall we find somewhere to eat on our way?'

'I reckon if we order a couple more drinks, we'll get more of these.' Flora pointed to the now empty plate where moments before the croquettes had been.

'Good plan. What would you like after that?'

'I'm thinking it might have to be a Martini.'

'I'll make that two.'

* * *

An hour later they left the bar, the cool, damp November night air hitting their gin-and-vermouth-flushed cheeks immediately. Rounding the corner of the narrow street, the sight before them brought them both to a stop. An almost deserted St Mark's Square seemed to be waiting just for them.

The lights from the buildings lining the square shone brightly, reflected back in the water on the ground left by a recent high tide, and ahead of them, beyond the square, lay the five domes of St Mark's Basilica, the clock tower to its right. They stood, trying to take in the size and sheer splendour of the sight.

'Oh, my goodness, it's just as I remember it,' Flora whispered.

'How old were you when you came here?'

'I can't remember exactly, maybe seven or eight. Tell you what I can remember: Billy running across here shouting at the pigeons. He'd yell at them, telling them to go away. Then get really cross when they'd take off and land again after a few seconds.' She pictured him, white-blond hair, blue stripy jumper, running ahead but always looking back to make sure Flora was in sight. She liked being back here, in a space she'd once shared with him.

'Look, there are people going into the church. Shall we go and have a look?' Johnny motioned up ahead.

'It's worth a try.'

They crossed the square and slipped into the church through the just-open door. Inside, it was in total darkness. Johnny could just make out some folding chairs in front of him. He grabbed Flora's hand and they took a seat as quietly as they could. Loud whispers in Italian seemed to come from somewhere in front of them.

Suddenly, enormous lights came on at the very front of the church, one after the other. Above their heads the roof turned to gold before their eyes. Then, gradually, as more lights came on, the entire ceiling was revealed, endless domes covered in mosaics now soaked in light.

They sat for a moment, staring at the ceiling, lost in the wonder of it all.

Suddenly, a voice called to them in Italian.

'*Scusi?*'

Moving their gaze down from above their heads, Flora and Johnny looked across to see a stern-looking Italian woman walking towards them. Her tour group, sitting quietly either side of her, now all turned to look at the pair of uninvited guests at the back.

'Sorry!' Johnny called back, raising his hand and deploying a smile. He looked at Flora. 'Time to make a swift exit, I think.' He raised an eyebrow.

Together they sprang up and made for the door at the back, out and into the square.

'This way!' Johnny walked quickly, pulling Flora behind them. Turning right and right again, they were soon back in the narrow alleys walking away from the square and on into the maze of streets beyond.

'I think we lost them,' Flora panted. She stopped to catch her breath, laughing as she did.

'I think we did.' Johnny laughed too.

With air in her lungs and a flush in her cheeks, Flora felt a rush of energy. Maybe it was just the Martini, but she was happy to be feeling something – anything – that wasn't sadness.

'You sure you don't want to find something to eat on the way back?'

'Actually, I could do with something a bit more substantial. Can we find a plate of pasta somewhere?' She pushed her hair back from her face.

'I think we're in the right place for that.' Johnny took out his phone and punched in a few words. He scrolled down and read for a few moments. Flora looked in the window of a shop where they stood, filled with carnival masks.

'It's like they're watching us.' A shiver ran through her.

'This way.' Johnny pointed and headed off. 'It says it's open.'

They walked through the streets, over a few more bridges and across small squares, their now-growing appetites calling them on. Flora looked longingly at some of the restaurants they passed, the smell and warmth of food wafting from doors, but Johnny kept going. A few dead ends later, they arrived at the place he'd been looking for.

'Here we are,' he said, looking up at the sign above the door, the name in wooden letters over the double-fronted window. Inside, couples and families sat at small wooden tables, the walls covered with a jumble of pictures and photographs. 'This is the one.'

'It looks perfect.' Flora was greeted enthusiastically by the owner. She assumed being a tourist would mean the same haughty treatment as at the previous bar but that certainly wasn't the case here.

They were shown straight to a table near the back and handed two menus. Flora picked a half-carafe of house Valpolicella, conscious of the considerable amount of alcohol already flowing through her veins. She eyed a plate of *spaghetti alle vongole* on its way to another table. 'Gosh, that looks good.'

The wine arrived and was poured quickly into tumblers on

the table by the young waitress with a friendly smile. Flora marvelled at the cherry pop of colour and the bright, juicy flavours of the wine as she took a sip.

'What are you going to have?' Johnny clinked her glass before also trying the wine.

'I think I'm going to have...' she looked down the menu, all in Italian, 'this one. I'm not entirely sure what it is but I think it's a local speciality, spaghetti and anchovies.'

Johnny screwed up his face. 'Seriously, I don't know how you eat those. They're so salty.'

'Well, good, then I don't have to share.' She grinned back at him.

Johnny realised he'd not seen that look for a while. 'In that case I'm going to ask for whatever the meat special is and have it even if I don't know what it is. Mack said that's the best thing to do here.'

Flora laughed. 'Did he now? Well, you're braver than I am.'

They ordered their food and Johnny topped up their glasses. 'So, what do you fancy doing tomorrow? Anything you want to see in particular?'

'I'm so happy walking and seeing what we find. I mean, we should maybe do a museum, don't you think? And I'm sorry but we've got to do a gondola ride at some point. We didn't do that when we came before. I remember Dad saying it was too expensive and buying us a lolly each instead. Billy was thrilled.'

'You are such a tourist!'

'Well, we can't come all this way and not go for a gondola ride, surely.'

'We'll ask at reception in the morning if they recommend any particular ones. What about going out to one of the islands? There's the glass one Mack mentioned.'

'We've only got tomorrow. I'd rather we just walk around.'

Their food arrived. A plate piled with thick spaghetti was placed in front of Flora, the smell of sweet onions and a faint salty tang punching the air as it passed.

'And today's special for you, sir.' The owner put down Johnny's plate. '*Figà àea Venessiana,*' he said with a flourish. 'Enjoy.'

Flora waited until he'd gone. 'Do you even know what it is?' she whispered.

'Not exactly...' Johnny looked down, the meat sitting on a pool of creamy polenta. 'But you know what, it smells incredible.' He took a forkful into his mouth.

'This, too.' Flora lifted her fork, now holding a mound of spaghetti. She shovelled it in, the texture of the pasta and the salty-sweet coating of the sauce making her sigh with pleasure.

'I'm not exactly sure what it is but whatever, it's so good,' said Johnny, still chewing, pointing at his plate with his fork.

As they wiped the last of the sauce from their plates with pieces of bread, cocooned in the warmth of the trattoria, Flora felt a fleeting sense of something she'd almost forgotten existed.

'Johnny, do you think it might be possible to be sad and happy at the same time? I don't mean to sound dramatic, but I think I'm beginning to understand how I'll have to learn to live with feeling sad about Billy – all the time, probably – but that maybe, just maybe it might be possible to live with it alongside happiness too. Does that make any sense?' She looked at her husband across the table.

'I think so.' Johnny tried his best to appear convinced.

'It's just that, I don't know... before all this happened, I thought grief was about crying, sobbing, falling to the floor, you know? I just wasn't expecting it to be so... well, quiet.'

'Now that does make sense.' Johnny thought back to the time in the hospital waiting room, the long walk out of the hospital, no one able to say even a word, just stunned silence. 'Flo,' he took her hand across the table again, 'it's going to take time and I don't think it'll ever go away. But we have so much to look forward to.'

Flora blinked back the tears. 'I knew I shouldn't have had that Martini.' She smiled at him across the table. 'Gin always makes me cry.'

## 22

The sound of bells found its way through the heavy curtains and darkness to Flora's ears. She turned and looked at the clock: a little earlier than she'd hoped, but the thought of a cup of tea in bed almost made up for it. Padding across the room to the small table with a tray of assorted teas, cups and a small kettle, she stubbed her toe on the edge of the bed. 'Ow.'

'What time is it?' Johnny croaked. 'Ow,' he said, clutching at his head with both hands.

'I know. Me, too.' Flora rubbed her eyes. 'It's eight o'clock. Tea?'

'Yes, please.' He turned on the bedside light and propped himself up on the pillows.

She flicked the switch of the small kettle and walked back towards the bathroom. Turning on the tap, she splashed cold water on her face, peering at herself in the mirror. She realised she was looking more like her mother every day. Oh God, her mother. Thoughts of their last conversation came flooding back, Kate's words in her ears. She made a mental note to avoid using the word 'fine' when talking to her in future.

She thought of her parents, sitting as they did at the table, her father at one end, her mother at the other, and Flora resolved to talk to Johnny about her predicament with her father. Then at least she could weigh up what to do. But not quite yet... She pushed the thought back down, along with all the other feelings she wanted to ignore for now, and set about making two cups of tea.

Johnny stretched and yawned noisily. He reached over and picked up his phone. 'So, you sure you're happy just walking about today?'

'Definitely.' Flora carried the two cups back to the bed, handing one to Johnny. She put hers down, then climbed back into bed. 'Well...' Johnny yawned again. 'I worked out a route that takes in two churches and a museum, as you suggested.'

'When did you do that?' Flora laughed.

'When you fell asleep, about two seconds after we got back here last night.'

Flora looked at him. 'Oh God, sorry.'

'Don't apologise. I'm just happy you slept well.'

Flora stretched out under the covers, finding his feet with hers. 'Thank you, I did.' She couldn't remember the last time she'd slept without waking up at least a couple of times in the night.

After breakfast they headed out and over the narrow bridge by the hotel. The pale blue sky was clear, and Venice looked impossibly beautiful with the winter sun on its face. They headed away from the Grand Canal into a warren of quiet streets lined with ochre, orange, yellow and pale pink buildings. Shutters remained closed, the shops not yet open. A few empty tables and chairs sat outside cafés. Flora felt quite disorientated, the painted signs on walls for '*Al Vaporetti*' the only clue as to the direction of the canal. After a few dead ends the streets began to widen a little

and before long they'd crossed a wide square, empty except for
the few Venetians, heads down, crossing it with purpose on their
way to work.

They passed a church, over another quiet canal lined with
empty boats, catching another glimpse of the Grand Canal as
they crossed the bridge. Then, with a sharp right followed by a
sharp left, they walked alongside another small canal and a great,
imposing church loomed into view. Flora looked up at the vast
red-brick walls, positively plain compared with the intricate lace-
like front of St Mark's Basilica.

'Is this the one we're looking for?' Flora looked at Johnny.

'Yep, this is the one. It's Gothic, apparently.'

Stepping inside, they saw the space was overwhelming. A vast
marble floor spread out before them, chequered with orange and
white squares. Stone pillars stood solidly, their size drawing
Flora's eyes up to the ceiling. Unlike the painted gold domes of
the previous evening, this church roof was a seemingly endless
web of arches and beams. Stone figures peered down on her
everywhere she looked. Huge paintings hung on the walls, each
one forcing visitors to stop and look.

A small boy ran across the empty space in front of them, the
smack of his sneakers on the stone floor echoing around them.

Flora and Johnny walked slowly towards the altar at the end,
passing another open door on the left. 'That's one of the Titian
paintings, *The Madonna of the Pesaro*,' Johnny whispered to Flora,
pointing.

Flora looked suitably impressed. They stopped to soak the
picture in, the vivid red, gold and blue colours making it stand
out despite its grand surroundings.

'That's St Peter in the middle and to the right, Mary. And the
family on the bottom left are the Pesaros, whoever they were.'
Johnny glanced from his phone back to the picture.

There was something about the way the baby in the picture played with his mother's veil, his foot raised playfully, that drew Flora's eye. He looked so lifelike, she thought he might step out of the picture at any moment.

They carried on walking towards the altar through a stone arch and into a chamber lined with carved wooden pews. Just before she reached the front, Flora caught sight of a line of candles flickering on a small shelf against a wall off to one side. She made her way towards them and stood for a moment looking at the flames, watching them dance as if to an invisible tune. She dropped a coin into a wooden box and picked up an unlit candle, lighting it from another before placing it alongside.

'You look like your heart is broken.' An older woman stood beside Flora. She wore a black down coat, her glossy brown hair pulled back in a ponytail. She smiled kindly, her green eyes glinting.

'It is.' Flora spoke without hesitation. 'My brother died, quite recently, actually.' She looked back at the candle she'd just lit, its flame now joining the others in their dance. 'Unexpectedly.'

The woman lit her own. 'My brother died, too, a long time ago.' They both looked at their respective candles for a moment. The woman spoke softly. 'Hearts stay broken. But I promise it gets easier to bear.' Flora searched for the right words to reply but before she could find them, the woman smiled, turned and walked away.

'You OK?' Johnny was now at her side.

'I think so. A weird thing just happened.' She looked around to see if she could see the woman again but there was no sign of her anywhere. 'I was just lighting a candle, thinking about, you know... and a woman came up to me, looked at me and told me: "Hearts stay broken"...'

'Wow, that's quite an opening line.' Johnny looked around for the woman as well.

'Yes, but then she said it gets easier. She lost a brother too, apparently.'

'How long were you two talking? You were only gone a moment.'

'Well, that's just it. That was pretty much all she said. I just stood there, I didn't even say thank you.' Flora looked again. 'And now she's not here.'

'Are you sure you're all right?' Johnny gently tipped her face back to his.

'I am. I'm OK.' And in that moment, she really meant it.

They walked on, up towards the painting that hung above the altar at the front of the church. Another Titian, Flora guessed, the colours as bright as those of the other one, the same movement in the clothes and bodies so beautifully captured in oils.

The space around her felt calm, peaceful. The words spoken by the woman sat in her mind. For months she'd been wishing the feelings would stop. Sometimes pain, sometimes a kind of numbness. Often it could leave her feeling physically sick. And she constantly felt so, so tired. But then there were days when she felt so completely wired she wondered if she would ever sleep properly again.

But if hearts really did stay broken then, perhaps, she needed to learn to carry that grief. To live with it, instead of waiting for it to leave. She thought of the kindness in the woman's eyes again.

'Shall we go and find coffee?' Johnny whispered.

Flora looked up at the painting one last time, then back at Johnny. She smiled. 'Perfect timing.'

\* \* \*

They walked slowly through the quiet streets of the Dorsoduro, with its tiny, unexpected squares and houses that seemed to hint at having seen better days. The occasional washing line crossed the narrower alleys from one house to another, high above their heads. The quiet canals here were charming, lined with houses of pale yellow, faded red and orange, empty window boxes clinging to the sides of the buildings below dark green shuttered windows. An old wooden barge loaded with fruit and vegetables sat beside one of the bridges, the easy conversation of the locals with the sellers on the barge reaching Flora and Johnny's ears as they crossed.

They passed windows of mask shops and jewellery shops, their shiny displays a challenge to the eye with so much detail to take in all at once. Standing aside to let people pass, Flora noticed there were more locals than tourists in this part of town.

A wine shop caught her eye on the other side of the canal, a scalloped-edge green awning hanging over faded gold letters spelling its name. 'How about we forget coffee and go straight to a Spritz?'

Johnny looked at his watch. 'Well, it is after eleven.'

They crossed the small bridge and walked into the *cantina,* where bottles of wine jostled for position in the window and on shelves on either side of the entrance. Inside the shop, bottles sat all the way from the tiled floor to the wooden-beamed ceiling, and on the right-hand side there was a long glass-fronted counter lined with small plates piled with *cicchetti.* Crostini, their precariously piled toppings held in place by toothpicks, tempted Johnny over for a closer look. Figs and parmesan, salmon and mascarpone, tuna and leeks, whipped salted cod and plump prawns flecked with paprika – the choice was seemingly endless. Cherry tomatoes were skewered on sticks alongside chunks of creamy mozzarella the size of golf balls, and pieces of Gorgonzola were topped with slices of pear and drizzled with thick, glossy balsamic vinegar.

Flora had gone straight to the wine shelves, drawn by the display of bottles. Each one bore a handwritten price tag on the neck, the selection of local Soave, Valpolicella and Amarone unlike anything she'd ever seen. She moved on to the Chianti and Super Tuscans before coming to the big-ticket Barolo and Barbaresco wines. She stared in wonder. Seeing some of the names of places and winemakers she'd studied writ large on wine labels was thrilling, despite the price tags putting them quite some way out of her reach.

Two men stood behind the counter, the younger one with his back turned as he cranked the coffee machine while the older loaded up small plates with yet more freshly made *cicchetti* from a silver tray. Johnny ordered a plate of assorted ones to try, along with two Spritzes.

'This is a wonderful place you have here.' Johnny smiled at the man putting his selection on a paper plate, gesturing to the shop.

'Thank you.' The man nodded, placing the plate on the counter followed by two paper cups, now filled with bright, effervescent liquid, ice and a wedge of orange. 'She likes the wine?' He looked towards Flora, still walking slowly along the shelves, peering closely at bottles.

'We run a wine shop where we live, in England. But we've only just opened. You look like you've been here much longer.'

'One hundred and twenty years.' The man chuckled, his eyes wrinkling at the edges.

'Well, you're obviously doing it perfectly.' Johnny picked up the drinks and the plate. 'Thank you. Is it OK to take this outside?'

'Please.' The man gestured to the door. 'Hang on, I forget your olives.' He skewered a couple of salted olives with toothpicks and popped one in each of the Spritzes. 'There you go.'

Johnny set down the cups and plate on the wall outside over-looking the canal and perched on it, waiting for Flora. He watched her move along the shelves, turning the occasional bottle round to look at the back label. He sometimes felt helpless, knowing how much she must be hurting. Most of all, he felt help-less at being unable to make it better. But seeing her now, lost in temporary wonder, he felt sure that she would, in time, feel happy again.

She came to the door. 'There's a bottle in there I'm going to buy, one I know we'll never get our hands on back at home. I'm going to take it back with us and we're going to drink it in the sun in the garden in the spring.' She clapped her hands in delight at the thought. 'Won't be a minute.'

'Well, don't be long or I might have to drink your Spritz.' He took a sip. The bittersweet sharpness of the Aperol made his mouth water.

Back inside, Flora put the bottle on the counter, a Soave Clas-sico from a small producer she'd read about but had never had the chance to try.

'Good choice.' The old man looked at her. 'You know this wine?'

Flora beamed. 'Actually, no. But I have heard about it and always wanted to try it.'

'The family have been making wines for over four hundred years. And the vines that grow the grapes to make this one,' he tapped the label, 'are more than seventy years old. The wine is amazing. The secret,' he tapped his nose this time, 'is in the soil.'

'Thank you, I can't wait to try it.'

'You have a wine shop, too, your husband tells me.' He started wrapping the bottle in tissue paper.

'Yes, we do. Yours is really special.' She glanced around the shop again.

'You are very kind. It's not always easy but, you know, wine is life.' He shrugged his shoulders. 'There you go. Hope you enjoy back in England.'

'Thank you so much.' Flora smiled at him as she took the bottle. 'We will. *Ciao*.'

Flora went to join Johnny, putting the wrapped bottle carefully in her bag as she left the shop. She picked up her Spritz and took a sniff, then a sip, first tartness, then sweetness, then a hit of salt, the bubbles prickling her tongue. 'You see, why don't we always have one of these at home before noon?'

Johnny laughed. 'I'm not sure we'd get much done in the afternoon if we did.'

'I'm talking about just the one, like the Italians. It's such a civilised custom.' The cool liquid ran down her throat. She picked up one of the crostini. 'Want to share?'

'No, I picked that just for you. I thought it looked right up your street.'

It was the pear and Gorgonzola one, and Flora devoured it in two bites. 'Oh, my goodness, that's so good.' She spoke with her mouth full, eyes bright. 'Want to split that?' She pointed to the one with prawns on the top.

'I think that's also got your name on it.'

'I was hoping you'd say that.'

She popped it into her mouth. They sat, sipping their drinks, taking in the sights, sounds and smells of this quiet corner of Venice.

'Maybe we should do something like that in the shop, with

the food?' Johnny picked up the last of the crostini, offering it to Flora.

She shook her head. 'No, you have it. How funny, I was just thinking the same thing. We could definitely try that, maybe for summer next year when the town's a little busier.' She tipped up her cup, draining the last of her Spritz. 'And I tell you what, these are definitely going on the menu.'

## 23

The early afternoon sun shone down, the blue sky now dotted with clouds. Their Spritzes had put a prosecco-fuelled spring in their step. Flora and Johnny headed through the streets back towards the Grand Canal and, on Flora's wishes, to the Guggenheim Museum. Kate had always talked about it as one of her favourite places in Venice but all Flora could really remember was sitting outside on a bench with Billy, waiting for their mother to finish looking around inside.

'Let's just have a quick look. I'm dying to see a Jackson Pollock in real life,' Flora pleaded, knowing Johnny's love for modern art did not run deep.

They wandered the calm white corridors of the museum, small statues on plinths around every corner and instantly recognisable paintings hanging in every room, from Magritte to Miró, Picasso to Pollock, much to Flora's obvious delight.

She stood in front of one of his paintings – a mass of splattered paint, so far as Johnny could make out.

'I don't get it, Flora, I really don't.' He peered closer.

'You don't have to. It's just not the painting for you.' She sat down on the small bench in front of it. 'I like looking at it, and that's enough for me to enjoy it.'

'But... doesn't it make you think you could have done that?'

'But the point is, I didn't. He did. You could say that about anything.'

'I suppose.' Johnny sat down beside her, his eyes still on the painting. He reached across and took her hand. They sat for a while, just looking, both lost in their own thoughts.

Johnny hoped the change of scene had lifted her spirits a little, that perhaps this break away would bring Flora back to him.

All Flora wished was that she could hear Billy's voice again.

They left the quiet of the museum and stood on a small terrace overlooking the Grand Canal, now busy with *vaporetti* carrying tourists as they snaked their way through the city's canals.

'What's going on there?' Flora pointed to the right where a makeshift bridge bobbed on the water, supported by floating jetties. People streamed across, mostly in their direction.

'I didn't think there was another bridge after the Accademia. Hang on...' Johnny tapped at his phone.

Flora gazed across the water at the famous Gritti Palace, the hotel's unassuming pale orange brick façade barely hinting at the decadent and luxurious interiors she'd once seen in a magazine. Bright blue poles lined the front of the building, sticking out of the water sentinel-like.

'It says here the bridge is a temporary one, there for some kind of festival. The Salute festival, something to do with celebrating the end of the plague. Apparently, the locals flock to light a candle in that church up there, Santa Maria della Salute, the big white one we saw from Harry's Bar last night. Want to go and have a look?'

Flora watched the Venetians crossing the bridge, wrapped up against the chill in thick coats and scarves.

'Let's walk past, shall we, but then can we find something to eat? I'm getting hungry. Again.' She smiled at Johnny before kissing him briefly.

They left the museum and joined the moving crowd of people walking towards the church, the enormous white dome of the Basilica towering above them. The sound of the crowd was gentle. People walked and talked quietly, an air of contemplation around them. They rounded a corner to find the huge steps of the church fanning out from the door at the top like a bride's train, and covered with people. Temporary market stalls lined the water-front with traders selling votive candles, their calls to potential sellers punctuating the thrum of the assembled churchgoers. Families greeted one another with waves and gentle hugs.

Flora and Johnny passed the crowds, walking along the front of the church and on towards the point. 'They're not afraid to remember the dead, are they?' whispered Flora.

'Not by the looks of it.'

'I mean, the English barely talk about it. It's like we don't know how to, but this feels more like a party.'

Johnny stopped. 'Flo, you know you must talk about Billy as much as you'd like to. The more, the better, in fact.'

'Maybe, but I worry it makes people uncomfortable.'

'Too bad. If it makes people uncomfortable, you're with the wrong people.'

'But, Johnny, I'm talking about my parents. I can't avoid them forever.'

'Oh, I didn't realise you meant them specifically. But I'm sure, with time, they will want to talk about Billy more. They'll want to remember all the good times you had as a family.'

Flora sighed. 'I hope so, but right now all Mum seems to want to talk about is how he died. It's like I can't find any common ground for us to talk about him.'

'I know. But she's hurting and that's her way of dealing with the pain. You just have to give her a pass on that, for now at least.'

'There's something else I need to talk to you about, actually. About Mum. Well, about Dad, to be precise.'

'Is he OK?' Johnny looked worried.

'He's not ill or anything. But,' Flora sighed, 'can I tell you when we're sitting down? I think I need a glass of wine for this one.'

'Of course, come on. There's a place just around the corner from here.'

They walked on ahead, rounding the point at the end, the wide stretch of water between where they stood and the island of Giudecca in front of them. The myriad of tiny streets behind them suddenly felt like a make-believe miniature world compared with the expanse of wide buildings and enormous domes dotting the skyline opposite them.

The crowds thinned as they walked away from the Basilica and the sun threw light onto their faces and across the pale stone of the pavement beneath their feet.

Johnny swiped at his phone. 'It's just up here.'

'Won't it be horribly expensive if it comes with these views?'

'You could be right, but we can just skip starters. Come on, we never go out at home. We're on holiday, even if we've only got half a day left.'

Up ahead, a restaurant terrace covered with a multitude of canopies seemed to be waiting just for them. Only a few of the tables were taken, books and cameras on the tables giving away the occupants' tourist status. On the other side of the pavement sat the restaurant building itself, packed with tables of Italian families finishing, by the looks of it, very good, long lunches.

Flora and Johnny were quickly shown to a table at the front, nearest the water, and handed two menus by a smiling young waiter. 'Is a good view, no?' The waiter looked out across the water.

'Amazing,' they chorused.

'Can I get you a drink?'

'Could we have a look at the wine list, please?' said Flora.

'Of course. We have a few specials today, seafood *zuppa* and *spaghetti alle vongole*. Also, we have some lobster today but,' the waiter lowered his voice, 'I wouldn't bother, is very expensive. Go for the *vongole*.'

'That's exactly what I'd like, the *vongole*.' Flora smiled at the waiter.

'No starter for you?'

'No, thanks, just the *vongole*.'

'Of course. And for you, sir?'

Johnny looked at the menu, hoping to find a dish at a price that didn't start with a three. 'I think...'

'I can recommend this one.' The waiter pointed at the menu. 'It's very good.'

'Yes, I'll have that one.' Johnny has no idea what it was but it was considerably cheaper than the other dishes on the menu.

'Perfect. I'll be back for your wine choice in a moment.'

Flora looked at the list of wines, the number of local ones running to a whole page. 'I'm going to order two glasses, a white and a red and we can try them both. What was that you ordered?'

'I have absolutely no idea.' Johnny poured them a glass of water each from the carafe on the table. 'I'm just doing what Mack said.'

Flora's eyes widened. 'But what if it's, I don't know... tripe? Isn't that a speciality here?'

'Adds to the excitement, I suppose.' Johnny laughed. 'You order the wine. I'll be back in a mo. I'm desperate for a wee.'

Flora ordered and a few moments later the waiter returned with two glasses of wine. The glasses were short-stemmed but generously sized.

'The Custoza,' the waiter said, putting the white wine on the table. 'And the Valpolicella.' He put the glass of red down too.

'Thank you.' Flora picked up the glass of white and took a long sniff as she looked out across the water. The scent of orange blossom and jasmine filled her nose, flavours of citrus followed by a touch of spice spreading across her mouth as she took a sip. It was just right for that moment, crisp and alive on her taste buds. She broke off a piece of the still warm focaccia the waiter had left on the table, popping it into her mouth. She chewed on the bread, the taste of rosemary mingling with the traces of lemon left by the wine. Taking a breath, she exhaled slowly.

Noting the flavours, the smells around her, the feel of the sea air on her skin and the sound of boats on the water, she began to feel as if she was resurfacing at last. Her shoulders felt lighter, her mind more present.

Johnny took his seat next to her, picking up the glass of white. 'What's this? Is it good?' He went to sniff the wine.

'Very good!' Flora winked at him. 'It's a local wine, Custoza. Lovely, isn't it?'

'Really good.'

Johnny managed to hide his surprise when his dish arrived, octopus, legs akimbo as if trying to escape the plate, and they talked easily, unrushed. They shared the glasses of wine, the white working with the *vongole* like a dream, and the bright cherry fruit pop of the Valpolicella matching the meaty octopus perfectly.

But, later, as they sipped on their strong espressos, Johnny noticed Flora had drifted in her thoughts. 'Would you rather we head back to the hotel, have a rest before going out for one last time later?'

Flora looked at her hands in her lap, then at Johnny. 'It's my parents, Johnny. There's something I've wanted to tell you for ages, but I just couldn't face saying it out loud.' She sighed. 'I think, well actually, I know... Dad's been having an affair.'

'Flora! What makes you say that?' Johnny couldn't hide his surprise. 'Are you sure? Your father adores your mother!' Robin had always struck him as so steady, dependable. Certainly not someone you'd put down as the kind who would have an affair.

'I saw him, at the station. With a woman. Johnny,' Flora fixed him with her eyes, 'they definitely weren't just friends.'

'How do you know?'

'Well, if I saw you kissing a friend goodbye like that...' Flora shook her head. 'Trust me, they were more than just friends.'

'Well, did you say anything?'

'Not at the time, but I have told him I know.'

Johnny waited. 'Go on.'

'Well, I said that either he stops it, or I'll tell Mum.'

'And what did he say to that?'

'He didn't say anything really. Although to be fair to him, he didn't have the chance. It was at the end of the launch party and someone came up to talk to us – Tilda, I think – just after I'd told him I'd seen him.'

'Look, it's not your problem to fix, it's theirs. But, Flora, I really hope you're wrong about this.'

'I hope so, too, Johnny, but my dad didn't deny it. What if my parents split up? I mean, I'm not sure either of them would cope without the other now...' Her voice broke.

Johnny felt a surge of anger rising in his chest. Flora had enough to deal with, without this to worry about too. 'Listen, it's up to them to sort it out. They're adults, Flora; somehow you have to leave them to deal with it. But I'm glad you've told your dad that you know rather than having to keep that to yourself. Now, let's just enjoy these last few hours without worrying about it, shall we? I promise you it will be all right in the end.' He squeezed her hand across the table.

Flora drained her coffee cup. 'I hope so, for both their sakes.'

They spent much of the rest of the afternoon back at the hotel, a tangle of limbs and sheets, their lovemaking gentle and indulgent. Later that evening, they crossed the Grand Canal by *traghetto*, standing as the locals did. They walked, hand in hand, along the quiet streets of Cannaregio, stopping for a glass of chilled, pear-scented prosecco at a small bar on a corner by a canal, another plate of *cicchetti* between them.

'We never did take that gondola ride.' Flora spoke between mouthfuls of fresh olive tapenade on crunchy crostini, the bitterness bumping up deliciously against the off-dry froth of the prosecco.

'Well, we've still got time. I'm sure I read somewhere you can do them at night. Why don't we do one after this?'

A while later they floated on the water, street lamps casting light onto the pale terracotta stone walls of the buildings on either side of the canal. Together they looked up at the stars. The air was cold now, kept from their bodies by a thick blanket given to them by the gondolier. The stillness in this hidden part of the city was quite magical. As they glided under a small bridge, a couple stood watching them. Flora looked up, catching the smiling woman's eye just before they disappeared from view. She caught her breath, turning back to see. But the couple had gone.

'That was her, Johnny,' Flora whispered, as she craned her neck.

'Who?'

'The woman in the church. The one who said, "Hearts stay broken." You remember I told you earlier?'

'Yes, and she also said it gets easier. Don't forget that.' Johnny kissed Flora's forehead.

'But don't you think that's a bit of a coincidence?' Flora looked back again but there was no sign.

'Could be. Who knows?' Johnny drew the blanket round them. 'You warm enough?'

Flora hugged him tighter. 'Venice feels like another world, far away from everything,' she whispered.

'It really does.'

'When we get home, will you remind me that I felt happy again? Just in case I forget.'

Johnny took her face in his hands and kissed her gently. 'I will, I promise.'

## 24

It was barely light when they made their way to the airport by taxi, crossing the bridge to the mainland. The flight back was uneventful, and Flora slept for most of it. As London came into view through the clouds, she thought of the children, of the hugs she'd give them. She smiled to herself. It had been barely forty-eight hours but she'd missed them more than she'd realised.

She glanced across at Johnny, reading a newspaper, his forehead furrowed.

'Anything interesting?'

Johnny quickly closed and refolded the paper, putting it on his lap. 'Oh, it's old. Someone must have left it on here yesterday. Nothing that interesting, the usual.'

Flora felt sure something was amiss but she couldn't quite put her finger on it. 'Can I have a look?'

'Honestly, it's all so depressing nowadays, you're better off not looking.' He went to put the paper back in the pocket of the seat in front of him.

'Johnny, please. I'm not so bad I can't handle reading the news. You don't have to protect me from everything.' She reached across and took the paper from the pocket. She hardly ever read a paper during the week any more, only the Sunday papers. Glancing at the front page she saw a picture of an ageing actor, topless in the sea on some tropical island with someone at best half his age. She turned the page and scanned the headlines, more to pass the time than for actual information.

'What do you want to do today? I thought I'd go into the shop this afternoon; perhaps you could pick the kids up from school?' Johnny went to take the paper from her.

'What are you doing?' Flora laughed, looking at Johnny. 'Let me, for once, read a whole paper. Even if it is a bit rubbish it's a total luxury to be able to do it without being interrupted by a child!' She laughed and went back to the page.

'Seriously, Flo, we need to have a plan. We've got things to do.'

Flora looked at him again, seeing worry on his face. 'Johnny, what's going on? Why are you being so weird?'

'I'm not!' He tried to look normal but they both knew he was failing, badly.

Flora slowly turned the page of the paper. There, looking up at her, was a familiar face. One she knew so well but couldn't square with being there on the page. Her stomach flipped. Billy.

'Flo...' Johnny reached his arm across her shoulders. He spoke softly. 'You don't have to read it.'

She stared at the page again, her brother's face staring out at her. She forced herself to read the words, but it was almost impossible. They rushed at her from the page out of order, out of focus. Tears clouded her sight, but slowly, she pieced it together. A picture of another man sat next to Billy's. She wanted to look away but found she couldn't. His name was right there. Stephen Hirst. Eighteen years old. She'd never seen this man's face before, which had been a conscious decision she'd made when Billy died. But here he was, looking right at her. And all she could think was: you are so young.

'Flora, why don't you—'

'It's fine, Johnny, really. I want to.' Flora didn't look up from the page. She read on, the words hitting her like sucker punches, blow after blow, again and again.

*Mother, Denise... devastated... family declined to comment...*

'Why is it in the paper now?' Flora's voice was flat.

Johnny spoke quietly. 'It's because the trial starts soon. He was charged with death by careless driving and pleaded not guilty, so...' Johnny sighed. 'Look, hopefully it'll be over quickly.' He held her gaze.

Flora knew that. She remembered the police coming to her parents' house back in those early days, just after Billy had died, to explain that the driver had been charged. She could remember the officers' voices but not their faces.

And now the trial was happening in a matter of weeks. She looked again at the picture of Billy. He'd been so full of life. Bursting, in fact, as if he'd taken more than his fair share of energy, of brilliance. She shut the paper and put it back on Johnny's lap. She closed her eyes as they came in to land, the face of the boy in her mind. She tried to replace it with Billy's, but her mind kept going back to the boy and the name of his mother. She thought of her own mother, too.

Would she or her mother ever feel like they were living properly again? Or was it only when Flora escaped real life that she wouldn't feel quite so sad? The image of those still, quiet waterways came into her mind, along with the words of the woman in the church. Deep down, Flora knew she had to learn to live with her broken heart. She just wasn't sure how.

* * *

Robin woke early but Kate was already gone, the sheets on her side not even warm any more. He slipped out of bed and went to the window, pulling back the curtain to look down across the lawn to the river below. There, at the end of the garden, sitting on the old stone bench, sat Kate wrapped in her dressing gown. It looked cold outside, too cold to be sitting like that. Robin quickly threw on some clothes and went downstairs. He made a fresh cup of tea and went down to his wife, mug in hand. The air was still, and there was a slight frost on the ground.

'Darling, you must be freezing.' Robin stood behind her, holding the cup forward.

'I like it out here this early. It's so peaceful.' She looked up at him, smiled a little and took the still-steaming mug. 'Thank you.'

Robin walked round the side of the bench and took a seat next to her.

He took a breath, then spoke gently. 'Kate, I think we need to talk.'

She laughed a little, keeping her eyes on the view in front of them. 'Don't you think it's a bit late for that?'

'Kate, please. We can't go on just not speaking about it.'

'About what, exactly?' Kate turned to look at him, her eyes not giving anything away.

'Well, about everything that's happened. About Billy...'

Kate looked away again. She took a sip of her tea. Then she spoke, her voice soft but steady. 'How about we talk about your affair instead?'

Robin was blindsided. His mind raced. How did she know? How long had she known? He looked at her, stunned.

'Lost for words, Robin?' Kate put her cup down. 'Did you really think I didn't know?' Her voice was flat, the words slow and deliberate.

'Kate, I'm so sorry…' Robin looked at her, wishing he could say something to make everything different.

'How long has it been going on for?'

He opened his mouth to speak.

'I said, how long, Robin? How long has it been going on for?'

'Kate, please…'

'Oh, for God's sake, Robin, just tell me. I want to know how long I've been taken for an idiot.'

'You are not… Kate, I never—'

'Years? I know it's been at least five. Please don't tell me it's more.'

'Well, yes, it has been about that.' Robin turned to face her. 'But please, Kate. It's over now.'

'Damn right, it's over.'

'Oh, Kate, no. Please can we talk about it first?'

'I don't think there's anything to talk about, Robin. You've been having an affair. For years. And I've known about it for years. I don't know who she is and, frankly, I don't care. I know that since Billy died you haven't seen her, and I thought that I might be able to live with that. But as it turns out, I'm not sure I can. So, I want you to leave. And I want a divorce. Not right away but once we get the court case over and done with, I want you gone for good.'

Robin went to reach for her hand. Before he could, Kate stood up. 'And I'm going to see Flora tomorrow, just so you know.'

'What will you say to her?' Robin looked terrified.

'I haven't decided yet.' Kate turned her back on the river and started walking up to the house.

Robin watched her striding away, her dark red velvet dressing gown blowing behind her in the wind.

After Billy had died, he knew he wouldn't ever leave Kate. It just hadn't occurred to him that Kate already knew about the affair. Or that, if she did, she wouldn't want to him to stay.

He looked back down towards the river. The thought of not living the rest of his life with Kate filled him with dread. He'd lost a son. Now he faced losing the woman he had loved for as long as he could remember. To risk it all had been the worst decision he'd ever made. Robin put his head in his hands and wept.

---

## 25

'Mummy!' Pip squealed as Flora stood in the playground, rushing up to meet her with Tom following close behind.

'I've missed you so much!' Flora hugged them both. 'Have you been good for Tilda? Did you have a nice time?' Flora looked around, spotting her friend coming towards her. 'Tilda, I can't thank you enough. Were they good?'

Tilda hugged her friend. 'They were brilliant. We loved having them. How was it? Was Venice as heavenly as I imagine?'

'It was really lovely, thank you. And honestly, it was so good to spend a bit of time together away from it all.'

Tilda put her hand on Flora's arm. 'I'm glad. Will you show me pics? I've got to run now but I want to hear all about it. Shall we get together on Friday?'

'Definitely, but you come over to me with the kids. I owe you.'

'Don't be silly, you don't owe me anything.' Tilda smiled.

'I really do. I'll make sure I have something nice in the fridge, promise.'

'You'd better, otherwise I'm not coming.' Tilda laughed and turned to go.

Flora blew a kiss to her friend. 'See you on Friday.' She called to her children: 'Right, let's go home. Daddy will be back soon and he's dying to see you, too. We missed you so much.'

'Tilda let us stay up much later than you do,' said Tom.

'Not that much later, really. Only half an hour,' Pip said, correcting him quickly.

'Oh, it was much more than that.' Tom looked at his sister, daring her to argue back.

'Come on, let's go. We've got to go via the supermarket, I'm afraid.'

'Oh, please can we not? I hate going shopping; it's so boring,' Pip pleaded with her mother.

'I know, I'm sorry but we'll be really quick. What do you fancy tonight? How about I make some pasta like we had in Italy?' She remembered the bowl of pasta on that first night in Venice, the taste and texture still fresh in her mind.

'Fish fingers!' It was Tom's turn to plead.

'But I hate fish fingers,' wailed Pip.

'No, we'll have those on Friday. Pasta tonight.' As she clambered into the car, her children still fighting over what they wanted to eat, Flora closed her eyes and took herself back to the gondola in Venice. The peace and stillness of the memory soothed her.

'Mama, are you OK?'

Flora opened her eyes to see Pip looking up, a worried expression on her face.

'Yes, I'm fine. I'm just a bit tired. It's been a long day.' She looked at them both, staring back at her expectantly, and smiled. 'But I am very happy to be home.'

The phone was ringing as she came back through the door. It had to be her mother on the landline. Flora dropped the bags on the floor in the hall and went to the kitchen to answer it.

'Mum, hi!'

'Flora! You're back. Did you have a wonderful time?'

Her mother sounded perky – too perky. 'We got back late this morning and I made it to school to pick the kids up just in time. We had a great time, thanks.' Flora thought of the last time they'd spoken. She'd assumed her mother would still be holding a grudge so Kate's jolliness was disconcerting.

'So, come on, tell me all about it. Where did you stay?'

Flora looked down the hall to see the children rummaging through the bags of shopping. 'Can you just wait until it's unpacked, please?' The children didn't even look up. 'Sorry, Mum, can I call you back? I've literally just walked through the door. I just need to get stuff sorted, then I'll call you right back.'

'Actually, I was calling to ask if you'd mind if I came over to see you tomorrow. There's something I need to talk to you about.'

'Is it about our last conversation, Mum? If so, I'm really sorry, I didn't mean to be unkind. If it's any consolation I've been feeling awful about it ever since.'

'No, it's not that, Flora. We'll talk properly when I see you. If I come for about ten o'clock, how does that sound?'

Flora had hoped to go to the shop but knew now wasn't the time to refuse her mother.

'Yes, that's great. I'll be here. We can go for a walk on the beach, if you like, if it's not raining.'

'That sounds perfect. I'll see you in the morning. I'm dying to hear all about your little holiday. Bye, darling.'

Before Flora could even ask another question, her mother was gone. It was not the conversation she'd been bracing herself for, to say the least, and for that she was grateful. She went to pick up the bags, collecting various escaped items of shopping along the way.

Later that evening, Flora filled Johnny in. 'Maybe,' she twisted her fork around the spaghetti on her plate, 'she's coming to talk to me about the court case.'

'Do you think you'll go?' Johnny poured some white wine into their glasses. It was a subject Flora had largely managed to avoid until now.

'I really don't want to. I'm worried I'll learn things in the courtroom I don't want to know.'

'I can understand that. Then don't go.'

'But if Mum wants me to, and I think she might, then I should go.'

'Well, see what she says. You don't have to give an answer there and then. You can always say you'll think about it.'

'True. Maybe I'm just burying my head in the sand. Which is basically what I think Mum was trying to say to me before.'

'Flo, just wait and see. You don't know she's going to say that. This is lovely, by the way.' Johnny took another mouthful of pasta.

'Thanks, Venice clearly inspired me.' She smiled at him, deciding not to mention the anchovies in the sauce.

* * *

Tilda plonked herself down on the sofa, glass of red wine within reach. Pete was putting the children to bed so she picked up her mobile and called Susie.

'Hi, love.'

'Is this a good time?'

'Yes, great actually.' Susie sounded bright. 'Julian's away tonight so I've got the house to myself.' Tilda could hear shouting from the children in the background. 'Well, apart from that lot, but they're only arguing about what to watch on TV. Everything all right?'

'I'm fine, but, well, I am a bit worried about Flora. I mean, obviously she's still going to be feeling down, given everything that's happened, and honestly, I think we just need to really keep an eye on her. Just without telling her. She'd hate to think we're having this conversation about her.'

'I know. It must be so hard. The shock of it all was awful. But I agree with you, she seems – how can I put it? – just quietly sad.'

Tilda picked up her glass. 'I think that's exactly it. And I don't think she wants to talk about it particularly either. I mean, I know she loves talking about Billy, but she told me she can't bring herself to actually think about what happened with the accident. And the court case will be coming up soon. There was something in the paper about it, apparently. Pete saw it on the train. And I'm just worried that until she goes through it, dealing with his death... she won't be able to move forward. Does that make sense?'

'I think we just need to make sure she knows we're here. If she wants to talk or not talk, whatever. I'm not sure we can force her to face up to the accident itself if she's not ready.' Susie sighed. 'Do you think we should mention the court thing to Flora, so she knows we're aware?'

'No, I don't think so. Unless she brings it up, of course. Maybe when the trial starts, we should let her know we can do whatever she needs to help. Poor thing.' Tilda closed her eyes, shaking her head. 'She obviously had a lovely time in Venice but the sadness in her eyes when I saw her today, Susie – it's heartbreaking.'

'That's exactly what it is.'

'We've just got to be there for her.'

'And we will be. I was thinking, shall we all go to the cinema next week? I'll see if I can find something uplifting for us to watch.'

'That's a brilliant idea. And let's do another walk soon too, when we can.' Tilda sighed again. 'You know, I wish I'd known

Billy better. I met him a few times and he really was larger than life. I know that sounds like a cliché but it's the only way to describe him. Flora absolutely adored him. I think they'd always been close, probably because it was just the two of them. Fuck, it's such a bloody waste.' She wiped her eyes.

Susie sat on one of the uncomfortable bar stools Julian had insisted upon, her wine glass clattering gently on the spotless marble counter on the kitchen island as she put it down. 'I wish I'd known him too. Sounds like he knew how to live life properly.'

'Here's to doing that.' Tilda raised her glass.

Susie did the same. 'Speak tomorrow?'

'Speak tomorrow.'

* * *

The noise of the television woke Denise with a start. She sat up in her chair, realised she must have fallen asleep where she was. Slowly, she reached forward to pick up the remote control from the low table in front of her. Her body felt heavy, her mind a muddle. She turned the television off and the flat fell silent. Glancing at her watch, she saw it was well after midnight.

She made her way to the kitchen, spotting a strip of yellow light seeping out from the bottom of Stephen's bedroom door. She listened for a moment, trying to hear if he was still awake. She knocked softly. 'Stephen?'

There was no answer. She waited a few seconds before knocking again, this time a little louder. His voice came back, muffled.

'Can I come in, love?'

'If you want.'

Denise opened the door. Stephen sat on his bed, staring at his phone in his hand. He didn't even look up at her. He was pale and drawn, his eyes dark. Denise had tried everything she could think of to try to encourage him out of his room but he'd refused to see or speak to any of his friends since he'd been charged. Whenever she tried to talk to him about the accident, or about what might happen at court, he shut the conversation down.

He'd pleaded not guilty to the charge of death by careless driving as instructed by his lawyer, but Stephen was so ashamed of what he'd done, he wished he'd pleaded guilty. In his darkest moments, he wished he'd been the one that had been killed.

'Come on, it's late. You need to try and get some sleep.' Denise smiled at him, trying not to show the fear in her eyes. She was scared of what lay ahead for him, knowing there was nothing she could do to change it. His fate was in the hands of others now. 'Maybe tomorrow we can go for a walk, get some air in those lungs of yours.'

'I'm not leaving here, Mum.' Stephen turned away from her onto his side, facing the wall. 'Not until I have to.'

She stared at his back for a moment, his shoulders hunched. She saw them shake but there was no sound.

Denise searched for something to say.

'Please leave me alone, Mum.' His voice trembled.

'But—'

'I said, GO!'

Denise closed the door as softly as she could, then held her hands to her mouth so he wouldn't hear her sob. Slowly, she walked away, resolving to try again in the morning.

## 26

Kate arrived the next morning on the dot of ten o'clock. Since returning from the school run Flora had spent the next hour clearing up, or in other words hiding piles of washing and picking up stuff off the floor. It wasn't that she was particularly house-proud, but her mother had a way of scanning a room that always made Flora feel like she lived in complete chaos.

She'd managed to get the coffee on and was two cups in when Kate walked through the door.

'Hel-lo-oh!' Kate called as she came through the door.

'Hi, Mum.' Flora came to greet her, kissing her briefly on both cheeks. Flora was immediately struck by how together her mother looked, hair up and with perfectly applied make-up. The last time she'd seen her mother, she'd looked quite different, tired and drawn. Flora winced a little as she looked down at her own attire, which consisted of tracksuit bottoms and an old wool jumper of Johnny's with holes in both elbows.

'Oh, I'm sorry, you obviously haven't had a chance to get properly dressed yet.' Kate gently brushed Flora's hair away from her face with her fingertips.

'Yes, I just threw this on for the school run, and I've just not had a chance.' Flora hoped this excuse would fly.

'Don't you worry. I know how busy you are.' Kate moved through to the kitchen. 'So, how is everyone?'

Flora followed. 'We're all good, Mum. Everyone's happy and healthy. The kids are doing great at school…'

'And Johnny, how's he?' Her mother took a seat at the kitchen table, hanging her coat on the back of the chair.

Flora sat opposite and poured Kate a mug of coffee. 'He's good, too. Things are really picking up now at the shop. You know, with Christmas coming.'

'Oh, that is good to hear. I always knew you were on to something there.'

Flora bristled but managed to stop herself from commenting. *Come on, Flora. She can't help herself.* 'How are you both? How's Dad?'

Her mother waved her question away. 'I'll come on to that in a minute. First, I want to hear all about Venice. Did you have a wonderful time? So sweet of Johnny to think of taking you there. Did you remember it at all?'

Flora smiled. 'Bits of it, yes. We barely had two days, but we walked a lot, ate a lot.' Flora laughed. 'And when we went to St Mark's I had such a vivid memory of Billy chasing pigeons, do you remember that?'

Kate nodded, staring at her coffee mug, clearly lost in a memory at the very mention of it. 'Yes, I really do.' Her eyes were sad. She closed them and shook her head, then looked back at Flora, a smile back on her face. 'Did you go on a gondola ride?' Kate picked up her mug, blowing gently.

'Of course. It had to be done. But we went at night. It was a bit cold but, honestly, Mum, it was gorgeous. So quiet. And the splendour of the place! Well, a kind of faded glamour. I don't really remember that. It was more about the ice cream when I was little.'

Kate laughed. 'Yes, it was mostly about the ice cream for you two back then. Anyway, it sounds like you had a wonderful time. I hope to go back there one day.' Kate put down her mug.

Flora waited for her mother to speak. It still felt strange to be talking about anything when their world had been so utterly shifted. She knew they had to talk about it at some point so, before she changed her mind, she took a breath and spoke.

'So, Mum, is this about the court case, because I've been thinking, if you want me to go—'

'No, Flora. It's not about that.'

Flora couldn't hide her surprise. 'Oh, but I thought—'

'Darling, whether you come or not is up to you. I'm not going to force you to do something you don't want to do.'

Flora was confused. 'So, what is it, then?'

Kate put both her hands on the table, looking at them. Flora shifted in her chair. She sensed she wasn't going to like what her mother was about to say.

Kate took a deep breath. 'I'm afraid it's about your father and me.'

Flora gasped. 'Oh God, Mum, please don't...' She put her hand to her mouth. She thought back to seeing him as he'd – they'd – walked up the steps at the station, the way they'd kissed and smiled at each other. She'd tried so hard to forget that image but now, sitting opposite her mother, she saw it more clearly than ever.

'I'm sorry, Flora, I know we've all been through so much, but I've asked your father to leave.'

Flora felt as if time had stopped. 'This can't be happening.' She didn't even know if she'd said the words out loud.

'I'm afraid it is. I wish it wasn't, but there we are. Not immediately, of course – I'm not going to be unreasonable – but I've asked him to find somewhere else to live, sooner rather than later.'

'But why?' Flora felt guilty even asking. She hoped her mother couldn't tell she already knew the answer.

Kate glanced down at her hands again. 'We've just grown apart in recent years and now, more so than ever, I realise I need to live the rest of the life I have in a way that makes me happy.'

Flora watched her mother's face, her lips pressed tightly together as she always did when determined not to say what she really wanted to say. Flora wanted to scream the words at her mother, but she, too, swallowed them. If her mother didn't know about the affair, she wasn't going to be the one to tell her. If anyone owed Kate an explanation, it was Robin.

Flora reached across the table to take her mother's hands. 'Did something happen?' She felt ashamed for asking when she knew the truth, feeling her cheeks redden as she spoke.

Kate looked at her daughter. 'No, nothing happened. I just think it's time we did things differently.' Kate's gaze was steadfast, despite her eyes filling with tears.

'Oh, Mum, please... you and Dad have been so happy for so many years. Is it really what you want?'

'For now, I think it is. I'm sorry, darling.' Kate's voice was practically a whisper.

They were both silent for a while, neither knowing what to say.

'So, what happens now?'

'I'm not entirely sure, darling. I mean, we're not arguing. I'm too tired to argue, anyway. Your father knows I want him to leave and I'll give him time to do so. He'll do as I say.' Kate sounded firm once more.

Flora shook her head gently, as if trying to shake out the

words that had been said. More than anything else, she wanted Billy to be here.

'Oh, Flora, I'm sorry. Please don't look like that.' Kate reached for Flora's hand.

'Mum, I'm sorry. I just can't... Can you really not find a way to...?' Flora struggled to speak, desperately trying to hold back the tears that were threatening to fall.

'I wish I could say it was all fine, Flora. But it hasn't been fine for a while now. And we can't stay together just because of what's happened. Losing Billy was devastating – I'll never get over it – but that's not a reason to stay when I'm not happy. In fact, it gives me more reason than ever to change things.'

'But, Mum, whatever's going on, or happened,' she felt her cheeks burn again, 'can you not, I don't know, work through it?'

Kate twisted the rings on her fingers. 'It's more complicated than that and I promise you it's not a decision I've taken easily. I'm sure your father will talk to you, too, but I wanted you to hear it from me. It's my decision.' Her face was resolute.

'I'm so sorry,' Flora whispered, looking at her mother across the table.

'So am I, darling. But that's just how it's got to be for now.'

As Flora waved Kate off, she felt more lost than ever.

\* \* \*

'Mack, I'm just going to sort out these deliveries for later,' Johnny called from the back of the shop.

'Thanks, Johnny.' Mack stood behind the counter, working his way through the day's post, strong coffee at his side. He'd been happy to see Johnny back in the shop, not realising quite how much he'd miss him and Flora until they weren't there. They'd obviously had a wonderful few days away and Susie had been a great help in the shop when she'd popped in as promised. Mack hadn't seen Flora yet, but she was due in just after lunch and he was looking forward to seeing her.

Just then the phone rang. Mack put down the letter he had in his hand and picked up the receiver. 'Hello?'

'Mack, it's Flora.'

'Hello, Flora, how are you? Are we seeing you later?'

'Actually, Mack, is Johnny there? Something's come up so I might not be in today after all, if that's OK. I'm so sorry.'

'Yes, hang on, let me get him for you.' Mack called through to the back of the shop. 'Johnny, Flora for you.'

'Thanks, Mack.' Johnny took the phone. 'You OK?'

'Johnny, Mum's just been. She's asked Dad to leave.'

'What? Why?'

'Well, she didn't say exactly why, and I'm not sure if she knows about the affair or not. It was awful, Johnny.' Flora sat down at the kitchen table. Her mother had barely been gone a few moments and Flora wondered whether the conversation had really happened; it all seemed too much to be real. 'I'm sorry but I just can't come to the shop right now.'

'Don't be silly, Flo. You don't have to. We've got it covered today. I'll be back home as soon as I can.'

'Don't hurry, I'm fine. I think it's just a bit of a shock. Actually, there's something I want to do, if you don't mind. I want to go and see Billy. At the church, I mean. I think I just want to sit there for a bit, see if I can get things a little straighter in my head. Would you mind? I'll be back in time to get the kids from school.'

Johnny pictured his brother-in-law's grave, a spot in a beautiful churchyard in the small village not far from Flora's parents' house. Flora and Johnny had got married in that same church and, most recently, Billy's memorial service had taken place there. Afterwards, Johnny and Flora had sat together on a wooden bench under an old cedar tree, a small plaque with the name of a long-gone parishioner behind them. He knew that was where Flora wanted to be.

'Of course, you go. And don't worry, I can pick up the kids.' Johnny looked at Mack, who nodded back with a thumbs up.

'Thank you. I'll text you when I'm leaving.'

'Drive carefully.'

Johnny put the phone down.

'Is she all right?' asked Mack, concerned.

'It's her parents. It's not great news. They're, well, separating.'

'Oh, poor girl, I'm sure that's the last thing she needs.'

'I know. It's so sad. They were always such a close family, but Billy's death has really knocked them all sideways.' Johnny shrugged, shaking his head. 'Anyway, I'll do the deliveries now, if that's OK with you. Then I can get the children.'

'Yes, of course. We're good here. It's not going to be busy today, looking at that weather.' Outside, fat drops of rain splashed onto the pavement at the front of the shop.

'We can go through the accounts list tomorrow. There are some new leads I need to follow up but could do with your help on wine suggestions to get them to agree to a tasting.'

'Sounds good. Now go, or you'll run out of time.' He shooed Johnny away. 'Go on.'

'Thanks, Mack.' Johnny drained his coffee cup. 'Catch up later.'

* * *

Flora drove the familiar route away from the coast and across the gorse-covered heath towards the village not too far from her parents' house. It was usually no more than half an hour's journey but the rain had slowed everyone down. As she made the last few turns into the village and back out the other side towards the church, the rain eased. Flora got out of the car, gave the door a shove and paused to take in the view of the top of the river behind her, before turning and walking up the long path towards the church. Even though she'd seen that view countless times – so familiar and yet always changing with the seasons and the tides – it never failed to take her breath away. Best of all, there didn't seem to be another soul around, just as she'd hoped.

She'd never really taken any notice of the headstones in the graveyard until Billy's was one of them. Now, as she passed, she read each name, thinking of the stories behind them, the families they'd left behind. She turned off the path and headed across the grass towards the spot where a cremation headstone marked Billy's grave. As she got closer, she looked ahead at the tree and the bench beneath it. Her heart sank. Someone was already sitting there.

All she'd wanted to do was sit there a while and tell Billy how furious she was with their parents. Now she couldn't, at least not alone.

Flora walked across to the stone and laid down the small bunch of garish flowers she'd bought on the way. 'I'm sorry, it's all they had at the garage.' She shrugged, speaking quietly.

She looked at his name, carved into the pale stone, the date of his birth and death painfully close together. She looked up at the sky, then back to the stone. 'I know you're not exactly here,' she tapped her foot on the headstone, 'but I know you're here.' She looked around. 'And I really need to talk to you.'

Before she could stop them, tears began to roll down her cheeks. 'Mum says she's leaving Dad and, Billy, I feel terrible because I know he's having an affair. And I don't know if Mum does. I can't say anything. Well, I could, but I'm worried that'll make it worse, although I don't know how it could get much worse.' She wiped at her face. 'God, Billy, I really wish you were here. I miss you so much.'

Suddenly conscious she'd been speaking out loud, she looked around. She could see the figure she'd spotted before, a woman sitting at the bench, wrapped in a thick black coat, a yellow scarf around her neck. Her grey hair was short, her cheeks pink with cold. Flora smiled.

The woman hesitated, then smiled briefly back. Then she stood and turned quickly, walking away towards the car park.

Why did she look familiar? Flora couldn't place her but felt sure she'd seen her somewhere. Maybe she had seen her visiting the graveyard before? Flora looked back towards the stone in the ground. 'Who was that?' She looked around again, but the woman was gone.

## 27

'Flo?' Johnny called out as Flora came through the door.

'Hi, how is everyone?' She walked into the kitchen just as the children scraped the last bit of ice cream from their bowls. 'On a Tuesday?' She put her head to one side.

'Hey, my tea, my rules. That's all they've had: their body weight in ice cream.'

'Johnny!'

'I'm kidding. Sausages.'

'Slightly burnt sausages,' Pip laughed.

'All right, no need to give me away.' Johnny ruffled the top of his daughter's hair. 'So, everything OK?'

'Well...' Flora laughed. 'We'll talk later. But yes, I feel much better for going, actually. Thank you.' She kissed her husband.

'Ew.' Tom pulled a face as he went to get down from the table.

'Not at all. I'm glad you went.'

'The weird thing is, I saw someone else there. At the church.' Flora sat down, picking up a leftover chip and dunking it in the ketchup left on the plate.

'What, someone you know?' Johnny went to the fridge. 'Want a glass?' He held up the bottle from the fridge door.

'Yes, please. I honestly don't know who it was, but she looked so familiar. I've been trying to place her all the way home, but I just can't. At least it stopped me thinking about my bloody parents, I guess.' She reached out to take the glass Johnny had poured for her. 'Ooh, that's good. What is it?'

'South African Chenin. Got it in the supermarket for six quid.' He held up the bottle triumphantly.

'Johnny, what are you thinking? That's our competition!' Flora looked mock-horrified.

'I know, I just wanted to see what they had in their range and this was on offer. Couldn't resist.'

Flora screwed up her nose. 'It's brilliant, annoyingly.' She took another sip. 'Anyway, I'm pleased I went. After seeing Mum this morning, I just needed to clear my head a bit.'

'Hey, you two, why don't you go and stick the telly on for a bit so I can talk to your mother.' Johnny picked up the empty plates from the table.

'Put your bowls in the dishwasher before you go, please,' said Flora.

With the children gone, Johnny sat down next to Flora. 'So, go on, what did she say?'

'Not much, really. Just that it was complicated. And that she was sorry.' Flora shrugged.

'So she definitely doesn't know about your father seeing someone else?'

'I don't think so. At least she didn't say anything about it. I'm thinking I need to tell him he's got to do everything to try and make it right.'

'Flo, we've been through this. You can't expect to be able to fix it. You've got to trust them to sort it out themselves.

Maybe, with a little more time, they might be able to get back to normal – well, as much as they can. I mean, after the trial...'

'Oh my God, that's it!' Flora banged her glass back down on the table. 'That's who the woman was at the church!'

'Who?' Johnny didn't follow.

Flora shook her head fiercely. 'I think it was the mother of the boy who killed Billy.' She stared at Johnny, wide-eyed.

'But... how do you know? You've never seen her, have you? There wasn't a picture in the paper.'

'No, but it was her. I know it, Johnny. It was the way she looked at me.'

'How can you be so sure?'

'I'm telling you it was her. She just disappeared when she saw me. Practically bolted, in fact. Seriously, I think she'd gone to see Billy's headstone.'

'Isn't that a bit... insensitive?' Johnny trod carefully, not wanting to say the wrong thing.

'Maybe. I don't know... She must feel wretched, though. I mean, her son is likely to go to prison for what he's done. It's not like actually mourning the death of a child, but living with the guilt – well, isn't that a sentence of sorts?'

Johnny could practically see her mind racing. 'Hang on, why do you think she would go there?'

'It would be easy enough to figure out where the church was, given newspaper reports of the accident or the memorial service or whatever. And like I said, I think she must feel so awful, guilty even. I mean, you'd just be stuck with it forever. Honestly, she looked so, so sad.'

'I still think it's a bit odd to go, knowing she might bump into one of you.'

'Well, it was a rainy Tuesday afternoon. I'm sure she didn't want to be seen. In fact, definitely not, given that she bolted as soon as she could once she'd seen me.'

'Do you think she knew who you were?'

'Johnny, I was standing by Billy's headstone talking to him like a lunatic! I'm sure she knew who I was.' Flora laughed at the thought of that. 'Poor thing, she must have felt terrible.' She shook her head.

Johnny topped up her wine glass. 'Hey, why don't you take this and go and run a bath. I'll make us something to eat. Go on, you've had a long day.'

'Eventful, that's for sure.' Flora smiled at Johnny. 'Well, I'm not going to pass that offer up, thank you.'

As she lay in the bath, her limbs flushed pink by the hot water, she kept thinking of the woman on the bench. She remembered the hair, the cheeks, the thick coat and scarf. But most of all she recognised the look on her face, that of someone haunted by something terrible.

* * *

'Mum?'

Denise closed the door gently behind her. She took off her coat and hung it on its peg, putting her handbag over the top of it.

'Just a minute.' She peered at her face in the mirror on the wall, wiping at the streaked mascara on her cheeks.

'Where've you been? You didn't say you'd be out all day. I was worried.' Stephen looked up from where he was sitting at the table by the window. The flat was almost in darkness save for a small circle of light from a lamp in the corner.

'I'm sorry, I didn't realise it was quite such a long way.'

'Who were you seeing again?' Stephen knew the answer but there was something about the way his mother had been behaving that made him wonder if she wasn't telling him the truth.

'I told you, I went with Jenny to see her sister.' Denise walked over to the kitchen and put the kettle on.

'Where?'

'I'm not quite sure exactly where it was, to be honest. I can't remember the name of the village.' Denise busied herself making a cup of tea, hoping Stephen wouldn't ask too many more questions.

'Right. So, how was she?'

'Who?'

'Jenny's sister.'

'Oh, fine. It was just good to get out, have a change of scene. She wanted the company on the drive. And I knew her sister years ago. We were at school together.' Denise hoped the questions would stop. She hated having to lie but she knew she couldn't tell Stephen where she'd really been. She knew he wouldn't understand.

Ever since Stephen had been charged with careless driving shortly after the accident, she hadn't been able to stop thinking about the man who had been killed, about his family. Night after night she lay awake in bed, thoughts of their anguish and suffering almost crushing her. She'd seen a photo of the man, who was not that much older than her own son. His face had smiled out at her from the picture in the paper, his eyes kind. Denise couldn't stop thinking about how he'd had no idea what lay ahead that night as he drove home.

Over and over again she'd wished she'd stopped Stephen sooner. Not just going out that night – she knew that what he was doing wasn't right – but stopped him from seeing those people. They weren't his friends. He'd been too keen to please, desperate for them to like him. But she hadn't been able to bring herself to say that to him. He was her son. And now it was too late.

Just like it was too late for the man he had killed, who was someone's son.

Finally, unable to bear it alone, Denise had confided to her friend and neighbour how she felt, and Jenny had agreed to Denise's request to drive her to visit the grave of the young man. Of course, Denise hadn't told Stephen; he had been in a terrible way since the accident. He hadn't wanted to talk about it, certainly not with her. Not that he saw anyone else, in fact had refused to see anyone since it happened. It just sat between them, an unbearable truth that neither knew how to deal with. She certainly didn't expect him to understand her need to do this.

Jenny had tried to talk her out of it, but Denise was adamant. 'I just want to go there, to say I'm sorry.' And so Jenny had agreed to drive her friend to the churchyard in the village where the family was from. Denise had seen the name in the paper and she guessed the grave would be there. No one else had to know; no one had to see her. That had been the plan, anyway.

Denise had felt quite calm on the journey there, watching the view through the car window change from the suburbs where they lived to open countryside. But then the rain started falling and by the time they got there it was pouring. She made her way alone to the churchyard, leaving Jenny in the car, in the car park. There wasn't another soul to be seen.

The fresh flowers on the ground gave away the location of those whose ashes were most recently interred and soon Denise found herself standing near the stone bearing the name of the man killed by her son. She looked at it for a while, from a slight distance, her feet rooted to the spot. She felt absolutely wretched for this man and furious with her son all at the same time.

Rain dripped from Denise's face, her hair sticking to her forehead. She moved to sit on a bench under a tree to collect her thoughts. She looked up, spotting a figure walking towards the churchyard. The woman had her head down, eyes averted. Whether she was avoiding Denise or simply hadn't seen her, Denise couldn't tell, but she watched with horror as the woman walked across the grass, straight towards the headstone near where she'd been standing moments before. Denise looked at her, wrapped in a long dark padded coat, a pink woollen scarf around her neck. The woman turned and smiled. Denise waited until her back was again turned, then stood and walked as fast as she could back towards the car.

'Can we go?'

'Are you OK, Den?'

'Please, can we go?' Denise did up her seat belt.

Jenny looked at her friend. She was clearly terrified. 'Yes, of course.'

Jenny tried to get her to talk. After a while, Denise spoke, her voice strained.

'I'm so sorry, Jenny.'

'Please don't apologise. I'm just worried this wasn't a good idea.'

'I had to come. I had to. I just... didn't think I'd see anyone.'

'Who was that woman?'

Denise looked ahead. 'I've no idea.' But the sadness on the stranger's face had given her away immediately. Denise knew exactly who she was.

## 28

The sound of the bell brought Mack out from the back of the shop. Colin, resplendent in top-to-toe rust red stood before him, a book in his hand and a big grin on his face.

'Colin, how are you today?'

'Excellent, thank you. And thrilled to say I've taken delivery of a book that I've been longing to share with you. I have my own copy, of course, but I've been trying to track one down for you for some time.' Colin handed the book to Mack with great care. 'It's quite old, as you can see.'

Mack held the book away and adjusted his glasses. '*Chats About Wine*.' He opened the front cover.

'Written by a chap called Hawker back in 1907. I came across it a while ago and have been meaning to recommend it to you for ages. He – Hawker, that is – refers to wine as "the elixir of life". Here, let me find his description for you. It's quite wonderful.' Colin turned a few pages over and pointed to the text. 'There, read that.'

Mack cleared his throat.

What then, it may be asked, is this wonderful elixir of life, which is almost as old as the world itself and yet is overflowing with the exuberance of youth; which restores and invigorates us when the powers of life are low; uplifts and cheers us in days of sorrow and gloom; evokes and enhances our joys and pleasures; and which, by the inherent force it is endowed with, gives animation, energy and inspiration to every sense and faculty we possess?

'Wine, that's what!' Colin laughed. 'I think you'll enjoy reading that, Mack. There's a whole chapter about the importance of having a good wine merchant in your town. It could have been written for you.' Colin looked very pleased with himself.

'Well, what can I say? That's very kind of you, thank you.' Mack was genuinely touched by the man's kindness. 'Can I repay you with a bottle of something?'

'Absolutely not, but you can point me in the direction of a bottle to have tonight. I'm making something special for dinner, a classic French daube. I'm just picking up the last few ingredients and need a bottle of wine to use in the stew and one to drink with it later.'

Mack went towards the French wine section, reaching down for a bottle of Côtes du Rhône. 'Use this one for cooking,' he handed the bottle to Colin, 'and this one to drink with it.'

Colin took the second bottle. 'Vinsobres...' He sounded unsure.

'It's the most northerly of the Southern Rhône top spots and this particular producer has vineyards only a stone's throw from the Alps so the altitude gives the wines incredible flavour. And because it doesn't have one of the big appellation names on the front like Châteauneuf or even Gigondas, it's better value. In my opinion, that is.'

Colin held the bottle away from him, squinting at the label, turning it around. 'Well, with that recommendation it sounds like just the thing. I'll take both.'

Mack wrapped them in paper and put them in a box for Colin. 'Here you go. I haven't charged you for the cheaper one – and don't argue about it.'

'Well, that's very kind, thank you.' Colin tapped his card on the machine. 'How's Flora doing? I haven't seen her for a while.'

'Ah, she's hanging in there. It's not been the easiest time for her, obviously, but she seems to be getting back to normal life a little bit more now. She's in here a few times a week now but still working from home, too.'

'Poor thing, I do feel for her. Must be hard, losing someone like that, so suddenly. You know, here one minute, gone the next.'

Mack tried to change the subject. 'So, how long are you cooking the beef for?'

'About three hours all in. It's all in the quality of the meat. And the wine, of course.' He nodded knowingly at Mack. 'When is the court case? For the boy, the one who killed Flora's brother? I saw it reported in the paper a few weeks ago.'

'Soon, I think. Apparently, the police were hoping it would have happened by now, according to Johnny, but things are a bit slow at this time of year. Still, hopefully it can all be over before Christmas and they can at least put that bit of it behind them.' Mack handed Colin a receipt. 'There you go, let me know what you think.'

'Oh, I will, thank you, Mack.' Colin picked up the box. 'And say hello to Flora for me when she comes in, won't you?'

'Of course, thank you.' Mack waved as he left the shop.

A few moments later the bell rang again. Mack looked up to see Flora.

'You've just missed...'

'Colin. I know. I saw him come in. I'm sorry, Mack, I know he's a lovely man, but I just don't want to... well, I'd rather not bump into anyone too chatty at the moment.' She looked at Mack and pulled a face. 'I'm sorry, that's probably a dreadful thing to say.'

'Not at all, I know exactly what you mean. He means well, though.'

'I know. Ooh, is that fresh coffee I smell?'

'It certainly is. I'll pour you one.'

'Lovely, thank you. So, Mack, don't faint but I think I've finally finished the online wine-course material. Just to warn you, Johnny's insisting that you and I do some short videos for the website, like an introduction, for example.'

Mack looked horrified.

Flora laughed, 'I know, I know. I had the same reaction. But he promises they'll be really short, he'll film them and do all the editing and we just have to talk wine for a bit. Honestly, if I'm being made to do it you have to do it, too.'

Mack raised his eyebrows. 'Well, if you think we should...'

'If we don't, we'll never hear the end of it, Mack. Let's just do it and then he'll leave us alone.' Flora took the coffee from him. 'Lovely, thank you. Right, I'll get on with those new tasting cards for those wines that came in last week.'

'It's lovely to have you in the shop, Flora.'

'I want to keep busy.' She smiled at him.

'I know you do. You get sorted. I'll fetch you some blank cards; they're in the back somewhere. No doubt Johnny's put them somewhere sensible and I won't be able to find them now.'

Flora spent the next hour writing short tasting notes for the new wines to go on the shelf. It had always been one of her favourite jobs, finding the words to describe the aromas, flavours and textures of wines, and thinking about the best type of food they'd go with. But this time she struggled to find the words, no matter how hard she tried. Instead, her thoughts kept returning to the woman on the bench. And the more Flora thought about her, the more she realised she wanted to talk to her. Why, she wasn't quite sure. She just knew that the need to meet her wasn't going away and sooner or later she'd have to do something about it.

* * *

Kate sat opposite Robin at the table, the house quiet except for the sound of the grandfather clock in the hall. The midday chime rang out. Robin looked up from his paperwork, not that he could concentrate. Kate was seemingly lost in her book, a weighty tome on Shakespeare's wife, Monty curled up on her lap.

Ever since delivering her news to Robin, life had gone on in a strangely normal way, their daily routine not that different from before. But the subject of his affair was a closed one, as far as Kate was concerned. Whenever he tried to broach the subject, Kate shut the conversation down. It just hung in the air, around but ignored, like an unwanted guest at a particularly hideous drinks party.

'Can I make you something for lunch?' Robin ventured.

Kate didn't look up. 'No, thank you. I'm going to pop out in a bit to pick up some shopping. I'll get myself something then.'

'Kate...'

'Robin, if this is about her, I don't want to hear it.'

'It's not. I mean, of course I want to talk to you about it, tell you it's over and how sorry I am...'

'Robin, I've said I don't want to talk about it and I haven't changed my mind.' She looked up at him, her eyes impassive.

'I know. I'm sorry. It's not that. I wanted to talk to you about next week.'

'You mean going to court?'

'Yes.'

'Well, obviously we've got to go to the wretched thing, but it doesn't really make any difference to Billy, does it? It's too late now.'

The words thumped onto the table.

Robin took a deep breath. He wanted to say so many things but was unable to find a way to bring the words out. 'If I could change what's happened I would.' 'I feel wretched.' 'I miss Billy.' 'I'm sorry.' 'I love you.' But the words stayed buried.

Kate closed her book, putting it on the table. She lifted Monty onto the floor and stood, brushing off her long navy needlecord skirt as she did. 'I'll see you in a bit.' She picked up the car keys from the dresser and left the room.

Robin couldn't tell if she'd been talking to him or the dog.

## 29

Tilda sat in Flora's kitchen, an empty pot of tea between them. Having taken the children to the beach for a runabout after school, they'd returned to Flora's house and the children had plonked themselves in front of the television in the sitting room next door.

'It's almost six – can we have a glass of wine now?' Tilda looked at Flora, hands pressed together.

'I'll see what's in the fridge.'

'Flo, I hope you don't mind me asking – please say if you'd rather not talk about it – but is there any news on your parents?'

'Not really. Mum hasn't changed her mind. I haven't spoken to Dad for a bit; I honestly don't know what to say. I feel if there's anyone who should have my support first it's her, really. After all, she didn't do anything wrong. But I don't want it to be about taking sides. And with everything we've gone through recently...' Flora poured out two glasses.

'Ooh, fizz! Really?' Tilda tried not to sound too excited.

'Napoleon said in victory you deserve champagne. In defeat you need it. Something like that, anyway.' She passed Tilda a glass. 'Well, this is actually an English sparkling wine but whatever, cheers.' They clinked their glasses. The toasty bubbles washed across Flora's mouth, leaving a streak of orchard-fruit flavours in its wake.

'Can I ask you a technical question?' Tilda took a sniff of her glass.

'Go ahead, caller.'

'Why don't you use flutes? I noticed you always use a normal wine glass even for fizz.'

'Because you can't stick your nose into a flute like you can a wine glass. And smelling it is one of my favourite bits, so I don't want to miss out.' As if to demonstrate, Flora swilled her glass, and stuck her nose in, taking a big sniff. 'See? Gorgeous.'

Tilda did the same. 'I suppose. But I usually forget to smell it anyway.' She grinned at her friend.

'I know, Tilda, you're a lost cause.' Flora laughed. 'So, to answer your question, no news on my parents. But it's the trial next week so maybe after that I'll talk to them about it again. As Johnny's told me a million times, it's not my problem to fix. They're grown-ups, too, apparently.' Flora couldn't help but roll her eyes.

'You know, if you do decide to go – to court, I mean – Susie and I can help out with the kids if you need us to, or one of us could come with you, if that would help?'

'You're very kind. Thank you.' Flora took another sip of her wine. 'But I'm not going.'

'Oh, OK.' Tilda sipped her wine.

'I want to save as much space in my head as I can for Billy, not fill it with things I don't want to know.'

Tilda nodded sympathetically. She couldn't help but feel that ignoring it wouldn't make it any easier, but Flora seemed adamant. 'Whatever you think is right for you, Flo. But just to say, we're here for you.'

'Thank you, lovely friend.' Flora raised her glass to Tilda once more. 'Now, I need to ask your opinion on something. And be honest because I think maybe I'm going a bit mad.'

Tilda shifted in her seat. 'I'm all ears.'

Flora sat back down, placing a bowl of crinkle-cut crisps between them. 'No judgement, OK?'

'No judgement.' Tilda tried to look serious, then reached for a crisp.

'So, I drove down to the churchyard near home earlier this week. To visit Billy's headstone.'

'I thought—'

'I know, I didn't think I'd grow to like going there either but it turns out it gives me a chance to think. Anyway, I was standing there, you know, just kind of... taking in the view and I turned and saw a woman sitting on the bench under the tree. The one where I sometimes like to sit. I know it's not my bench but I realised I'm not used to sharing it. Whatever,' Flora waved her hand, 'she was sitting there, the woman. I've never seen her before but there's something about her that seems instantly familiar. And I can't put my finger on it. I'm thinking, have I met you before? But then I think, she's just here to visit someone, too. But when I turn again, she's gone. Like, literally vanished. And when I get home, it hits me. It's the mother of the boy who hit Billy's car.'

Tilda practically spat her wine out. 'How on earth do you know? *Have* you seen her before?' She wiped at her mouth.

'No, but it's her. I know it. And I think she'd come to see Billy's grave, too.'

'So did you say anything to her?' Tilda took a slow sip from her glass.

'I didn't get a chance to, and I didn't really put two and two together until later that day. But now I'm thinking that I want to talk to her. Tilda, it's all I can think about.'

Tilda's eyes widened in surprise. 'But I thought you said you didn't want the details.'

'I don't, not of what happened. I can find those out after the court case if I want to. No, this is more about me wanting to understand why, not what. Do you see?'

'Sort of.' Tilda tried her best to look as if she did. 'But if that's the case, why not ask him, not his mother?'

'You mean the boy who did it?'

'Yes, surely he's in the best position to tell you.'

'Maybe he is. But there was just something about seeing her that made me think that I could speak to her, one mother to another, you know? Perhaps one day I could speak to him, too, but at the moment, that feels too brutal. I'm not sure I could face him. No, it's her I want to talk to.'

Tilda wasn't sure if she really understood, but nodded even so. 'I see what you mean.'

Flora smiled at her friend. 'I realise this might not make sense.'

'Oh, Flora, can you tell I'm struggling?' Tilda laughed apologetically.

'You're an open book, Tilda. Look, I feel like I've been shattered into a million tiny fragments over the last few months but if I'm to try and keep going, I've got to learn to live with what's happened. With Billy, I mean. I'm not sure I have the energy to care what happens to my parents' marriage at this point, to be honest.'

'Oh, Flora, you don't mean that.'

'No, I'm sure you're right, but this is about making sense of what happened to Billy. Or at least trying to.'

'That makes a bit more sense. Sorry, Flora, I'm probably not saying the right things at all.'

'No, you're saying exactly the right things. Everyone's so worried about saying the wrong thing, they end up not saying anything at all.' Flora topped up their glasses. 'I guess what I'm saying is that I know it's not going to be easy, but I want to try to move on. No, not move on. That's the wrong phrase. I think I just mean... I want to go on. Yes, that's it. I want to find a way to go on, and not feel sad all the time. But to do that I need to have some sort of understanding from somewhere.' Flora popped a crisp in her mouth, the loud crunch breaking the small silence that had fallen between them.

'Fuck me, Flo. That's quite heavy.'

Flora burst out laughing, closely followed by Tilda, and once they'd started, they couldn't stop. They laughed until tears rolled down their faces.

'What's so funny?' Pip stood by the kitchen door, a half-smile on her face.

'Oh, I don't know, darling. We were just talking and, well, sometimes you've just got to laugh.' Flora wiped the tears from her face.

'Amen to that,' said Tilda, draining her glass.

## 30

'Stephen, are you awake?' Denise knocked on the bedroom door, gently. A muffled reply came from the other side of it. 'I've got you a cup of tea.'

'Yeah, come in.'

She turned on the light and put the tea down on the small table by his bed. 'How are you feeling?' She looked at him as he rubbed his eyes, his hair sticking up, looking unbearably young.

'Thanks, Mum.' He reached across for the tea, spying his one and only suit hanging up on the back of his cupboard door as he did, a stark reminder of their day ahead.

She perched on the end of his bed. 'I'll make you a proper breakfast, if you like. I think you should eat something before we go.'

'I'm not...' He looked at his mother's face, expectant. 'Thanks, that would be lovely.'

'Eggs and bacon?'

'Yes, please.'

Denise stood up to go.

'Mum?'

She turned to her son, his ashen face looking up at her.

'I'm sorry.'

'I know you are, Stephen. Let's just get this done. We'll be all right.' She smiled at him, hoping she looked more reassuring than she felt. She went to the kitchen and put some bacon under the grill. Then she broke eggs into a glass bowl, slaking them with a knife. As she stood there, the sound of metal rhythmically hitting glass, she closed her eyes and sent up a silent prayer. Their lives had been shattered that August night, the days afterwards a blur. She thought back to that small, stuffy room at the police station, where an appointed lawyer, Mr Sawyer, had explained that Stephen should plead not guilty to a charge of death by careless driving.

She'd watched her son retreat into himself ever since, Denise trying to find the right things to say, but the hideousness of what had happened was always there. She'd barely slept more than a few hours at a time, for months. She often felt as if in a dream, or rather a nightmare, wishing desperately for someone to wake her.

Now they sat in silence, Denise drinking more tea whilst her son pushed his breakfast around his plate.

'You need to eat.'

'I can't.' He didn't look up, his voice breaking.

'Come on, you need strength for today.'

'Mum, I killed someone.'

'I know. And I wish we could change that, but we can't. So, you just need to tell them what happened, in the courtroom. Just as Mr Sawyer said. That's all you can do.'

Slowly Stephen raised his eyes. 'Mum, I don't think I can do it.'

'I'm afraid you don't have a choice. But no matter what happens, I'll be there. Now, try and eat. I'm going to go and get ready; we're being collected in about an hour.'

'OK.' His hand trembled as he tried to scoop up some eggs with his fork. He let it drop to the plate with a clatter, blinking back tears. Pushing his plate away, he stood and went back to his room, sat on the edge of the bed and looked at the suit. Next to it, on the floor, was a bag he'd packed the night before, together with his mother's help. It contained some clothes, a pair of trainers and a washbag. Denise had insisted he take the earplugs she'd bought him, along with a stack of paper and stamped envelopes with their address on the front.

Stephen had known this day would come, had even told himself he was prepared to face it. But all he wanted to do, right then and there, was shut the door and never come out of his room.

They sat in the taxi, Denise trying to answer the driver's questions politely whilst giving nothing away. Stephen looked out of the window as the court buildings loomed into view, drab and unassuming. The day was grey and overcast, the air heavy.

Mr Sawyer greeted them as arranged, carrying bundles of paper. He was a large man, the buttons on his shirt struggling to hold the strained material in place, his eyes jet black like a shark's. Together, Denise, Stephen and Mr Sawyer made their way inside and, after going through a lengthy security check, were shown into a small room off to the side of the courtroom.

Mr Sawyer hung up his overcoat on the back of the door. 'Right, we might be here for some time, just to warn you. The hearing is due to start at nine thirty but we'll see. For now, we wait. Can I get you some coffee?'

'No, thank you.' Denise managed a small smile.

Stephen shook his head, too, his gaze fixed on the floor.

'Right, well. I shan't be long.'

'Actually, do you mind if I just go and find the ladies first?'

'No, of course. Right out of there, down the hall, second on the left.' Mr Sawyer gestured which way Denise should head.

'Thank you, I won't be a moment.' As she walked along the corridor, she passed an older couple coming down a flight of stairs, flanked by another man carrying papers. Denise looked at them, her eyes meeting the woman's for a fleeting second. The woman hadn't even noticed her, but Denise knew. She had similar features, the same bright eyes as the woman she'd seen in the churchyard. She watched them disappear as they walked on down the long corridor in the opposite direction. She felt suddenly weak and her vision blurred before black started to close in around her. Then nothing...

* * *

'Mrs Hirst, can you hear me?' Denise tried to focus. She could just make out a face, the words coming to her as if through a fog. 'How are you feeling? You gave us a bit of a scare there.'

Denise took a sip of the water from the paper cup being held to her lips. She swallowed slowly. Things started to come back into focus. She could make out Mr Sawyer in a chair opposite and, to his left, Stephen.

'You OK, Mum?'

'Yes, I... don't know what happened.' She tried to speak but her lips felt like cotton wool.

'You fainted. We found you lying at the bottom of the stairs.' The kind woman spoke again. 'Here, try and drink some more water.'

Denise did as she was told.

'Mrs Hirst, are you sure you don't want to have a lie down? At least until we go into the courtroom?' Mr Sawyer failed to keep his mild irritation from his voice.

'No, really, I'll be fine. I'm feeling better already.' She tried her best to sound convincing, a little chirpier. 'I think I just should have eaten more this morning, that's all.'

'Well, I'll leave you to it, then.' The woman went to leave. 'Just shout if you need me again.'

'Yes, thank you. We will.' Mr Sawyer shut the door behind her. He waited a few moments whilst Denise sipped slowly from the cup. 'Now, listen. I need you both to be strong. Stephen, do your best to speak clearly, answer the questions as we've discussed. Denise, you'll be sitting to one side but it's not a big room: you'll be able to see Stephen quite clearly. We've been through all the "what ifs" but let's go in there with the right attitude. Are we clear?'

They both nodded.

There was a knock at the door.

Mr Sawyer called out, 'Thank you.' He looked back at them and clapped his hands together. 'Time to go.'

\* \* \*

Flora sat at the tasting counter in the shop, tapping at her laptop, a line of unopened bottles in front of her. She tried to concentrate on the words on the screen, but the cursor had been in the same place, blinking furiously at her, for what seemed like an age.

Mack came down the stairs into the shop carrying a tray. 'I thought you could do with these.' He walked across to her, putting a plate of biscuits down in front of her.

Flora looked at the plate. Normally, she'd have fallen on it. She looked up at Mack. 'It's the court case today.'

'I know, Flora. I see you're trying to distract yourself with work but why don't you take advice from an old bugger like me and go for a walk on the beach? It's never not a good idea to go for a walk on the beach.' He looked at her over his glasses.

'You're right. I'd thought I could do something to distract myself but it's not working. When did Johnny say he'd be back?'

'He said around two-ish, so you go. I'm fine here.'

'Excuse me?' A man who'd been browsing the expensive clarets called over to Mack. 'Have you got anything really old?'

Mack walked back towards him. He'd been quickly brushed off by the man when he'd first come into the shop. 'Well, I think we've got a '92 in the back.'

'But 1992 is hardly old.' The man scoffed.

'It's 1892, sir.' Mack pushed his glasses up his nose, smiling.

'Ah, right. Very good. What sort of price are we talking?'

'Around eight.'

'Hundred?'

'Eight thousand.'

'Maybe something a little younger?' The man seemed to deflate a little.

Flora stifled a laugh. She closed her laptop and shoved it into her bag, waving at Mack as she slipped out of the shop. She decided to head to one of her favourite spots, a stretch of beach reached by a small path through the hedge just off a lay-by. Somehow it had remained a secret, even among locals. She put the radio on, voices talking about an opera singer she'd never heard of. Hitting the button, she switched station and suddenly the car was filled with the sounds of one of her favourite songs. She turned up the volume, the music taking her back to a time in her parents' garden when the most fun to be had involved a hosepipe and a sprinkler. She remembered the way she and Billy would race through the spray, watching as the water threw rainbows in the air. She could hear him calling her name, pleading with her to watch as he jumped over the sprinkler, dissolving into fits of laughter as they both got soaked.

She pulled up by the side of the road and headed down to the beach. The tide was out, leaving islands of slick, glossy mud on show, small channels of seawater running between them. Great puffy clouds scooted across the blue sky and the wind carried the scent of salt with it.

Flora buttoned up her coat and walked into the cold wind, the sound echoing in her ears. The waves moved quickly towards the shore, one after the other after the other. She moved from the pebbles onto the sand closer to the shoreline, enjoying the feel of it sinking under her feet. She glanced behind, seeing her footprints being washed away just seconds after leaving them.

As she looked out to sea, the words of the woman in the church in Venice came back to her, so clear it was if the woman was standing right next to her. 'Hearts stay broken,' Flora whispered, her words taken out to sea by the wind.

She felt her phone vibrate in her pocket. She grabbed it and pulled it out, turning it to see the screen. She stood for a moment as she pulled off her gloves in order to unlock the phone, tapping in the numbers of her wedding anniversary.

The message flashed up from her father. It took her a moment to take it in. She looked at the message again, wanting to make sure she was reading it right. Tears clouded her eyes.

She rang Johnny's number. He picked up immediately.

'Have you heard from them?'

'Yes, Dad's just texted.'

There was a pause. 'And what did he say?'

Flora looked down at her boots in the sand, her feet now wet. She hadn't noticed the waves washing up over her feet.

'He, um... was found guilty. He's got eighteen months in prison.'

'Wow. Are you all right? Where are you?'

'I'm at the beach, the bit by the old lighthouse.'

'Are you with anyone?'

'No, I wanted to come on my own.' Flora walked back towards the shingle on the beach. 'I'm going to head back in a bit. I'll see you at the shop.'

'Flo, why don't you go home?'

'Actually, I think I might go to my parents'. I think I should see them.'

'Well, it's up to you. But they will have had a long day, I should think.'

'I know, which is why I'm thinking I'll take them some food. Actually, would you mind if I stayed there tonight? I'll come back first thing in the morning.'

'Of course, whatever you think. But, Flo, you sure you're up to driving?'

'I'm fine, Johnny. I promise. I'll call you later.'

'I love you.'

'I love you, too. Thank you. Tell the kids I'll see them tomorrow.'

She put her phone back in her pocket and looked out at the vast sky in front of her. She thought of the rainbows in the air as the tears rolled down her cheeks.

## 31

'Thank you, Jenny.' Denise leaned in through the car door.

'It was the least I could do. I wasn't going to leave you on your own there now, was I?'

'Guess I've got to get used to the house being empty.' Denise shrugged. She hadn't dared herself to think ahead as to what might happen if her son was sent to prison. But she really didn't think she was going to feel like this. After the shock of the accident and the constant worry of what might happen, the unthinkable had finally come true. Her overwhelming memory of the day was watching Stephen and the back of his head as he was taken out of the courtroom by two police officers. He'd turned and given her a small wave just before he left and then, before she could even wave back, he was gone.

She walked back into the dark, empty flat. She hung her coat on its peg, turned on the hall light and went to the kitchen. She topped up the kettle then stood, watching it boil.

She thought of Mr Sawyer's words as they'd left the court. Eighteen months didn't mean eighteen months. It would be more like nine months and the rest on licence with a fair wind behind them, whatever that meant. Denise knew she should have been grateful to know Stephen wouldn't be in prison for as long as they'd thought, but still, she was devastated. Then her mind turned to the couple she'd passed that morning at court. She'd not taken her eyes off Stephen once they were in the courtroom but part of her knew she hadn't dared to for fear of meeting theirs. She thought of them sitting there, listening to see what would happen to the man who'd killed their son. Their lives had been shattered because of her own son's actions. Because he'd been stupid enough to take a stolen car and drive his friends – not that they were really his friends, not one had been anywhere near Stephen since the accident – in the hope of impressing them. In order to fit in. She thought back to him as a little boy, always with his head down, not wanting to draw attention to himself.

What should she have done differently? Was it her fault that he wasn't strong enough to stand up for himself? Had she loved him enough? Did she love him too much? The same old questions crashed into her head, one after the other, not even bothering to form an orderly queue. They were familiar now. She hadn't been able to think of anything else for months.

Denise poured hot water into a mug, splashing it onto the kitchen counter as she did. It took a few seconds to register she hadn't put a teabag in. Leaving the mug on the side, she went to the table by the window. The street below was now quiet. Far away, the sound of a siren made her think of her boy. She closed her eyes, put her hands together and prayed.

* * *

Dinner at her parents' house had been quiet. Flora had called ahead, telling them she was coming with something for them all to eat. Kate had protested, saying she had something in the freezer, but Flora had insisted.

'Please, Mum. Just let me do this for you.'

Her father had answered the door. They'd hugged. 'You OK, Dad?'

He'd nodded, then gestured to the bags Flora was carrying. 'Let me take those.'

She smiled. 'Thank you.'

'Hey, Mum, how are you?' Flora crossed the room and hugged her mother.

'Well, just glad that's over, to be honest.' Kate sighed.

'I'm sorry I didn't come.'

Kate passed her a glass of wine. 'You had your reasons to not want to be there.'

There was a pause. Flora was about to fill it when her mother continued.

'So, what did you do today?' Kate put some plates on the table.

'I went to the beach.' Flora wanted to tell her she'd cried until her eyes hurt.

'That sounds nice. More for you, Robin?' Kate proffered the bottle across the table to her husband. 'Actually, if you don't mind, I'm going to go and have a bath. I am feeling absolutely exhausted. I'm sorry, Flora, I know you've brought food but I don't think I could eat a thing.'

Flora went to protest but her mother was already on her way out of the room. She turned just before she left. 'Come up and see me before you go to bed, Flora.'

'I will.' Flora waited until she heard her mother's footsteps disappear up the stairs. 'Dad, what's going on?'

'What do you mean, darling?' Her father busied himself getting cutlery out of the drawer.

'Oh, come on, Dad.' Flora couldn't help but laugh.

Robin stood up and went to the kitchen dresser. He picked up the whisky bottle. 'Fancy one of these instead?'

Flora nodded. Robin poured out two measures of whisky into tumblers and handed one to Flora.

'Thank you.' She brought the glass to her nose and sniffed it gently, the smell of smoke and sea filling her nose. 'Dad, please talk to me. I don't understand what's going on.'

'I'm not sure I do either. I have ended my relationship with... her.'

'Who?' Flora wanted her father to spell it out to her. It might be over, but she wanted him to squirm at least a little.

'You know who. Ally.'

'How long?'

'Flora, please...'

'I said, how long?'

'About five years.' He looked at his glass, unable to meet his daughter's eyes.

'Why, Dad?' Flora hissed at him.

'I don't know, Flora. I know that's not good enough, but I honestly don't know. If I could go back and change it, I would. It was a really, really stupid thing to do.'

'And it's really over?'

'Yes, it really is. Sadly, though, I don't think that makes any difference to your mother.'

'But, Dad, you can't just let it go like that! She's clearly so hurt, and desperately trying not to seem like it – you know what she's like.'

Robin looked at his daughter, knowing that she was right. 'I'm not sure she wants me to stay. Not now. After everything that's happened, I just don't think she can forgive me.'

Flora fixed him with a stare. 'Look, after everything that's happened you have even more reason to make sure you change her mind. You need to show her that you're sorry, that you want to make things better.'

'She doesn't seem to want to try.'

'Dad, that doesn't mean she doesn't want *you* to try.' Flora rolled her eyes.

'Right.' He took another sip of his whisky.

'And I tell you what, if Billy were here he'd be telling you to do the same thing. To do something rather than nothing.' Flora held her father's eye.

'I know he would.'

'He'd also be furious with you.'

'I know that too.'

They looked at each other for a moment. Flora smiled at her father. 'It's not too late, Dad.'

Robin sighed. 'I hope you're right.'

Kate sat in the bath hugging her knees. The water was lukewarm, the bubbles long gone. She could just about hear their voices below, the words muffled but the tone unmistakable. Flora was clearly giving her father a talking-to.

Kate felt drained. Her limbs ached, her eyes were heavy. She closed them for a second, seeing the courtroom once again. It had been such a strange day, the functionality of it all at odds with the emotions she'd had to keep in check.

Seeing the man who'd killed her son for the first time in the flesh had been harder than she could have possibly imagined. He'd looked so normal, not the monster Kate had imagined at all. In fact, he was still a boy really, and he had looked so lost and scared. And seeing the woman she assumed was his mother, the back of her at least, sitting there, seemingly not taking her eyes off her son for even a second, was almost unbearable. It made the whole sorry story feel like such a waste.

Kate pulled the plug and stepped out of the bath, wrapping herself in a warm white towel. She crossed the bathroom into the bedroom and sat on the edge of their bed, reaching for her night-gown and putting it gently over her head. There, in a frame on the bedside table, was a picture of Flora and Billy as small chil-dren, sitting in a sea of daffodils. She'd taken that picture one sunny day in their garden, down near the river. Robin was just out of shot and the grins on the children's faces were directed at him, clowning around for Kate to get the perfect picture. Kate could remember the sound of their laughter, fits of pure giggles, even now. Moments afterwards, Robin had grabbed the camera and taken some pictures of Kate, smiling into the camera. One of them sat framed on his bedside table, his favourite photo, as he often told her.

She reached for the picture, picking it up and holding it in her lap. Their life together had been so happy, for the most part. How could he have betrayed her like that?

Monty poked his nose around the door and, at her call, came trotting across the bedroom. She reached down to pick him up.

'Come on, then.' She put him in the middle of the bed, where he promptly circled a few times before settling down into his perfected position, curled up with his paws crossed. He looked up at her, his brown eyes sad. She stroked the top of his head, his coat gloriously soft. 'You're not helping, Monty.'

There was a gentle knock at the door. 'Mum?'

Kate looked up to see Flora standing there, holding a mug. 'Come in.'

'I brought you some hot water and lemon.' Flora walked over to put it down on the table next to Kate. She spotted the picture in her mother's hand. 'Oh, Mum.' Flora sat down next to her mother and put her arm around her shoulders. 'I'm so sorry. It must have been awful for you today.'

'It really was, Flora.' Kate finally let herself cry the tears she'd been holding back all day. 'It just made everything seem such a dreadful, dreadful waste. All of it.' She sighed. 'And I don't understand why it had to happen to us. I mean, it could have been anyone. Why did it have to be Billy?' Kate looked at Flora, tears streaking her face.

'I don't know, Mum. I wish I knew, too.' Flora hugged her tightly.

'And seeing that man. Well, boy really.' Kate took a deep breath. 'He looked so... normal.'

'Mum, like you said, this doesn't bring Billy back. But at least the trial is done.' Flora took the picture from her mother's hands, studying it. 'He looks so happy there.' She looked at Billy's face, his head back, laughing. 'He was beautiful.' She placed it back on the bedside table. 'Mum, can I just ask one thing of you?'

Kate wiped her eyes. 'Yes, of course.'

'I know it's not your doing, but please, please don't give up on Dad.'

Kate waved her hand. 'Oh, Flora, I'm too tired to even think about that.' She slipped under the duvet, pulling it up around her.

'Mum, please?'

Kate sighed. 'The truth is, darling, this isn't just about forgiving your father for what he's done.'

'But—'

Kate put her hand on Flora's arm. 'It's not just about his actions. I've lost a son and that's devastating. But I've also been betrayed, and I have to learn to live with knowing I'm not good enough for the person I love, the person I thought loved me.'

'Mum, that's not true...'

'I'm afraid it is. And the worst thing about being rejected by someone is that it doesn't make you hate them. In fact, it makes you love them even more.' She looked up at her daughter. 'I just need some time, that's all. To figure out what I want to do. Which is why I've asked him to go, so that I can do that without him here. I'm sorry, I know that must be hard for you, especially after...' Kate shook her head, then looked up at Flora. 'But it's just how it's got to be, for now, at least.'

Flora nodded slowly. The pain in her mother's eyes was almost impossible to bear. She hugged her again, then kissed her mother's head and turned to leave. Just before she left the room, she turned back. 'Mum?'

'Yes, darling?' Kate reached for her mug.

'I love you.'

'I love you, too. Sleep well.'

Lying in her bed in her old room that night, Flora found that sleep refused to come. She couldn't stop thinking about seeing her mother like that. Flora grabbed her phone and tapped out a message to Johnny, the screen lighting up her face in the dark.

I miss you x

She put the phone back on the table and turned towards the window, the shapes in the dark so familiar even after all these years. The bears on the windowsill, the dressing table covered in half-used bottles of perfume, photo frames crammed with images of her teenage life, all still just as they were when she left home. Her phone pinged. She turned back and tilted the screen towards her.

I miss you too x

## 32

'Pass me the tape?' Tilda pointed at the roll of Sellotape in the middle of the table. 'Actually, pass me the wine first.'

Flora, Tilda and Susie sat around the marble-topped island in Susie's kitchen. Not that it could be seen for all the wrapping paper and bags of sweets piled up in the middle.

'So, tell me again how exactly we got lumbered with this job?' Flora topped up the wine in Tilda's glass, then Susie's, then her own, draining the bottle. Their second, she noted. It seemed to be going down like water for all of them, even Susie.

'It's Tilda's fault.' Susie pointed at her without looking up from her present wrapping.

'Oh, come on. At least we don't have to bake anything. This way we just have to wrap a few presents for the kids whilst, I'd like to point out, drinking really nice wine.' Tilda had volunteered them to do present wrapping for the children for the School Christmas Fair. She'd chosen to ignore the no-sugar rule in the guidelines promptly issued by the head of the PTA, instead clearing the shelves of small packets of sweets in the local supermarket.

'Susie,' Flora reached for the empty bottle, 'you do know this is a really expensive bottle?'

'Is it? I've no idea – first one I found in the fridge.'

Tilda picked up her glass and sniffed. 'Now you mention it, it does smell expensive. How much would this go for?'

Flora looked at the label, noting the producer. 'Well, the producer is a bit of a cult figure. I think this goes for around forty pounds a bottle.'

Tilda choked. 'Bloody hell, really?'

Flora laughed. 'Yes, really.' She looked at Susie, who carried on sticking down paper as if she hadn't heard. Flora caught Tilda's eye for a second.

'Well, I'd rather do this than make mince pies any day.' Susie looked up at them, picking up the empty bottle from the table. 'Shall I get another one?'

Soon, the wrapping was done. They sat around, piles of wrapped sweets stacked neatly into boxes, their cheeks flushed with wine and laughter. Tilda finally broached the subject Flora wanted to but didn't dare.

'How are things with Julian? I take it he's not coming back tonight?' She glanced at the clock. It was nearly eleven.

'No, he's staying in London again. You know how it is.' Susie shrugged. A silence followed. Clearly, Susie wasn't going to give anything away, not yet.

Flora, suddenly made brave with the wine, sat up. 'Actually, Tilda, I've got a favour to ask you. Given your second-to-none skills at stalking people online...'

Tilda did a mock bow. 'Thank you very much.'

'I need to know where to find a woman called Denise Hirst.' Flora took another small sip.

'Isn't that...?' Tilda looked at Flora, her forehead crumpling a little.

'The mother? Yes.'

'But isn't that, well... illegal?'

'No, not that I know of. According to my father any contact between them and us is meant to be through the Victim Liaison Officer, but the thing is, I don't want my parents to know about it. And it's not like I want to see him, just his mother.'

'Are you sure that's a good idea?' The look on Susie's face told Flora she quite obviously didn't think it was.

'I've seen her before, actually. In the churchyard, where Billy's ashes are buried.'

'What was she doing there?' Susie sounded astonished.

'Well, your guess is as good as mine, but she practically ran as soon as she saw me. And the thing is, I couldn't help but feel... not sorry, but something for her. I haven't been able to stop thinking about it ever since. I know it sounds weird but I would like to talk to her.'

'What about your parents?'

'I'm not planning on telling them.'

'Oh, Flo, are you absolutely sure?' Tilda looked worried.

'Listen, they've got their own stuff going on at the moment. I promise, I've thought about this a lot and, yes, I'm sure. She can always say no, but I thought I'd write to her, see if she'd be willing to meet me. Just for a cup of tea, perhaps.' Flora looked from one friend to the other. 'Please don't look at me like that. I'm feeling much better than I did, honestly. Well, generally, anyway. I still have my moments.' She thought of one just a few days earlier, when a song on the radio had brought back memories of Billy in such a rush, she'd had to pull the car over to the side of the road and wait until the sobs had passed.

'It's just that, well, she might not say what you want to hear.' Susie spoke softly.

'But that's just it. I don't know what I want to hear. I just need to ask some questions. And she can always say no or not answer them, but if I don't ask, I'll never know. And then I'm stuck, and I really, really don't want to be stuck any more.'

Tilda sighed. 'Well, I still think it's a little insane, but, yes, give me a home town and I'll try and find an address for you. Strictly between us.'

'Thank you.' Flora smiled at her friend.

Susie scooped up the empty glasses. 'Right, come on, you two, chucking-out time.' She looked up at the clock. 'Do you want me to call you a cab?'

'I ordered one earlier.' Tilda looked at the clock, too, squinting to make it come into focus. 'Shit, how did that happen?' Just then her phone rang. 'Yes, we'll be out in a minute, thanks.'

'Thank you, as ever, for your wonderful company. It was just what I needed.' Susie hugged each of them in turn.

'Take care.' Flora hugged her back, feeling the bones of Susie's shoulder blades through her jumper.

'I'm properly worried about her,' Flora said urgently to Tilda as they sat in the back of the taxi on the short drive home.

'I know. Me, too. He's obviously an arsehole. But hopefully she'll wake up one day and realise life doesn't have to be like that.' The taxi pulled up outside Tilda's too soon for them to continue their character takedown on Julian.

'If only it were that easy.' Flora kissed her friend. 'See you tomorrow.'

She watched Tilda wobble up the path to her door, fake leopard-fur coat swinging off her shoulders, red platform boots proving quite the challenge after all that wine. Tilda fumbled in her bag, holding her key up in triumph after a moment, grinning back at Flora.

'Looks like you ladies had a good evening,' the taxi driver said, looking into his rear-view mirror.

'We did, thank you.' Flora smiled to herself, counting her blessings to have friends with whom she could talk about nothing or everything, depending on what was needed.

She crept into the house and up the stairs, got undressed in the bathroom and slid quietly under the duvet into bed.

'Nice evening?' Johnny turned to face her.

'God, sorry. I thought I was being really quiet.'

'You were,' he lied.

She curled into his body, the warmth of his skin warming her own. They lay in silence for a moment.

'You know I mentioned finding that woman?'

'Yes.' He couldn't help but sound sceptical.

'Tilda's going to find her address for me. I'm going to write her a letter.'

'Are you sure that's what you want to do?'

'I'm absolutely sure.' She nodded into his chest.

'OK. Now, can you stop talking so I can do this?' He kissed her gently on the mouth.

'I can.' She tried to speak, laughing.

'I said, stop talking.' He kissed her again, his hand running softly, slowly up and down the length of her torso. She moved in closer and closed her eyes, letting her body respond and her mind drift upwards.

# 33

Kate looked out on to the garden, a thin frost covering the ground. The December sky was grey, the wind whipping the tops of the waves on the river in the distance below. She had slept heavily, without help, for the first time in a while. Her head didn't pound as it usually did at this time in the morning.

She switched on the kettle, let Monty out into the garden and returned to the table a few moments later with a cup of tea. There, propped up against an empty vase on the table, was a letter. Just a simple piece of paper, folded in half, with her name written on the outside in Robin's handwriting.

She reached over to pick it up. Unfolding it with one hand, she held it out and pulled her glasses down from her head with the other. His words swam in front of her eyes. He was sorry. He didn't know why he'd done what he'd done. He wished he could take it all back. He loved her more than anything, more than ever. His affair had been a temporary madness and it would never, ever happen again. He hoped she would forgive him but he would understand if she couldn't.

Kate put the letter down on the table and slowly sipped her

tea. She thought of him, sleeping upstairs in the spare room where he'd been ever since she had confronted him in the garden. He'd done as she'd asked, not asked her to change her mind. But now, seeing his words down on paper, she knew something had to change. They couldn't carry on living in limbo. She'd asked him to leave but sitting there, his words in front of her, she knew deep down she didn't want him to, not really.

But could she really stay with him knowing what she knew? Did that not consign her to a life of feeling like she was second best? Monty scratched at the door. Kate let him in and he trotted straight across the kitchen to his bed by the foot of the Aga to warm himself, settling down with a contented grunt.

She thought of Billy, the familiar pang of pain in her heart at his not being here. Flora's words came back to her, pleading with Kate not to give up on her marriage. Outside, snow started to fall, slowly at first then faster until flurries of snowflakes danced outside the windows. She sat for a while, letting her mind wander down old alleyways full of memories of her life together with Robin. When they'd met, they'd had barely a penny between them but their dreams had matched in size and shape. How they'd married against all their parents' wishes, so young but so sure. How he'd encouraged her at every step to become the successful interior designer she wanted to be; she in turn supporting him through his professional life, attending endless company dinners, charming everyone as she went. How he'd been the most present of fathers, certainly compared with many of their friends back when the children were small.

Most of all, she thought of how they'd always been so happy in each other's company. When the children had grown up and moved away, it had felt like they had a whole second act to enjoy together.

So why had Robin decided to throw years of marriage away

for someone else? Kate had to know. She stood up and went to boil the kettle again, taking two fresh cups of tea up the stairs.

* * *

The phone rang, waking Denise from her sleep. Or rather, from her nightmare. In it, she could see Stephen, but she couldn't hear him. He'd been in a room, at the end of a long corridor, calling to her.

She sat up in bed and switched on the light, then reached for the phone.

'Hello, Mrs Hirst?'

'Speaking.'

'I'm sorry to ring so early. It's Mr Sawyer.'

'Oh, hello, Mr Sawyer. Is everything all right?' Her heart was immediately hammering in her chest. 'Has something happened to Stephen?'

'No, no. It's good news, actually. Which is why I'm ringing you this early. I thought you'd want to know as soon as possible. We've got a hearing date for the appeal. It looks like we'll be able to get Stephen out of there sooner than we thought. He'll still be there a for a while but hopefully not quite as long.'

Denise put her hand to her mouth. She almost didn't dare believe what she was hearing. She took a breath then spoke as calmly as she could. 'When will you be able to tell him?'

'As soon as I can, I will. I'll make an appointment to go and see him. And I'll keep you informed as soon as I have any more news.'

'I don't know what to say. Thank you, Mr Sawyer.'

She felt elated and exhausted all at the same time. All of her letters to Stephen had gone unanswered. None of her phone calls had been returned. She'd seen him only once since he'd been sent to prison; he'd refused to see her after that. They'd sat oppo-site one another in the large visiting room, Denise desperately trying not to show how horrified she was at his appearance, how horrified she was at the surroundings.

In turn, he'd barely said a word to his mother at that meeting, turning his head to one side to hide a violet bruise on his cheek-bone. His knee hadn't stopped moving up and down and his knuckles were scratched raw. He had looked so vulnerable to his mother and all her instincts screamed to get him out of there. But there was nothing she could do except try to reassure him he wouldn't be there for evermore, encourage him to keep his head down and do as he was told. Most of all, she had tried to remind him that she loved him and would be there waiting for him when he came home.

Denise put the phone back down and sat up. She put on her slippers and went to make herself some tea. There, on the table where she'd left it, was the letter that had arrived the day before, a small white envelope with her name in handwriting she hadn't recognised on the front. She took her cup to the table by the window, opened the envelope and took the letter out to read it again.

*Dear Mrs Hirst,*

*My name is Flora. Billy Fraser was my brother. I'm sorry if this letter comes as a shock to you, I honestly don't mean it to, but I'm wondering if you might be able to help me.*

*I'm trying to come to terms with Billy's death. I loved him so much and miss him terribly, every single day. I know I can't change what's happened, much as I wish I could. But daring to think like that only makes it more painful.*

*I'm hoping that talking to you might help me move forward just a little. It's not that I'm expecting you to say anything to make things better. In fact, I don't really know what I'm hoping for, but I think I saw you in the churchyard a while ago. And it made me think that things can't have been easy for you either.*

*Anyway, please don't feel you have to reply but if you ever do think you might be able to meet me, let me know at the address above.*

*Yours sincerely,*

*Flora Harper*

*PS. I hope you don't mind me finding out your address. I promise I won't write again.*

Denise sat and looked at the letter for a while with shaking hands, reading the whole thing over once more, then she folded it and put it back on the table. All this time she'd thought the woman she'd seen at the graveyard couldn't possibly have known who she was. She'd felt guilty for being there, almost as if she was invading the other family's space, their own private grief. But something had made her want to go. And she had known she couldn't move on until she did. Deep down, Denise knew she owed it to the woman to agree to meet her.

* * *

Tilda sidled up to Flora in the playground. 'Have you written the letter yet?'

'Yes, a few days ago, actually. She'll have received it by now. I've not heard anything, and I probably won't, but at least it's done. And I feel better just for doing it.' Flora had been trying not to think about it too much, but her heart had jumped when she'd heard the postman that morning. 'I sort of don't want to know how you do it but you're very good at online stalking.' Flora raised her eyebrows at Tilda.

'I should do it professionally, really.' Tilda laughed, then looked round and leaned into Flora. She lowered her voice. 'I've also found out some other stuff, about someone else, but I can't tell you what yet.'

'Oh, come ON, you can't do that!' Flora laughed. 'Who's it about?'

'No, I'm sworn to secrecy. But you'll find out soon enough.' Tilda pretended to zip her mouth.

'You're terrible, Tilda.' Flora gently prodded her friend on the arm.

'Thank you.' Tilda beamed.

'That's not a compliment, believe it or not. Right, where are those kids? I've got to get them sorted: gymnastics tonight.' Flora rolled her eyes.

'Lucky you. I've got two hours by the side of a football pitch and it's bloody freezing.'

The children ran out of school and across the playground like animals being let out of a zoo.

'Hi, Mum!' Pip ran towards Flora, a great plastic model in tow.

'Wow, what's that?' Flora tried to look enthusiastic.

'The Eiffel Tower!' Pip tried to hold it upright, the weight of the plastic bottles making it collapse on its side.

Flora looked again. 'Oh, yes, of course it is. How brilliant!'

'Look what I've got!' Tom pulled at Flora's coat on the other side. He held a tiny eggshell cupped very gently in one hand.

'Oh, look at that. Where did you find it?'

Tom looked serious. 'I found it near the bushes over there at break time. I thought it meant the bird had died but Miss Scott told me it just means it hatched and flew away, probably a long time ago. And it'll be having a lovely time by now, flying about high in the air.'

Flora gently stroked Tom's hair. 'I think she's absolutely right.

Come on, let's get you home so we can get food inside you all before we take Pip to gymnastics.'

'Oh, no, please, not gymnastics,' Tom wailed. 'It's so boring.'

'Well, maybe it's not so much fun to watch, but I keep telling you to give it a go. I think you'll love it. Think how high you bounce on that trampoline at home. The ones at gymnastics are bigger and better and way, way bouncier.'

'But gymnastics is for girls.'

'Says who?' Flora looked at her boy, cheeks pink with cold.

'I don't know. It just is.'

'Rubbish. Gymnastics takes real skill and determination, not to mention strength.'

'Can you win money doing it?'

Flora laughed. 'Well, I'm sure you can but I don't think that's the point. Why, is that a deal-breaker for you?'

'Well, if I can make money doing it then I can go on holiday to Venice, too.' He looked at her solemnly.

'Oh, I see. You're still cross we didn't take you to Venice.' She laughed. 'In that case, yes, you can win money if you're really, really good at it.'

'I'll think about it, then.' Tom nodded thoughtfully.

## 34

'There you go, Mrs Russell. I think you'll love that one, I know how you like your Gavi.' Mack wrapped the bottle in tissue paper.

'Oh, I do, Mack. Reminds me of holidays many years ago.'

'And isn't that one of the best things about wine? Even on a chilly day like today it can take you to sunny places.' Mack put the bottle carefully into a bag. 'Thank you. See you next week?'

'Yes, I'm sure I'll need topping up before Christmas. Bye!'

Mack waved. Mrs Russell had always been one of his favourite customers, not least because of her fairly expensive taste for good Italian wines. He called out to the back of the shop, where Flora was busy packing up orders to go out later that day. Johnny was already out and about making deliveries to local restaurants. Business had really picked up over the last month as people geared up for the festive season. Everyone seemed to be in the mood to celebrate a little more than usual.

'Hey, Mack. All well?' Flora's flushed face appeared at the door.

'All good, Flora. That was Mrs Russell, she'd come in for more Gavi. Do you need a hand?'

'No, I'm nearly done, thanks. We're shifting a lot of wine this week. I think preparing those mixed festive cases was a great idea. People don't even have to think about it.'

'Yes, they've been a success. And how's the take-up been for the wine courses?'

'Pretty good, actually. We should be able to run a full four-week block in the new year. I've roped in a couple of my friends for the first one but hopefully once word spreads, I won't have to rely on them every time.' Flora smiled at the thought of Tilda's face when she'd reassured her she wouldn't have to spit the wine out if she didn't want to. Flora pushed her hair back from her face and put her hands on her hips, packing tape in one hand, scissors in the other. 'It really does look brilliant, you know.' Strings of tiny lights hung across the ceiling and down the sides of the shelves, and the window display was a wonder, boxes of wine peeping out of a giant fake snowdrift. She had mentioned the idea almost as a joke, but in no time Johnny had located a source of fake snow from a company that made it for film locations. Biodegradable, of course. Flora and Mack had overruled the request for an inflatable reindeer, much to Johnny's dismay.

'Are you back here after deliveries?'

'Yes, I'll pop back but I won't be in tomorrow, if that's OK? Johnny will be, obviously.'

'No problem.' Mack took a sip of his coffee.

She felt she owed him an explanation. 'I'm going to meet someone, actually. The mother of the boy who... well, the one who's in prison.'

Mack looked at her over his glasses. 'Right.'

'It's just that I saw her a while ago, from a distance. And she looked so sad. I don't quite know why, but I just feel a need to talk to her. Her son's in prison still, but I'm meeting her tomorrow near where she lives.'

Mack put his cup of coffee down on the counter. 'Flora, you know she might not give you the answers you're looking for.'

'I know, and I'm not looking for answers really. I just want to understand things a bit more. Maybe.'

'Flora, I say this as someone who knows, so please take it as I mean it. Bad things happen and unfortunately, especially for people like us, who've lost people we love too early, some things can never be explained.'

Flora sat down on the stool by the tasting counter. She closed her eyes for a moment. 'Mack, can I ask what happened to Jamie? I keep wondering why we've never talked about it. Is it still too painful?'

There was a pause. 'Leukaemia. Acute myeloid leukaemia, to be precise, which is very rare but, sadly for Jamie, incurable back in those days. It came on so quickly, we hadn't really noticed anything other than him feeling more tired than usual. By the time it was discovered, there wasn't much we could do about it. It was just a question of time.'

'Oh, Mack, I'm so sorry. I didn't know.'

'Don't apologise; I didn't tell you. I haven't really talked about it much since Elizabeth died. It took us a long time to learn to live with it. He was so young.' Mack sighed. 'But it's a question of accepting it rather than trying to understand it.' He shook his head. 'I spent years making that mistake.'

'I know what you're saying makes sense, but it doesn't make it any easier.'

'It won't, not yet, anyway. You don't wake up and suddenly everything has fallen into place. But one day, if you want it to, it'll find you.'

'What will?'

'Forgiveness.'

'Mack, I can't forgive what happened to Billy. That boy killed him. I don't see how I can ever forgive that.' Flora's voice shook slightly.

'You don't have to forgive anything if you don't want to. But forgiveness isn't the same as permission.'

'You know, when we were in Venice, I was lighting a candle for Billy, and a woman standing next to me was lighting one for her brother. And she said hearts stay broken.'

Mack nodded his head. 'I think she's right. But you learn to live with it.'

'Yes, she said it gets easier to bear. I can hear her saying now. So, do you think meeting his mother is a mistake?'

'Not if that's what you want to do, no.'

Flora thought about it for a moment, then drained her cup. 'I think I want to go.'

'Then go.' Mack shooed her away with his hand, smiling.

She stood and went to grab her coat. 'Thanks, Mack, I'll see you later.'

'Yes, see you later.' The bell tinkled as she left the shop. Mack found it heart-breaking watching Flora searching for something to ease the pain. But he knew, more than most, there was little he or anyone could do to help. It was just a matter of giving it time.

* * *

Susie sat alone on the bench, watching the children as they clambered over climbing frames and flew as high as they possibly could on swings in the adventure playground. 'Mummy, Mummy, watch!' came the cry, seemingly every five seconds.

'Hello, you.' Tilda grinned as she swiftly took a seat beside Susie. 'Go on, kids! Snacks after.' She shooed her own children away. 'So, you want the good news or the bad news first?'

Susie braced herself. 'Bad.'

'OK, well – and I think you already knew this, Suse – he's definitely up to no good.' Tilda put her hand on Susie's arm. 'I'm so sorry.'

Susie sat up straight, breathing what sounded more like a sigh of relief than one of shock. 'And the good news?' Susie fixed Tilda with her enormous eyes, her dark hair pulled back into its usual sleek ponytail.

Tilda pulled out her phone from her bag. 'Turns out he's been very sloppy about covering his tracks.' Tilda couldn't help but smile at this, a glint in her eye. 'Susie, if you needed evidence, it's all here.' Tilda pointed at her phone. She tapped the screen a few times, then swiped and tapped some more. She held the screen so Susie could see it. 'There.'

Susie squinted at the screen. 'May I?' She took it from Tilda to get a good look. 'Oh my God, I knew it. His old fucking girlfriend.' She started laughing.

'I'm not sure what reaction I was expecting, Susie, but it definitely wasn't laughter.'

'I'm sorry, but I should have known it would be her. He's far too lazy to actually put in any effort to find someone new.' Susie tapped at the screen again. 'Wow, she hasn't changed much.' Susie looked at the familiar features of her husband's old university friend. She'd even met her a few times, first at their wedding, then over the years at various landmark birthday parties. 'I never liked her.'

'Susie, I'm so sorry, but you did ask me to.'

'Please don't apologise. You did exactly as I asked. I don't even have a Facebook account any more so there wasn't a hope of me ever finding this stuff out. So how did you know?'

'Well, she goes on and on about being single, in a "lady doth protest too much" kind of way. Then I looked at her photos and sure enough, she's been in all the same restaurants as the ones he's been in on the dates you told me. Luckily, her serial posting addiction worked in our favour. And if you look at this photo, where she's taken a selfie...' Tilda scrolled to find the offending photo, 'you can see there's a hand on her thigh.' She zoomed in on the photo.

There, quite clearly, was a pudgy hand resting high up on the smiling woman's thigh. Susie got closer to the screen. 'He didn't even bother to take his wedding ring off.'

'You sure you're OK?' Tilda put her phone back in her bag.

'Well, it's hardly a surprise. I just hadn't envisaged being a divorcee.'

'You mean that's it? No second chances?'

Susie smiled with relief. 'No second chances. This is my ticket out.'

## 35

Flora had arrived early, not wanting to risk getting lost or stuck in traffic. It was still over half an hour until the agreed meeting time. She found a quiet table at the back of the café suggested by Denise, ordered a pot of tea and a toasted teacake and went to the table with her tray.

The café was busy with people coming and going, the constant buzz of conversation meaning that individual ones couldn't be heard. Thank goodness, thought Flora.

She'd parked not far away, walking through the streets of the unfamiliar town, Christmas lights twinkling overhead and in shop windows. The high street was busy with shoppers carrying bulging bags, the sound of a brass band in the air. But now, sitting here, a teacake she suddenly had no appetite for in front of her, Flora wondered what on earth she was doing. What had made her think that meeting this woman would make any difference to how she felt about losing her brother? Flora looked at her watch. Fifteen minutes until the meeting time. She still had time to make a run for the door and forget the whole thing, if she was quick. She put her arms back into her coat and reached down, looking for her bag on the floor.

By the time Flora looked up again, someone was standing opposite her, an older woman. Same grey hair, a small smile on her face. 'Hello.'

'Oh, I...' Flora stumbled on her words, embarrassed.

'I'm Denise.' The woman's voice trembled a little.

'I'm so sorry, I just...' Flora shook her head. 'I'm Flora. Please, sit down.'

Denise did so, unravelling her scarf and putting it with her coat on the back of her seat.

'Can I get you some tea?'

'No, thanks, I ordered some on the way in. They're bringing it over in a moment.'

They looked at one another, neither sure of what to say next.

'So,' Flora began.

'So,' said Denise.

Flora took a deep breath. 'I guess I need to start by saying thank you for agreeing to meet me.'

'Honestly, it's the least... I feel I owe it to you.' Denise wanted to reach out her hand but stopped herself, worried about saying or doing the wrong thing.

'I'm not expecting you to say anything to make me feel better. I think I just want to... I don't know.' Flora sighed. 'I'm sorry, Denise, I don't know what I want.' She laughed nervously.

Denise looked at her. 'Listen, this is an awful situation for us all. You've lost a brother and I am so, so sorry for that.' Her voice trembled again. 'More than you will ever know.' She put her hands together, letting them fall into her lap. 'And my son is in prison for doing what he did.'

'Why did he do it?' The words were out of Flora's mouth before she could stop them.

Denise took a breath and held it for a few seconds before she spoke. 'I wish I could tell you. I lie awake every night asking the same thing. Wondering if there's something I could have done, should have done to change things.' She nodded her head slowly. 'The truth is, when I ask Stephen the same thing – which, believe me, I've done over and over again – he doesn't have an answer either. He knows it was stupid. If he could go back, of course he'd do things differently.'

Flora blinked, trying to keep the tears behind her eyes from falling.

Denise continued, 'Please don't think I'm making excuses for him. I'm not. He'll have to make his own amends when he's… when he can. But in the meantime, please know that I am so, so sorry for what's happened. I don't expect you to forgive him for what he did, but…' Denise paused, searching for the right words, '… I hope that he can make sure his past doesn't determine his future. He owes it to your brother to do so.'

There was a long silence. A tray with a teapot, cup and saucer and small jug of milk appeared. 'Can I get you anything else?' The waitress smiled at them both.

'Yes, please, can I ask you to warm up this teacake?' Flora proffered her plate.

'Thank you.' Denise looked at Flora, smiling gently. 'Think I might join you and have one of those, too.'

'And another one, please,' Flora asked the waitress. 'And, please, can I have some extra butter?' She turned back to Denise. 'Best bit.'

Denise nodded, still smiling. 'So, can you tell me about your brother? I'd love to know what he was like… only if you want to, of course.'

Flora wiped at her eye, the thought of him making her smile, too. 'I'd love to tell you about him. He was brilliant, actually. I was lucky that he wasn't just my brother, he was a real friend. We were always close, from a young age – perhaps because it was just the two of us – but even though he was a bit younger than me I always looked up to him. He was so secure in his own skin, happy to take what life threw at him. And he always seemed to be able to make the most of it. I think what I really loved was his fearlessness. He was just never afraid, no matter what. It was if it never occurred to him that something bad would happen.'

'Oh, Flora, I'm so sorry...'

'No, I don't mean the accident. He was like that his whole life: just lived, you know, totally unafraid. I wish I could have been the same.' She smiled to herself, remembering how he always teased her for worrying too much, about being caught swimming in the river, or creeping back into their parents' house late at night. 'In a way, I'm glad he didn't know what was coming. It was like he lived his life just as he wanted right up until that point.' Flora stirred her cup of tea slowly. She looked up at Denise. 'I just miss him.' Her voice was barely audible.

'I can't imagine how terrible that must feel. I'm so sorry, Flora.'

Flora looked up. Denise looked absolutely heartbroken. 'Tell me about Stephen.'

'Well, it's quite a different story I'm afraid. He was... is,' Denise corrected herself, 'he's always seemed to find life hard. It was always just him and me. His father left years ago. Stephen was too young to even remember him. He struggled as a child to make friends and of course I've always wondered if that's my fault. Did I make him too...?' Denise searched for the words. 'I don't know, I worry that if I'd done things differently, none of this would have happened.'

Flora remembered Mack's words to her in the shop earlier that day. 'You know, a friend of mine said that living your life trying to change the past will keep you stuck in the same place forever.' Flora smiled. 'Something like that, anyway.'

Denise reached across the table and squeezed Flora's hand. 'He sounds like a good friend.'

'He really is.' Flora nodded. 'How is he doing? In prison... if you don't mind me asking.'

'He's doing OK.' Denise decided Flora didn't need to know any more than that, wanting to spare her the details of the scars that would no doubt stay long after the bruises had gone. 'I just want him home.' Denise caught herself. 'Oh, Flora, I'm sorry. That must sound so insensitive.'

'No, I know what you mean. I'm just glad we're able to talk. It's not been easy for either of us, in different ways, I suppose. I can see that now. And maybe what's happened might change the course of your son's life in a good way.'

'I will do everything I can to help make that happen.'

They looked at one another. Flora reached for Denise's hand, taking it and holding it in her own. 'Thank you.'

The two women left the café together and as they stood on the street preparing to say goodbye, unsure quite how to do it, snow started to gently fall. Flora spoke first. 'Well, I'm going this way.'

Denise gestured in the opposite direction. 'And my bus stop is that way.'

'Thank you again. I really appreciate you coming.' Flora held out her hand.

Denise took it with both of hers. 'Thank you, Flora. I'm really glad you asked me.' She shook Flora's hand. 'You take care.'

'And you.'

They parted not knowing if they would see each other again, but for now, it was enough.

That evening, as Flora lay on the sofa, she told Johnny how the meeting had gone.

'It's so weird to be bound to someone by events out of the control of either of us. The sad thing is there are no winners. Everyone loses. But Denise is determined to try and help Stephen live a better life after he's released, and that's good to know.' Flora looked at Johnny. 'Honestly, it was awful seeing the pain on her face. Literally etched into her face.' Flora touched her own.

'She didn't lose a son.'

'Yes, but she's obviously living through her own kind of hell at the moment. That's what I mean. There are no winners.'

'Are you going to tell your parents about meeting her?'

'Maybe one day. In fact, I think Mum might like to meet her. But not just yet.'

'Come on, finish this,' he handed her the last drop of his whisky, 'and let's go to bed. You look shattered. Lovely, obviously,' he laughed, 'but shattered.'

She was knackered, all right, but her heart felt lighter than it had for a long time.

* * *

'Do we really have to go?' Pip looked longingly at her mother.

'Yes, we do, and you know you'll enjoy it when we get there.' Flora tried to tame Pip's hair with a hairbrush that clearly wasn't up to the task.

'Ow!'

'Sorry,' Flora grimaced.

'Can't find my shoes.' Tom wandered past, dragging his coat.

'They're by the front door,' Johnny called after him. 'Hey, you sure you want to go? We can always say – I don't know – you're not feeling well?'

'I can't avoid them forever, can I?' Flora gave a slight shrug.

'I suppose not. Right, I'll see you in the car?'

'Out in a mo. I'll just grab a bottle of something to take.'

Flora went to the fridge and opened it, spying a bottle of Crémant de Limoux in the door. Crémant always reminded her of the time her father had opened a bottle to celebrate Flora and Johnny's somewhat surprise engagement. She thought of how happy he'd been at the news. Her mother less so, but deep down, she knew how fond of Johnny her mother was now. She grabbed the bottle and stuck it into her bag.

Flora hadn't seen her parents since her visit straight after the trial. She knew she should have made more of an effort to visit them but somehow it had been easier to just put in a phone call for the last few weeks, rather than actually go and face them. It made her sad to remember how close they'd once been, and how that had changed since Billy had died.

The journey passed with the usual bickering in the back whilst Flora and Johnny attempted to have a conversation over the noise. They soon gave up and cranked up the music instead, which resulted in a mass singalong as the tracks from one of their favourite musicals blasted out of the stereo.

'Best behaviour, please,' Flora reminded the children as they pulled up in the drive. 'And, Tom, please don't say yuck when Granny puts vegetables on your plate.'

'But she always gives us that green stuff.' Tom pulled a face.

'It's called kale and it's very good for you, I'll have you know. Just say thank you and suck it up, sunshine.' Flora pointed her finger at him.

'It's rude to point,' said Tom, cheekily.

'Hello, darling.' Robin stood on the doorstep, waiting to greet them.

'Hi, Dad, how are you?' Flora hugged him.

'Hello, Flo. Go on through, your mother's in the kitchen.' He turned to Johnny. 'How are you?'

Johnny shook Robin's hand. 'Good, thanks. Good to see you. Here, this is from us.' He gave him the bottle. 'Still cold, just about.'

'It's been a while. But we're very glad you're here.' Robin glanced inside to make sure Flora was out of earshot. 'How is she?'

'She's pretty good, Robin. We're busy at the shop so I think that helps, you know, keeps her occupied.'

'Go on through; we're in the kitchen.' He waited for them all to go ahead before following them in.

'Darlings!' Kate turned from where she stood by the Aga, throwing her arms open. 'I am so pleased to see you.' She crossed the kitchen and wrapped her arms tightly around Flora.

'Hi, Mum,' Flora said, her voice muffled by Kate's bright scarf. As she took in her mother's familiar scent, felt the softness of her cheek against her own, she was suddenly overwhelmed by how pleased she was to see her. Flora had braced herself for more tears or, even worse, silence. Instead, there was nothing but love and a kitchen filled with the delicious, unmistakable smell of a Sunday roast. 'How are you?'

'Very well. Darling,' she called over to Robin, 'can you give everyone a glass? And look at you two!' Pip and Tom stood beside Flora, smiles on their faces as instructed. 'You've grown since I last saw you! Haven't they grown?' She looked at Flora.

'Mum, it hasn't been that long...'

'Long enough. Now come on, let's hear what you've been up to. How's everything at the shop?'

'Actually, pretty good. We're thinking about opening up a small café next year. Well, not really a café, more a kind of snack bar so you can take your food and have it outside with a glass of something. We saw something like it in Venice and it got us thinking... Anyway, how about you?' Flora looked across at her father pouring out a glass of the Crémant for them all. She looked back at her mother. 'Is everything... OK?'

Kate lowered her voice. 'I think it will be. We'll talk about it later. You and I can walk down to the river for a bit of air after lunch.'

They sat and feasted on slow-roast lamb, Robin topping up Johnny's glass with a particularly good Rioja Reserva at regular intervals, given that Flora was the designated driver. Then followed a bowl of Barbados cream dolloped on top of baked plums, the warm spices filling the kitchen as they cooked.

Her parents seemed almost back to normal, much to Flora's surprise. She found herself relieved and unnerved all at the same time.

After lunch, as they walked down to the river, the children running ahead, Flora was finally able to talk to her mother alone.

'Mum, how are you really? How are you and Dad?'

'Well, it's not been easy, as I'm sure you gathered. But,' Kate took a deep breath, 'I did listen to what you said.'

Flora tried to remember. 'Um, what did I say exactly?'

'Well, you suggested I gave him a chance to explain, at least.'

'And?' Flora looked up, seeing Johnny and her father walking ahead, her father's walk slow and familiar.

'I'm not sure I'll ever be able to forgive what he did but I do believe him when he says it won't happen again. And how sorry he is. We were both at fault in our own ways. We lost each other for a while, maybe took each other for granted. But to be honest,' Kate sighed, 'I've loved him for too long to let him go now.'

Flora felt relief flood through her. She hugged her mother tightly. 'Oh, Mum, I'm so pleased.'

Kate put her hands to her daughter's face. 'We've all been

through so much. I just want to try and start enjoying the time we have again.'

They walked on ahead, catching up with the others at the riverbank. Together they stood for a moment, watching the tide coming in, the gulls wheeling overhead.

Flora stood with her arm through her mother's. 'Billy loved swimming in this river.'

Kate looked at her daughter. 'You miss him, don't you, darling?'

'So much it hurts.' Flora looked up at the sky. She thought of Ruby. They'd messaged a few times since the memorial; Flora couldn't bear the thought of how Ruby had glimpsed a future with Billy, only to have it taken away. She hoped that one day Ruby might want to meet up properly. Flora thought they could be friends. 'Mum, I have to tell you something and I hope you won't be cross.' Flora looked at her mother. 'I met up with Stephen Hirst's mother, Denise.'

Kate looked blank for a moment, then her eyes widened with surprise as she realised who Flora was talking about.

'When?'

'A few weeks ago. I wanted to tell you, but in person, to explain.'

Kate looked out at the river. 'You know, it's fine, Flora. I'm realising that we all need to deal with this in our own way. And that might not be the same way, but if that's what you needed to do, then that's OK with me.'

'Really?'

'Yes, really.' Kate nodded slowly. 'So, what was she like?'

'Sad.' Flora sighed. 'Really, really sad. She was also sorry, said she hoped he'd live a better life when he comes out of prison. You know, I think you might like to meet her one day.'

'Maybe. Just not yet.' Kate tucked a stray strand of hair behind her daughter's ear. 'You know, we still have each other. And he'll always be with us, just not right here.'

'I know, Mum.' Flora smiled.

The knock on the door brought Mack downstairs. It was half an hour before opening time, but someone had been knocking for a while. He walked across the shop and undid the lock on the door.

'Colin, you're keen.'

'Morning, Mack. I'm sorry to make you open up early, but I wanted to get these to you whilst they were still warm.' Colin, resplendent in camel, held up a tin. With a flourish he opened one corner. 'Smell that.'

Mack did as he was told, the smell of warm cheese and pastry escaping as Colin held the lid up for a few seconds. 'Oh, my goodness, you made gougères.'

Colin looked fit to burst. 'I did. And let me tell you, there is a real art to making them.' He explained, in detail, how his first batch hadn't been up to scratch, his second an improvement but by no means perfect. 'But this, my third batch, I'm pleased to say, is very good indeed.' He gave the tin to Mack. 'These are for you, for the party later.'

'Oh, Colin, you didn't have to do that.'

'But how could I not? It's your one-year anniversary since you relaunched the shop! How many have you got coming?'

Mack shuffled back to the counter and placed the box gently on top. 'Flora and Johnny have organised the guest list so I'm not absolutely sure. You know, friends and family, some of our regulars, the usual suspects. It should be fun.'

'Well, let me know if there's anything else I can do to help. You know I'm always happy to top up glasses.'

'I know you are, thank you, Colin. See you later, then. I think we've said six o'clock.' He glanced outside. 'If it stays like this, we'll be able to be outside.'

'Fingers crossed.' Colin gestured to Mack, crossing his fingers on both hands. 'See you later.'

Mack went to put the lock on again when Flora appeared. He opened the door. 'Why's everyone so early today? You just missed Colin.'

'Oh, no, did I? Is he coming tonight?'

'Of course, and he made these.' Mack pointed to the counter.

Flora went over and picked up the lid, peering inside. 'Oh, my goodness, these are my favourites!' She reached in to take one, popping it into her mouth in one go. The flavour of warm Gruyère cheese and soft choux pastry filled her mouth, making her almost weep with joy.

'Are they good?'

'Have you not had one?' She offered the now open tin to him. 'You have to have one now, whilst they're still warm.'

He took one and did the same, nodding at Flora as he chewed. 'So good.'

'Would it be wrong, Mack, to have a very small glass of something bubbly, just us two, whilst we polish off a few more of these?'

'I have just the thing.' Mack went to the fridge in the back, taking out a bottle. He removed the stopper. 'We opened this yesterday. It's new from a small grower near Avize. It's incredible.' He poured out two small glasses of champagne and took them back over to the counter.

Flora was now perched on the stool behind, half a dozen of the tiny cheese-sprinkled gems in front of her. She took the glass, lifted it to her nose and took a long sniff, the scent of freshly popped toast enough to make her mouth start watering.

Mack raised his glass to hers. 'Here's to us, Flora. Look what we did.'

She smiled back at him. 'Here's to you, Mack. Thank you for making me understand...' Flora swept her gaze across the shop, searching for the right words, '... that life goes on.'

They clinked their glasses and for the time it took for them to drink a few sips of champagne, nothing else mattered.

* * *

Just after six that evening the shop started to fill with family and friends, the party soon spilling out into the courtyard. The warm summer air carried the scent of wisteria, and music drifted from the old record player in the corner, set up by Mack with Pip and Tom in charge of changing the record from time to time. Flora and Johnny did the rounds carrying glasses of perfectly chilled pale Provence rosé, pressing them into their guests' hands.

Flora's parents had arrived early to help them set up. She watched as they laid out glasses, her mother unable to help herself then from doing a little emergency weeding in the beds in the courtyard. They looked comfortable together again, Flora noted. She'd never spoken about the affair with either of them again – and hoped she'd never have to. Her father had had a lucky escape, so far as she was concerned, but more than that,

Flora was surprised to discover that she admired her mother for refusing to give up. She wasn't sure she'd have been able to do the same.

Tilda and Pete arrived, Pete carrying a small magnolia tree in a pot.

'This is for the courtyard and to say congratulations, we're so proud of what you've done with the shop,' said Tilda.

'Guys, you shouldn't have… but thank you. That's so lovely of you. Here, take these,' she gave them each a glass of wine, 'and go through, I'll be out in a minute.'

The bell tinkled behind her. It was Susie. Flora did a double take. 'Bloody hell, Susie. You look amazing!' Her friend stood there, immaculate as ever, but there was something about the way she looked that was different.

'He's agreed to a divorce.' Susie beamed.

'Oh my God, that's fantastic!' Flora hugged her friend. 'I mean, you're OK?'

'I'm over the bloody moon.' Susie laughed. 'But I don't want to waste a second more thinking about it tonight. I want a massive glass of something delicious, please.'

'You're in the right place.' Flora laughed. 'Come with me.' She led Susie by the arm into the courtyard, handing her a glass on the way.

Johnny waved at Flora from the corner where he stood with a small crowd of regulars, signalling that he was coming over. 'I've just asked Mack if he'd like me to say a few words, but he said he's happy to.'

'Great, so long as I don't have to do it this time.'

The sound of spoon against glass brought the assembled crowd to a hush. 'Hello, can you all hear me?' Mack stood by the back door of the shop. 'I promise to keep this brief. Right, well, first I want to thank you all for coming, of course. I feel very lucky to be celebrating the first anniversary, which was actually a few weeks' ago, of our new, improved wine shop. As you all know, it couldn't have happened without two very special people, Johnny and Flora.'

The crowd cheered.

'Now,' Mack continued, 'it wasn't so long ago that I thought it was the end of the line for this shop. But then Flora – and Johnny, of course – came along and decided it wasn't the end. In fact, it was the beginning of a whole new story. Thank you both.' He raised his glass. 'To Flora and Johnny!'

The crowd toasted, followed by a round of whoops and applause. Johnny turned to Flora, kissing the side of her head. 'Want me to get you another lime and soda?'

Flora looked down at her swelling stomach. 'God, no, I can't face another one. I'll make do with tap water after this.'

Kate appeared at their side, her face a picture of pride. 'Well done, we're so happy for you.'

'Thank you, Kate,' said Johnny.

'Now,' Kate looked at her daughter, 'how's that Venice baby doing?'

Flora laughed. 'Mum, please stop calling her that. It really freaks me out.' She put her hands on her belly, feeling the baby turn like a jumping bean.

'Sorry, I can't help it. I'm just so excited.' Kate sighed. 'Right, I need to find your father. Luckily, he's driving tonight so I can have another one of these.' She held up her empty glass.

'Let me sort that out for you, then.' Johnny took it and went off to get her a refill.

'Mum, are you really all right?'

Kate took Flora's hands. 'Darling, I'm fine. Good days and bad days, you know.'

Flora nodded. She did indeed know. 'I miss him so much, Mum.'

'Me, too.'

Colin appeared with a fresh glass of rosé for Kate. 'Johnny sent me over with this.'

'Thank you, Colin.' Kate took it from him. 'That's a beautiful colour on you, by the way.'

'Thank you. It's sage green.'

Kate and Flora clinked glasses, their smiles tinged with sadness.

'He'd have been so happy for you,' said Kate, softly.

'I know.' Flora squeezed her mother's hand.

'Gougères?' Colin held a plate of them.

'Thank you, Colin. Mum, you have to try one, they're so good.' She turned to Colin. 'Why don't you tell my mother how you make them? I'm really sorry, but I've got to dash to the loo. Again.'

Flora crossed the courtyard into the shop, making her way upstairs. She saw the window at the back was open and went to it, looking down at the courtyard below filled with familiar faces, the sound of talking and laughter floating up towards her. She looked up at the pale silver moon overhead.

'Hey, little brother,' she whispered.

# BOOK CLUB QUESTIONS

1. Who did you most identify with in *In Just One Day?*
2. How well do you think Helen McGinn dealt with the mother/daughter relationship?
3. What made Billy and Flora's relationship so memorable?
4. Did you feel sorry for Denise or did you think she was to blame?
5. What did you think of the book's title?
6. Which character did you like most and least?

# AN INTERVIEW WITH HELEN

1. Flora is a wine buff - how much of Helen McGinn is there in Flora?

When it comes to wine, quite a lot. I didn't follow quite the same path as I've worked in the wine industry all my working life but I did all the wine exams as Flora does. Writing about that brought back lots of memories! And to this day I love pouring over wine maps. (I promise I'm more fun than I sound).

2. Who was the hardest character to write?

Probably Kate because she's such a contradiction. At first glance she seems quite chaotic but she's far more capable than she seems. Over the course of the story she loses so much but still comes out fighting. I want you to love her and find her infuriating all at the same time. Some of my favourite people are just like that.

3. How did writing this book compare to writing your first novel, *This Changes Everything?*

This was definitely more of a challenge. Obviously I had the experience of writing a fiction book under my belt but This Changes Everything was written over four years. This one was written in a year with three lockdowns! And of course the subject matter was different, more personal in fact. My little brother, Tim, died twenty years ago when he was just 26 so I know what losing a sibling feels like. Writing this one was an intense experience but the time was right. Grief is such a personal experience and I wanted to explore how it affects people in different ways. And how life can be good again, even if things are never the same.

4. How does Kate experience Billy's death as compared to how Flora experiences it?

Their reactions are so very different. Kate feels a lot of anger from the start whereas Flora feels as if she's underwater, almost disconnected from those around her. It takes a while but they come to understand that neither way is right or wrong, it's just how it is. And how you feel changes, often from day to day. Years ago, like a moron, I Googled 'how long does grief last'. I was desperate to know when it would stop hurting. Of course that didn't help but in time I realised the answer is learning to live with it and finding the positives wherever you can. Grief lasts forever but, eventually, it might not hurt quite so much.

5. Denise is such an interesting character. What gave you the idea to include her point of view?

I really wanted to explore the feelings of two mothers who had been affected by what happened and though Denise didn't lose a son, her life was changed too. The way she questions what she could or should have done differently to change the course of events was heart-breaking to think about. It certainly wasn't her fault but I wanted to show it was hard for her too in this situation. We don't often hear that side of the story.

6. How does Venice help Flora come to term with Billy's death?

Johnny knew she'd been there with Billy years before when they were kids, so he'd hoped it would bring back some happy memories as well as providing a much-needed change of scene. I went as a teenager many years ago when inter-railing with friends and again years later for our wedding anniversary. I love it but the fading splendour seems to lend an air of sadness to the city which fits with Flora's frame of mind. I like the idea that once the city has worked its magic, she's able to remove her mask and not feel she must put on a brave face. The woman in the church telling Flora that hearts stay broken is one of my favourite scenes in the book. It's sad but she does say things will get better. And she's right, they always do.

# ACKNOWLEDGMENTS

Thank you to my very special agent Heather Holden Brown, to Elly James and all at HHB for your constant encouragement and unwavering dedication.

Enormous thanks to Amanda Ridout and Team Boldwood, especially to my editor Sarah Ritherdon for being so completely brilliant at what you do. Thank you to Nia Beynon and Claire Fenby for bringing this book to life and getting it into people's hands. My thanks also to Yvonne Holland for making sure it all made sense, to Alice Moore for the beautiful cover and to Ross Dickinson, Sue Lamprell and Suzanne Sangster for all your help and support.

Once again, huge thanks to Charlotte Russell and Alie Plumstead for your honest feedback on my early drafts and to Chris Daw QC for your invaluable insights and expertise on the technical stuff. Thank you to Marina Cantacuzino MBE for taking the time to talk me through your incredible work and to Edwina Snow for making that happen. The Forgiveness Project had a profound effect on me and I'm forever grateful that our paths crossed when they did, Marina. Also, to my friend Liz Gough. Liz, this is all your fault and I can't thank you enough. Wine soon, please.

Talking of which, I must give a special mention for my favourite independent wine shop, The Solent Cellar in Lymington. Heather and Simon, thank you for inspiring the shop setting for this story (and for keeping everyone's wine racks topped up with such lovely wines)!

Thank you to my parents Christine and Ken, stepmother Jo, and in-laws Frank and Dru for your love and eternal cheerleading, and to my brilliant sister Alex for making the world a much brighter, funnier place to be. And to my little brother Tim, I miss you every single day.

To my husband Ross and to my children George, Xander and Alice, in the words of The Beach Boys, God only knows what I'd be without you. Thank you, I feel very lucky to have you all (but please can you not leave wet towels on the floor, kids. That's actually quite annoying).

Thank you to all the readers of my wine blog, The Knackered Mother's Wine Club. Your amazing support over the years is never taken for granted and I appreciate every comment / wineglass emoji.

Finally, thank you so much for reading this book, it really does mean the world to me. It was a tough one to write but I'm so glad I did. Life does indeed go on. X

# MORE FROM HELEN MCGINN

We hope you enjoyed reading *In Just One Day*. If you did, please leave a review.

If you'd like to gift a copy, this book is also available as an ebook, digital audio download and audiobook CD.

Sign up to Helen McGinn's mailing list for news, competitions and updates on future books.

https://bit.ly/HelenMcGinnNewsletter

*This Changes Everything,* another wonderful read from Helen McGinn is available to order now.

# ABOUT THE AUTHOR

**Helen McGinn** is a much-loved wine expert on TV and in print and an international wine judge. She spent ten years as a supermarket buyer sourcing wines around the world before setting up her award-winning blog (and best-selling wine book) *The Knackered Mother's Wine Club*. She is the drinks writer for the Daily Mail and regularly appears on TV's Saturday Kitchen and This Morning. Helen lives in the New Forest.

Visit Helen's website: www.knackeredmotherswineclub.com

Follow Helen on social media:

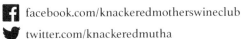 facebook.com/knackeredmotherswineclub
twitter.com/knackeredmutha
 instagram.com/knackeredmother

# ABOUT BOLDWOOD BOOKS

Boldwood Books is a fiction publishing company seeking out the best stories from around the world.

Find out more at www.boldwoodbooks.com

Sign up to the Book and Tonic newsletter for news, offers and competitions from Boldwood Books!

http://www.bit.ly/bookandtonic

We'd love to hear from you, follow us on social media:

facebook.com/BookandTonic

twitter.com/BoldwoodBooks

instagram.com/BookandTonic